"I wish you wouldn't push this."

But Grace wanted to push. It was something far more appealing than dealing with the fact she hadn't gotten over all her fears in seven long-ass years.

"I'm not pushing anything. If you don't feel anything for me, walk away."

Kyle didn't. Indecision played all over his face. From what she knew about Kyle, she imagined there was quite the internal war going on inside that all-too-active brain of his, but she could wait it out.

She knew what his lips would feel like on hers, but just the faintest of touches. She had a vague sense of what he would taste like, but their kiss from a few days ago had been so brief, so totally on her that it was really just a teaser, an appetizer.

And now, she was really interested in the main course.

Dear Reader,

It's rather surreal to sit down and write a "dear reader" letter for my very first Harlequin Superromance. I've been reading these from authors I greatly admire for years, and to now be one of them is...well, something I'm very, very proud of!

When I set out to write *Too Close to Resist,* I started pretty much as always—trying to write a story people can recognize or relate to. But I knew I wanted to do two things within that realm: first, I wanted to write two main characters who were fundamental opposites. As that idea grew, I realized I wanted them to have dealt with similar things in their pasts, and have that *cause* those differences. So it wasn't just that they had different personalities, they had completely different ways of dealing with traumatic events.

The second thing I knew, perhaps even before I knew who Grace and Kyle really were, was that I didn't want the hero to swoop in and save the heroine in any situation. I wanted Grace, whatever danger might befall her, to be standing in that moment alone. There would be no white knight saving her, but a partner who would stand beside her in the aftermath. Support her and comfort her, but not "fix" anything for her.

I couldn't be happier with how that turned out, or how much I love these two and the way they stand by each other. I hope you'll enjoy them too!

If you're on Twitter, so am I—probably more than I should be. I love to talk to readers, @NicoleTHelm. Visit my website at www.nicolehelm.wordpress.com.

Happy reading!

Nicole Helm

P.S. Keep an eye out for my upcoming titles from Harlequin E, coming later this year!

NICOLE HELM

—

Too Close to Resist

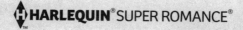

HARLEQUIN® SUPER ROMANCE®

Recycling programs
for this product may
not exist in your area.

ISBN-13: 978-0-373-60851-5

TOO CLOSE TO RESIST

Printed in U.S.A.

H HARLEQUIN®
™ www.Harlequin.com

ABOUT THE AUTHOR

Nicole Helm grew up with her nose in a book and a dream of becoming a writer or an artist. When her middle school art teacher poked fun at her stick figure birds, she decided to focus on writing. Luckily, after a few failed career choices, a husband, and two kids, she gets to pursue that writing dream. She lives in Missouri with her husband and two young sons, and writes her books one baby's nap at a time.

For my mom.
I've been waiting for the perfect book to dedicate to you. One that would mean something extra special, but as I thought about what that "extra special" might be, I realized, that was irrelevant. Every book I've written, every character I've come up with, goes back to you reading chapters out of *Charlotte's Web* and *Little House on the Prairie* to me. Every heroine with a backbone, a strong belief in herself and a sense of humor is because you taught me those things just by being you. Thank you for everything, always.

CHAPTER ONE

"THANKS AGAIN FOR doing this." Grace McKnight sat in the passenger side of her brother's truck and tried not to feel like a coward or a failure.

She wasn't succeeding.

"Happy to do it."

Grace fidgeted in her seat. Jacob's good-natured acceptance of her proposal didn't make this any easier. Nothing about Barry's getting out of jail had made life easier. Nothing.

Seven years after he'd beaten her into a three-day coma, Barry was still influencing her life. No matter how Grace tried, she couldn't find another alternative.

Going to live with her brother currently felt like the only option. Not only because of Barry and what he might do to the woman who'd testified against him, but also because living within walking distance of her parents was driving her insane, or at least turning her back into the jumpy weakling she'd been directly following her incident.

She couldn't go back to being that person. So

a little buffer from her parents was necessary, no matter how much it felt like running away.

Barry hadn't even been released before Mom and Dad started hovering. Dropping in multiple times a day at the gas station where she worked—even when they should have been at work themselves. Bringing her dinner or breakfast at her tiny house a few streets over from theirs. Filling in every second of her life with false cheer and barely contained worry.

Grace couldn't blame them, but she also couldn't handle it. It was hard enough living with the fear that Barry would try to seek some kind of revenge. Her parents' constant checking up and fake smiles, buying her alarms and talking to county deputies behind her back left her ready to head back to therapy.

She'd worked too hard and come too far to go back to being that woman who hid from everyone and everything.

So she'd stay with Jacob for a month or two, let her parents see that everything was all right. Give them some time to calm down and relax. If she lived with Jacob, they wouldn't hover as much. Jacob had a security alarm, a roommate. Grace would be safe, constantly surrounded by Jacob or Kyle. They would believe she was safe and looked after. They wouldn't be by her side constantly.

A few weeks and her parents would see that

Barry's being out of jail changed nothing. She could convince them. Had to. Because if she convinced them, she'd be that much closer to convincing herself.

And then maybe things could go back to normal. Maybe.

Grace moved her gaze to her tattoo. A Native American morning star, it symbolized strength and courage. A nod to Grandma Davenport, the strongest woman Grace had ever known.

Symbols had strength. Grace had to believe they'd give her some. Even when this felt cowardly. Even when it felt as if she was giving up, she had to let that symbol give her some comfort.

She was doing what she had to do. For herself. For her parents. For the life she deserved. It wasn't running away if it saved her sanity or kept her parents from worrying themselves into an early grave. Was it?

Grace took a deep breath and let it out, watching the small town of Carvelle fade away into cornfields and then into the larger town of Bluff City.

Grace preferred Carvelle's small-town charm, and the ability to survive without a car because everything was within walking distance, but Bluff City had its moments. The Mississippi snaked below the town, calm and lazy. The sun was shining and even some of the deserted brick buildings along the riverfront looked pretty instead of dilapidated or flood worn.

Or maybe that was just her appreciation for the damaged and neglected.

Jacob's house/office was an old Victorian nestled in the bluffs. Grace smiled as they approached the big building with curving edges and diamond windows. Five years had transformed it from a deserted, decaying eyesore to a shining white vision of the past. With the bluff to the side and the river beneath, it was downright gorgeous and a testament to the success of MC Restorations.

Her baby brother had built a business he loved. She tried not to let that be a source of bitterness for her. Sure, she spent forty hours a week cashiering at a gas station, but she also spent the rest of her free time happily painting. On occasion, she sold a piece, too.

She wasn't an abysmal failure, and she wouldn't let herself wallow in thinking she was.

Jacob pulled into the lot out back, and with the reality of the situation sitting in front of her, Grace tensed. Living with her brother was one thing; invading his business territory was another. Because Jacob didn't live or work in this house alone.

"You never did tell me how you got Kyle to agree to this." Jacob's business partner and roommate, Kyle Clark, wasn't her biggest fan. To put it mildly.

"He's a decent guy, Grace. I know you two rub

each other the wrong way, but he wasn't going to say no to this."

Grace stepped out of the car and looked up at the house that would be her home while she searched for some semblance of normal.

Yes, she and Kyle rubbed each other the wrong way. He was all repressed, cold impassiveness and she was, well, a normal human being with feelings. Feelings she expressed verbally and through her art.

She had no problem with people who were different from her, but Kyle was bound and determined to look down his nose at her and her choices. It never failed to rub her the wrong way.

Jacob gave her a nudge. "Come on. Let's get you settled."

It was cold enough to warrant wearing a coat, but Grace decided to tough it out without one. She hefted her bag onto her shoulder and pushed Jacob away from trying to carry her suitcase and painting-supply case.

They walked in the back entrance, which had once been meant for servants. The thought made Grace smile. She definitely belonged in the servants' quarters.

"Oh, do me a favor, don't tell Kyle about your gun. Not sure how well that one will go over."

She patted her bag. "Keep ol' Betsy on the downlow. Got it." Not a problem. She didn't go around announcing to the world that she could barely stand the thought of leaving her house unarmed. It wasn't something she was proud of. Fear lived and breathed inside of her, but shame and determination kept it buried.

Grace followed Jacob up the back stairs to the room he'd earmarked for her.

He stopped at the top of the stairs. "I had Kelly come in and do the interior design for your room."

"I told you not to do that."

He shrugged, pushing the door open. "The more rooms we have to show what we can do, the better. I just rearranged the order a bit."

"I'm sure Kyle loved that." The minute Grace stepped into the room, she forgot all about Kyle and his OCD tendencies. "Jacob, this is gorgeous." It was a tiny room—Grace had insisted on that. Not to mention its location had been the most practical choice in staying out of Jacob's and Kyle's hair. Their offices were on the other end of the long hallway.

Even if the room was tiny, it was absolutely perfect. She had a big window that overlooked the river. The light would be excellent to spend her mornings painting. The view was inspiring. Yeah, this was a little better than spending eight hours at Cabby's, then going home and painting by unnatural light in the basement of her little house.

Not that she'd had time to paint with her parents' constant hovering.

Grace took in the rest of the room. She'd expected the fuss and frills of the Victorian era, but it wasn't like that at all. The walls were a deep green with a gleaming white trim. The full-size bed was covered in a floral-print bedspread, but the little violets were so tiny and pale lavender, it didn't overwhelm the room. A small dresser stood in the corner with a ceramic lamp, delicately painted with more violets to match the bedspread. A lavender vase held a clutch of pink roses.

"I know it's a little girlie with the flowers, but Kelly said an artist could appreciate a little girlie. Even you."

Grace dumped her bags near the closet and grinned. No, she'd never been much of a girlie girl, but this was too pretty to resist. She was already planning out the colors she'd use to watercolor a hillside of violets to match the room.

"It's perfect. Perfect." She gave Jacob an impulsive squeeze. Leave it to her brother to make sure she wouldn't want to leave anytime soon.

"I even had Kelly leave the walls bare so we could put up something you paint here. Artwork inspired by the room itself. Clients will eat that up."

Grace was speechless and a little misty. She'd learned a lot in the past seven years, mainly how to protect herself, but she'd also learned firsthand that her little brother was one hell of a man when he wanted to be.

"You're here."

Grace turned and wrinkled her nose at Kyle standing in the doorway. It was a Saturday, and what was he wearing? Khakis and a button-up shirt. Who did that? If he ever deigned to wear jeans and a T-shirt, he might actually be kind of cute. In that preppy, brooding kind of way.

He'd filled out a bit since high school. Now instead of looking like a beanpole, he looked more as if he could be a marathon runner, lean but all muscle. He kept his blond hair cut very short, and his dark blue eyes always looked at her with the practiced disdain of royalty.

Which was crap because he was from Carvelle just like her and Jacob. Not only that, but he'd grown up in the trailer park while she and Jacob had lived in a small but cozy house in the nicer part of town thanks to two teacher parents.

But Kyle always went on about wine and opera and every pretentious thing under the sun with his clients, as though he was from somewhere cultured and fancy. He seemed to go out of his way to make people think he was something better, shinier and more important than a boy from a trailer park.

Grace wanted to feel sorry for him and what little she knew of his difficult childhood, but Kyle did everything in his power to pretend that his years in Carvelle didn't exist.

It rankled Grace's nerves the way he sneered

at her choice of clothes, or her tattoo, or the colorful strands of her hair. He seemed on a mission to make her feel like the gum he'd scraped off the bottom of his shoe.

She didn't deserve that treatment, and she'd never let him believe she did.

But he was agreeing to let her stay at his house. And she knew, mostly when her guidance counselor mother reminded her, that Kyle's attitude had to stem from some kind of insecurity. So she would try to be nice.

Try.

"Hey, Kyle."

"Grace. Welcome."

His tone was bland. He sounded like a butler in one of those boring British movies where nothing happens and people just look at each other longingly.

Whatever, Mr. Khaki Pants. "Thank you for letting me stay." Her gratitude was sincere, even if he wasn't one of her favorite people.

"Of course."

You're here. Grace. Welcome. Of course. Could the guy string more than two words together? Grace turned to the window and the pretty view below. It really was best now that he was so tight-lipped, because she had a bad habit of baiting him when he started talking about anything.

He shouldn't bother her. Grace knew that, but it

didn't change the fact that he did. All that conde-
scension and disapproval. It was human nature to
want to be contrary, wasn't it? She certainly wasn't
going to go the Kyle Clark route and dress and act
like some kind of stuffy, repressed robot just because bad things happened.

No. She lived in the moment, for the moment,
took everything she could from the moment. Screw
rules. If she wanted her hair to be fuchsia, so be it.
If she wanted to tattoo her face with an obscene picture, her prerogative. And if Mr. Stick-Up-His-Ass
frowned upon it, she most certainly did not care.

Grace flipped her hair over her shoulder, hoping
he noticed the cascade of color beneath the brown.

Mom's voice reminded her to play nice, and
Grace felt immediately contrite for her inner dia-
tribe. Sore nerve? Ugh. The guy was doing her a
favor; she was going to have to cut him some slack.
Or just avoid him at all costs. But right now, avoidance wasn't an option. "It's a great room. You guys
have accomplished a lot."

"Thank you."

Grace rolled her eyes at yet another two-word
sentence, but she bit her tongue. No need to get off
on the wrong foot her very first day.

Silence settled over the room and Grace sighed.
"All right, let's get this over with." She could feel
the pinned-up tension waving off Kyle and weigh-
ing heavily on the small corner room. She could

ignore it, or they could all get it out of their systems so the next few weeks went smoothly.

"What?" Jacob and Kyle asked in unison.

"Mr. Stickler over there probably has a list of rules for me while I'm here. Probably wants me to sign a blood oath I'll follow them, too."

Jacob looked at Kyle, then the ceiling. Obviously she'd been right.

"It's okay." She hopped onto the pretty bed, stretched out. "Lay 'em on me."

KYLE FROWNED. HE did have some ground rules for Grace, but even he wasn't rude enough to bring them up the minute she arrived. Especially when she was staying with them for such…sensitive reasons.

But Grace embodied everything Kyle worked so hard to rise above. No, she didn't just embody it, she embraced it. She flaunted it. He had a business to run in this house, and her image didn't match.

And if he kept telling himself that, he could ignore that Grace always put him off-kilter. Always prompted more response out of him than he wanted to give.

"I'm sure you have something to say about my tattoo," she offered. "You're always sneering at it."

He wanted to argue. He didn't sneer at it, per se. It was just so bright and…visible. That was fine for

Grace, it even kind of suited her, but Grace…Grace did not fit the ordered, muted world he wanted.

"Your tattoo is fine, but… Well, it's an image thing. We routinely have clients taking tours of the house. While your room will be off-limits for the duration of your stay, we may ask you to vacate it for scheduled tours. The kitchen and TV room are within the common areas. It's likely you'll be seen. Some people are put off by tattoos." Which was why no one ever saw his.

She lay back on the bed, resting her head on folded arms. The sleeve on her arm rode up so the tattoo was now almost completely visible. The faded T-shirt she wore had bunched up so that a smooth strip of pale skin was exposed.

Back in high school she'd been more curvy, but ever since her incident, as he preferred to refer to it, she'd changed. She was lean now, her body toned with muscle as if she'd spent a lot of time trying to purposefully bulk up.

Wasn't that what he'd done after his own… incident?

Kyle focused on the tattoo. "Well?"

"Well, listening to you talk reminds me of Mr. Mallory's boring science lectures. But I get it. Walk around in long sleeves to hide my off-putting tattoo. Next?"

He scowled. How did she manage to make his perfectly reasonable request sound so ridiculous?

"Next…" Kyle paused. She'd started this, but he was coming off looking like the jerk.

And that was why he hated to be around Grace. She always flipped things on their side. He could never control the situation. He'd spent eighteen years in a volatile, uncontrollable environment. He'd fought tooth and nail to get out, to make something of himself enough so that he was in control of his life.

Grace had an easy way of making him feel as though he'd failed.

"If you don't like my tattoo, I imagine you don't approve of my hair, either."

"It is rather colorful."

"And that's a problem?"

He tamped down his irritation. For whatever reason, Grace always pulled emotions out of him he usually found easy to repress. No one else in his life could do that even with their best efforts.

Well, except one person, but Kyle refused to acknowledge that little blip.

"*Problem* is a harsh word. Again, it's about image. We want our clients to look at this house, at us, and see professionals. Whether it's right or not, your tattoo, your hair, your clothes will reflect on us. It's not a professional look."

"Is this guy serious?" Grace demanded of Jacob.

Jacob fished his phone out of his pocket. "I

should call Mom. Tell her I got you settled in." He stepped out of the room.

"Coward," Grace muttered. She looked over at him now, her brown eyes assessing and obviously not impressed with the result.

"Bet you never thought you'd be alone in a bedroom with me," she said after a pause.

"No, I suppose not." Which wasn't exactly true. Before he'd left Carvelle determined to never, ever set foot in that hellhole again, he'd had a little thing for Grace. But like most things from his teenage years, Kyle had come to his senses and left it behind.

Grace let out a lengthy sigh. "I get it. You want me to be some business professional clone."

Kyle doubted it was possible. "Just during business hours."

She snorted, rolling onto her side and studying him. "Personality isn't a crime."

Personality Grace had in spades. She always had, but she'd changed over the past few years. Her personality had expanded, exploded, so that it was so big he felt choked when he was in a room with her.

"No, I suppose not."

"You could use a shot of it now and then." She grinned.

It was hard to take offense when she was right. He preferred not to have much in the way of personality. It was the best way for people to look at him as an efficient professional without wanting to get to know him better. Getting to know people always led to questions he didn't want to answer.

"Well, I'll leave you to settle in."

She nodded, closed her eyes. "Thanks for agreeing to this, Kyle. Really."

Kyle swallowed. It had taken some convincing on Jacob's part to get him to agree, so her thanks only made him feel like an ass. "No problem. I may be lacking in personality, but you're always welcome."

She might irritate him to no end, but he knew what it was like to go through trauma. Though he'd managed to keep them at a distance, the McKnights had always offered to help him. He owed the same to Grace. Whether he liked it or not. So he'd agreed to Jacob's one-month proposal, and hoped like hell that was all it took.

"Don't be so nice. I won't know how to act." She flopped back on the bed and took a deep breath, her chest moving up, drawing his eyes down to the deep V of her T-shirt. Quickly he stepped to the door and moved his eyes to the ceiling.

The last thing he needed to be noticing was his best friend's sister's breasts. Even if they were nice breasts. Well, weren't most breasts pretty nice? Good God, he needed to stop thinking about breasts.

He stepped out of the room before she could do anything else to put him off-balance.

Kyle walked down the long hall to his office. He didn't believe in wasting days on leisure. There was always something to work on for MC Restorations, and nothing made him more balanced than work.

Jacob was sitting at Kyle's desk, his battered sneakers resting on the gleaming wood. Kyle tried not to wince.

"So do I get an A plus?"

Jacob chuckled. "I give you a solid B. A for effort, though."

Kyle rolled his eyes. "Do you mind? I have work to do."

Jacob swiveled in the chair, planting his feet on the ground instead of Kyle's desk, thank God, but he didn't get up. "We've talked about this."

"Yes, we have, and we haven't come to an agreement. So you keep taking your weekends off and I'll keep working mine."

"You need to lighten up, dude. We made it. MC is doing great. We don't need to bust our asses with the seven-day weeks anymore."

"I'm light enough to suit me. And I work the amount of days I care to work."

"Come on. Tonight you should come out with me and Candy. It'll be fun."

"As fun as the last time you and Candy invited me out and I got ambushed by squealing Jenny?" As long as Jacob was dating Candy the Dictator, Kyle would be staying far away. He didn't understand Jacob's need for constant companionship. Being alone on a Saturday night sounded great to him, especially if Candy and her slew of single friends was the alternative.

Jacob held his hands up. "I had no idea that was Candy's plan until Jenny showed up. The squealing wasn't that bad."

"Every time the waiter brought something." Kyle imitated the horrible high-pitched squeal and Jacob hid a laugh with a cough. "It *was* that bad."

Jacob shook his head, but he was laughing. "You're too damn picky, man. Besides—"

"I'm not going. Shouldn't you at least be around on your sister's first night?"

Jacob frowned, swiveled back and forth in the chair. "Yeah, tell that to Candy. I tried to get Grace to come, too, but she and Candy don't get along."

"I can imagine." Kyle jabbed a thumb over his shoulder. "Now, if you don't mind."

Jacob rolled his eyes. "One of these days, you're going to have to let up."

"Well, one of these days is not today." Kyle slid into the chair Jacob vacated, feeling immediately better. This room, this desk, was indeed his happy place. Some people thought it was sad, but Kyle was perfectly content, so what did other people matter?

"I won't stay out too late, but keep an eye on Grace for me."

Kyle scowled. That was definitely not his first

choice, but he nodded if only to get Jacob out of his room. He had no doubt Grace could take care of herself.

Jacob left and Kyle booted up his computer. So it would be just him and Grace in the house tonight. Thank God it was a big house and Kyle had plenty of work to keep him occupied.

CHAPTER TWO

GRACE COULDN'T FOCUS on painting. She was restless and feeling a little weird about being in someone else's house, and Mom's constant texts kept interrupting her. Might as well give up.

She'd visited Jacob's place plenty of times, knew most of the house as well as her own, but she'd rarely spent the night. And she'd never been in the house knowing Kyle was around without Jacob to act as a buffer.

Grace poked her head out of her room. It shouldn't matter if Jacob was around or not. Kyle had agreed to let her stay, and even welcomed her, even if that welcome came with a set of rules.

Scowling, Grace tiptoed down the blue runner in the hall. "It's an image thing," she mimicked, stepping onto the second-story balcony. Who talked like that? Who thought like that? She didn't look like some crazed hobo. Tons of people had tattoos, many way more visible than hers, and the colored hair was definitely a trend right now.

Well, maybe not in Bluff City.

Of course, Grace could remember that Kyle's

parents hadn't dressed nicely and had been considerably inked, and his mother's hair had definitely not been natural. Even if Grace thought he should be over that connection ten years after they'd all gone their separate ways, maybe she kind of understood why they made him uncomfortable.

Grace took a deep breath of the cool April evening. She didn't want to think about Kyle anymore.

It wasn't quite dusk. The street below was narrow and lined with barren trees on either side, their bark rough and hewn from winter. Most of the houses on the street were the same sprawling Victorians as the one she was in, some still in good shape, a few not so much. She found them just as appealing with their vacant windows and fading paint as those MC Restorations had restored to be gleaming nods to the past.

It was a quiet little neighborhood on top of the bluffs, though the river was to the side of the house and she couldn't see it from here. Grace wondered why someone had designed a porch here. Had it been to watch the horses and buggies below all those years ago? Or perhaps to spy on the neighbors without having to talk to them.

Grace took a deep breath, smiling at the hint of spring she inhaled. Spring was the perfect time of year. Renewal appreciated warmth. She couldn't wait to see the uninterrupted sloping lawns turn to green, the trees slowly leaf out. The next month would bring a flurry of change.

And once things went back to normal, she would go home to Carvelle, to her little house in the middle of town. Her lawn would be green, too, and likely Mom would put a pot of pansies on her doorstep and plant some impatiens under her crab apple tree.

But...would things go back to normal? Would Barry finally be an unfortunate memory instead of a constant factor? Would her parents be the comforting, enjoyable people they'd been when Barry was in jail, or would she have to develop a more permanent plan? Or would she—

"Enjoy the moment, Grace," she said into the still around her. Why was it so hard?

A dot of red drew Grace's attention. Down the road a ways someone was jogging. Grace watched the figure, a man, get closer. Hmm. Not a bad view.

Despite the cool temperatures, there was a ring of sweat around his running shirt. He had broad shoulders and a body obviously—thanks to the skin-tight shirt—full of lean muscle. Loose gym shorts did nothing to hide the powerful legs that must have been used to a hard run. Grace never considered a man's legs particularly sexy, but watching muscles bunch and brace as his feet hit pavement, then pulled back up, might convince her to change her mind.

Leaning on the railing, Grace continued to enjoy the show and let her mind wander. Maybe he did this every night. Maybe she'd take up running, strike up a conversation. They could stretch each other out. Maybe...

Oh, crap.

So quickly she tripped over herself, Grace moved away from the railing. She squeezed her eyes shut and prayed fervently Kyle hadn't seen her ogling him. Kyle. *Kyle.* She knew he was runner skinny, but who knew that meant sexy and lean and yummy?

Oh, crap. She'd just called Kyle sexy. And yummy. She was going to be sick.

Well, it wasn't her fault he always dressed so formally she had no idea he was actually hot underneath.

Oh, crap.

Grace hurried back inside. She had to get back to her room as soon as possible. And maybe never come out again.

Of course, the universe wasn't done screwing with her, because she had to pass the top of the stairway she could hear Kyle walking up. Her brain went through a chorus of *oh, craps.*

Not knowing what else to do, Grace put her head down and powered past the stairs, determined to do one thing and one thing only: get to her room without falling any deeper into this weird alternate reality she found herself in.

"Grace." He sounded about as surprised to see her as she was to discover he was freaking hot.

Oh, crap. "Hey." She turned to face him. Beads of sweat dripped down his face. See? That wasn't sexy. He huffed in time with the beat coming from the headphones dangling from his neck. Not sexy at all. "Uh, good run?" Oh, God, she was an idiot.

He tugged at the collar of his T-shirt, looking about as uncomfortable as she felt. "Yeah. I... Yes." He nodded after the fact and kept fidgeting with his shirt collar.

"Great. I was just—" *plausible lie, plausible lie, plausible lie* "—going downstairs to make myself some dinner. Want anything?"

He shifted from one foot to the other, still holding on to his collar. What was that about?

"I usually just order in."

Grace waved that idea away, inching past him. He smelled like sweat and Irish Spring. Oh, crap. "I'll make enough for two. Feel free to help yourself." Why was her voice so weird and squeaky? And why the hell was she inviting him to spend more time in her presence?

"Sure. I, um, have to run through the shower first."

Well, now that she screwed herself out of re-treating to her room to determine what the hell had short-circuited in her brain to find Mr. Stuffed Shirt attractive, she had to go make herself, and him, some dinner.

Forcing one leg to follow the other, Grace took the first stair. She made the mistake of looking over her shoulder, accidentally making eye contact with Kyle, who was staring after her. She'd never noticed what a deep, pure blue his eyes were, and what the hell was wrong with her?

Grace whipped her head forward and took the stairs as quickly as possible. Distance seemed to be the best method to nip this crazy in the bud.

In the kitchen, Grace took a moment to lean against the wall and take a deep breath. This was weird, definitely, but not fatal by any means. So Kyle turned out to be more than just kind of cute. What did that matter? His personality hadn't changed.

Bolstered, Grace poked around in the fridge. Not much to work with despite the state-of-the-art appliances and an overall gorgeous interior. Aside from the stainless-steel fridge and stove, the room looked like it came right out of the 1900s. Dishwasher and microwave were hidden inside gleaming white cabinets with distressed brassy handles. Decorative copper pans hung from a pot rack above the oven, and the walls were decorated with antique prints of food. A display cabinet stood along one wall with a handful of old kitchen gadgets and green bottles.

There was a small restored table in the circular end of the kitchen, surrounded on three sides by windows overlooking the side yard and the bluff below.

Grace pulled out eggs and cheese and a green pepper for an omelet. It would be another great place to paint with the almost surrounding windows. She wondered if Mr. High and Mighty would deign to allow her to paint in this room, or would that ruin his precious image, too?

Grace smiled as she mentally patted herself on the back. She was back to thinking about Kyle in the normal way, not the "hey, my brother's stuffy best friend is surprisingly hot" way.

"I'm sorry we don't have much in the way of food."

Grace was startled, but hid it by pulling open a drawer blindly. She'd been in this kitchen quite a few times, but had never cooked in it. The pans had been easy enough to find, but she had yet to discover a spatula.

"I don't like to cook for one, and Candy's been keeping your brother busy the past few weeks."

"I'm surprised you cook at all." Was that mean? Was she being snippy? Suddenly she couldn't tell if she was engaging in banter or bitchiness. Not good.

But she was off-kilter. Not only had she never

seen him in shorts and a T-shirt during a run, but now he stood in front of her, hair wet from the shower, the smell of shampoo infiltrating her nose, and he was in track pants and a loose long-sleeved T-shirt. He wasn't even wearing shoes, just perfectly white socks.

It was downright…normal.

Grace opened another drawer at random, focusing on the task at hand. In other words, not think about Kyle as anything more than her brother's annoying roommate/business partner.

There were pretty little tea towels in this drawer. For a bachelor pad, it was quite the place. Of course, it wasn't a bachelor pad. It was their business, and no doubt their interior decorator had picked out the dainty towels.

"The drawer right next to the oven."

Grace looked up to find Kyle practically standing right next to her and only at the last second did she manage to keep herself from jumping away. "Huh?"

He opened the aforementioned drawer and pulled out a spatula. "Isn't this what you're looking for?"

"Oh. Right." She took it from his outstretched hand, being very careful not to accidentally make physical contact. That would just be weird. "Thanks." Grace avoided eye contact, instead focused on cracking eggs into a bowl.

"We keep a pad of paper in the cabinet over here for a grocery list."

Forced to look now, Grace turned her head and watched as he opened the cabinet and pointed to the pad of paper hanging on a hook inside of it. "Feel free to add to it."

"Sure. Thanks."

"I go Sunday mornings, so if there's anything you want for this week, you might want to get it down tonight."

Grace smiled a little at that. Of course he had a set grocery day. The guy was about as anal as they came. But he looked good in the casual outfit, though he didn't seem any more relaxed than usual.

He looked down at himself. "What?"

Heat stole up her neck so she quickly turned back to her omelet preparation. "What?"

"You're staring at me."

"Am not," she muttered before realizing she sounded like a whiny kid.

"I don't wear a suit to bed, if that's what you're thinking."

She snickered because he'd actually made a joke at his own expense, but it didn't last long because thinking about Hot Kyle plus what he wore to bed was bad news.

"Is that on your schedule, too? 'Wear normal clothes Saturday evening.'" She wouldn't be surprised. He probably even had a certain day of the week for sex. Oh, crap. *Danger! Danger! Do not think about Kyle and sex in the same sentence.*

She focused on the knife in her hand and the green pepper that needed slicing and willed every synapse of her brain away from images of Kyle's powerful legs; flat, lean stomach; serious blue eyes.

She almost squeaked when Kyle stepped behind her. She could hear him breathing as he watched her slice the green pepper. She felt as if she was in a cooking class and he was the teacher analyzing her technique. Which was good. When he was being all judgmental, she had no desire to picture him naked.

Oh, crap.

KYLE WATCHED AS Grace haphazardly cut up the green pepper. It took every ounce of control to keep from telling her she was doing it wrong, but knowing Grace she'd just do it even more haphazardly to annoy him if he pointed it out.

Since he'd already run five miles this evening because he couldn't focus on work thanks to Grace and all her innate Grace-ness, he wasn't about to let her get under his skin anymore.

She was just so unpredictable. And not the kind of unpredictable he could troubleshoot. He never knew when she was going to scowl at him, poke fun at him or smile brightly at him in a way that made him uncomfortable. A discomfort he'd spent a lot of time ignoring the past few years.

Kyle pulled out a dish towel and stepped toward

her to lay it on the counter so she would take the hint and use it instead of wasting another handful of paper towels. You'd think he'd slapped her on the ass the way she flinched.

He stared at the tattoo on her arm, because if he didn't he might be tempted to look at her ass, and, well, adult Kyle didn't do such things.

Besides, she was acting a little strange this evening. Jumpy. Maybe Barry being out of jail was getting to her. He should probably make a point to be nice, and make her feel that she wasn't alone. He still wasn't too happy about Jacob's bailing and leaving the responsibility to him, but Kyle wasn't selfish enough to not be honorable.

Grace had made the first step in being friendly, offering him some of the dinner she was making. So he would try to follow suit. Even if they were very different, they did have to cohabit for the next month, and Kyle would really prefer a smooth, non-confrontational thirty days.

And yes, he was counting down.

He collected two plates and silverware and set the table. What could they talk about over dinner? Jacob was about the only thing they had in common, and it seemed strange to discuss him when he wasn't here.

There was art, of course, but he'd tried that before. She always wanted to discuss the impressionists and modernism. Most of what he knew about art stemmed from his reading on the Renaissance period or still lifes. He'd never been one for the fanciful. "What would you like to drink? I could open a bottle of wine."

"Uh, I'll just have milk."

Milk. Well, a discussion of wine was officially off the table. It occurred to him that they could discuss their shared past. Growing up in Carvelle, high school, but Kyle had made the decision a long time ago not to talk about those things. Then he could pretend his childhood there had never happened. That he wasn't Kyle Clark of the Rosedale Trailer Park, where his parents were quite famous for all the wrong reasons.

"You okay?"

He blinked, realized he was standing in front of the open refrigerator not doing anything. "Of course." He pulled out the carton of milk and focused on pouring drinks and gathering napkins.

"Oh."

He turned to see what she was commenting on, but she just stood there, pan in hand, staring at the table. Then she laughed.

Kyle frowned, looking at the table himself. What on earth was she laughing at? "What?" he demanded.

She shook her head and stepped over to the table. Still laughing, she put half the omelet, which now resembled scrambled eggs with stuff in it because she'd done it wrong, onto his plate, then the remainder on hers. "You're just kinda weird, Kyle."

Irritated and defensive, he locked his jaw tight. He would not lose his temper, or point out that if someone in this kitchen was weird, it was most certainly not him.

"Actually, *weird* is a bit harsh. Quirky, I guess."

He stared. "I'm quirky?"

"You know, in a totally anal, rigid kind of way." She slid into a seat, didn't bother to put a napkin in her lap before lifting her fork.

"I see."

"Kind of odd for a guy who grew up in a double-wide." She shoveled in a bite of food, and though his stomach rumbled after his long, difficult run, he didn't make a move for the table.

This was one of the many reasons that, despite her unfortunate circumstances, he hadn't wanted Grace here. Of the very few people in his life who knew a little bit of his childhood, she was the only one who'd yet to take the hint that the topic wasn't open for discussion and never would be.

"You give them too much credit. It was a single-wide."

She blinked at him. "Wow. That's the most I've heard you talk about the past since you left Carvelle."

Irritated the comment had slipped out, Kyle scowled. "And it's the very most you ever will." He turned to the stairwell. He would go do some work. Work would calm him down. But before he could take another step, Grace's voice interrupted him.

"Aren't you going to eat?"

It was the last thing he wanted to do at the moment, but letting his irritation show only served to increase people's curiosity. Kyle returned to the table, telling himself to make sure bland Kyle was in fine form tonight. "Yes, of course."

As he droned on about foreign markets, boring even himself, Grace retrieved a pen and the pad of paper for grocery lists. She shoveled eggs into her mouth and scribbled intently until he was done with his monologue.

She pushed the paper across to him, and he was forced to look into her amused smile for a moment. She was like a tractor beam with that smile, all pretty, cheerful goodness. He could not let that get to him.

He looked down at the paper. It was a drawing, no, a caricature of him. She'd overemphasized his square jaw, drawn little money signs over his head, and in the background was a quick sketch of her with z's filling a thought bubble above her head.

He didn't want to smile, didn't want to find it funny. Hell, it was funny, and the smile won over the impassive expression he'd been working so hard to keep.

"Is that a little glimpse of a sense of humor?"

Grace feigned shock. Or maybe it wasn't so much feigned as exaggerated. He wouldn't be surprised if she was shocked.

"Don't know what you're talking about." He lifted a bite of egg to his mouth, trying to tamp down the amusement, the…lightness Grace seemed to infuse the room with.

She was a temporary visitor. This wouldn't become normal. He wouldn't let her so effortlessly invade his carefully erected protections.

No smiles, no jokes, no long, alluring legs could make him forget who he was. What he was. His soul was empty, and there was no chance of his risking filling it again.

At least he kept telling himself that, even as he folded up the drawing and put it in his pocket.

THE VOICES WERE LOUD. So damn loud, but then they always were. Kyle heard the sounds of crashing glass mixed with screams. Darkness morphed into the tiny room of a trailer and screams formed words.

"You stupid slut. Did you think I wouldn't find out? Who do you think you are, you whore?" A thud pounded against Kyle's bedroom wall. He closed his eyes, turned his music louder.

"You and your two-inch dick have screwed every willing meth addict in this damn place." More crashing glass. A scream.

"I'm going to kill you. This time I'm really going to kill you."

Kyle swallowed down the bile that rose to his throat. How many times had he heard that? Too many to count, but the sound of angry footsteps heading toward where he knew Dad kept at least two guns, loaded, struck real fear through him.

He was sick and wobbly, but he pitched to the door and stepped into the hall. He saw his father, a big, thick tree trunk of a man, weaving this way and that, drunk or high or both. Kyle had seen him this way before, but not with-it enough to have murder in his expression. Until now.

Something glass knocked into his father's skull, splattering glass and blood everywhere.

"You bitch!" his father howled, turning back to the front of the trailer. Even though blood dripped down his neck, he stalked back to where Kyle knew Mom was waiting.

Not sure who he was trying to save, if anyone, Kyle scrambled for his parents' bedroom. He fumbled with a drawer, pulled out the gun with his shaking hands.

End it, his mind whispered. *End it.* Fear was replaced by something steely and steady in his gut. His hands stopped shaking and his feet led him to the living room. There was no shock in seeing his father's hands around his mother's neck as her legs flailed and her eyes bulged.

Kyle walked right up to his father and pressed the gun in his back. "Stop." His voice wasn't steady, wasn't even a command, and his father looked over his shoulder at him and the gun with a sneer.

"You wouldn't shoot me, you pansy-ass piece of shit." Kyle jumped back as his father's hands dropped from his mother's neck and reached for him.

"Try me." He held the gun steady, trained on his father's head. He wanted this. He wanted to pull the trigger and end everything once and for all.

The sound of sirens stopped him and the world went black.

When Kyle woke up from the nightmare, he flipped on every light in his room. He sucked in a breath, let it out slowly. As nightmares went, it was tame enough. Nothing more than the truth. Nothing as jarring as when the dreams turned to fiction and he pulled the trigger. Killing his father and feeling immense satisfaction in it.

Kyle swallowed down the nausea rushing up his throat. Even though his legs were weak, he purposefully strode to his office. He flipped on every light there, too.

His hands shook, but he brought the computer to life and began to type a memo to Leah, Jacob's go-to electrician.

He worked for an hour before he was moderately confident the dream wouldn't return. Between his five-mile run and the two hours of sleep he'd managed before the dream, surely he'd be exhausted enough to sleep soundly now.

He shut down the computer and turned off the lights, but when he stepped into the hallway he heard a thud come from down the hall. From Grace's room.

Worry leaped to action, but reasonable Kyle kept it tamped down as he slowly made his way down the hall. Another thump was followed by a crash. Kyle jogged the last few strides and knocked on Grace's door, his heart beating too fast for comfort. "Grace?"

She mumbled something, there was another thump, and then she opened the door, light from her room pouring into the hallway. She looked disheveled by sleep, her hair a tangled mess, her too-thin tank top's straps hanging off her shoulders.

"Are you all right?" Since he was doing everything in his power not to look at her bare shoulders or below, he studied her face. She looked pale, and she was shaking. Kyle frowned. "What's wrong?"

She hugged herself and shook her head. "Nothing. I'm fine."

"Sit," Kyle ordered, pointing to the bed. He noticed her easel was upended and deduced that it had been the source of the crash. He also saw a half-empty water bottle on the floor, picked it up and shoved it at her. "Take a drink."

Surprisingly, she obeyed by taking a long, loud gulp. Because her damn shirt was practically see-through, he pulled the coverlet tangled at the end of the bed over her shoulders. "What happened?"

"I had a dream. That's all. It woke me up." She was still pale, shaking, lost. Since he knew the feeling all too well, he sank onto the bed next to her. Reminding himself it was just a friendly gesture, he put his hand on hers.

"What happened over there?"

"I was trying to get to the light, but I tripped." She let out a loud shaky breath. "And it hurt like a bitch," she squeaked, obviously losing the battle with tears.

He'd been there a few times himself. So he patted her hand and let her cry, one part of his brain telling him to comfort her, the other telling him to run away. Instead, he was frozen. Offering half comfort.

When she was breathing almost evenly again she pulled her hand away and mopped up her tears with the backs of her hands. "I guess bad things have a way of sticking with your subconscious."

As he well knew. What he didn't know was what to say. Actually, he did know what to say; words of commiseration fumbled through his brain. "Yes, they do."

"If I wasn't loud enough to wake Jacob, you must have been awake already. Bad dreams, too?"

She was close and smelled like paint and flowers, and the words fumbling in his brain wanted to get out, but he couldn't. If he let them out, they would never go away. And she'd know and… Kyle stood abruptly. "I should get back to bed. Early day tomorrow."

"Kyle."

But he couldn't stop. He had to be alone where he could beat back the words and images and everything else. Where Grace's pretty face and direct questions didn't tempt him away from the protections he'd built.

CHAPTER THREE

KYLE TRUDGED DOWN the back staircase, the smell of coffee a shining beacon after a terrible night. If he'd gotten three hours of patchy sleep he'd consider himself lucky.

Voices drifted up the stairwell, and when Kyle reached the bottom he found Jacob and Grace sitting at the kitchen table laughing over cereal.

His stomach cramped at the realization that mornings in the McKnight household were likely always like this. Bright, cozy laughter. With last night's dream still flashing vividly through his mind, it was hard to swallow.

What had mornings been like in the Clark trailer? Overpowered by the stench of alcohol or drugs and vomit or piss. A quiet so deep and lonely, but safe. Blissfully safe.

Without greeting, Kyle walked over to the coffeepot and poured himself a mug. He felt too sick to his stomach to take a sip.

"Hey, man, you okay? Looking a little green."

Kyle turned, tried to smile, but knew it came out a grimace as he saw two pairs of brown eyes staring at him. He didn't want to be studied or worried about at the moment. Especially not by two perfect people.

Not that either were *perfect* perfect, but they seemed that way in the aftereffects of a two-nightmare night. His encounter with Grace had left him primed and ready for nightmare number two, and he'd woken feeling vulnerable.

Kyle refused to do vulnerable.

"Kyle?"

"Right. I'm fine." He forced himself to take a sip from his mug. "Just needed a little jolt." He lifted the mug, attempted another smile.

Grace shook a box of cereal at him. "Going to eat?"

He had no desire to fill his already queasy stomach with sugary cereal to go along with the bitter coffee, but he also didn't want to appear rude. With a tight smile he retrieved a bowl and his own cereal, sans marshmallows, and took a seat next to Jacob.

"You even eat anal cereal," Grace said, shaking her head. She was still in pajamas—that too-thin tank top that allowed the white bra underneath to be visible, and way-short shorts that showed off a mile of pale, smooth leg. Kyle focused on pouring the cereal in his bowl.

Jacob snorted. "Anal cereal?"

"Okay, that sounded gross, but you get what I mean. The only person I've ever seen eat generic bran flakes is Grandpa. Do you buy them on double-coupon day, too?"

"No." Her syrupy sweet voice was meant to bait him, and no matter how raw he was feeling this morning, he would not give in to the urge to bite. "You know, on days we run a business here it would be best if you got at least half dressed before leaving your room." Okay, apparently he was going to bite.

"Not a morning person, then?" She lifted a heaping spoon to her lips, but his eyes were drawn to her pretty much bare leg swinging back and forth while the other was curled under her. Could those things she was wearing really count as shorts?

Kyle concentrated on pouring milk onto his cereal. "I prefer solitude in the morning."

"It's true. I usually can't get a word out of him before ten. Even for business. He'll just email me a memo."

Grace rolled her eyes, kept swinging that damn leg. "I bet Kyle sends a lot of memos."

"Thank God for email, or I'd be drowning in paper."

It took a lot more effort than it should have to tear his gaze from Grace to Jacob. "So from here on out should I expect the two of you poking fun at me to be my morning greeting?"

Jacob grinned. "It is the McKnight way."

"Wonderful." Kyle poked at his cereal. He wasn't

remotely hungry. Nor was his edgy mood from his dream assuaged any by Grace's and Jacob's teasing. So he would focus on what would. "The Porters sent pictures this morning. I uploaded them onto the website."

"You don't even take Sunday off from talking about work? What about it being the day of rest and all that?"

Kyle gave Grace a bland look. "Time is money. The more time I work, the more money I have to put into this business."

"Work, money, work, money." Grace dismissed it with a wave. "Snore."

"Yes, I'm sure doing your little paintings and calling it art is quite scintillating, but some of us do have to make a living." He knew the words were too harsh the minute they were vocalized. This was exactly why he preferred to be alone in the morning. Time and quiet to shore up his defenses.

"So is this what *I* have to look forward all month? You two going at each other?"

"I thought it was the McKnight way." Kyle rubbed his temple, where a headache was brewing. A perfect addition to the unsettled stomach and gritty-eyed lack of sleep.

Jacob shook his head and made a *tsk-tsk* sound. "Banter is the McKnight way. We poke fun at your anal-retentiveness. You don't fight back with an insult. You should make fun of my dating history or Grace's hair. You know, unimportant stuff."

"Hey, what's wrong with my hair?"

Jacob gave his sister a doleful look. "You've got a freaking rainbow in there."

Grace snorted. "It's called self-expression. At least I don't look like some low-end catalog model."

"See." Jacob grinned at Kyle. "Banter."

Kyle failed to see the appeal. Or the difference. "Yes, well, like I said, some of us have a business to run."

"I hope it keeps you warm at night, Kyle." Grace pushed away from the table. "Or maybe you're just part robot. A very lifelike C-3PO." With that parting comment, Grace sashayed out of the kitchen, hips swinging in those foolish tiny shorts.

He wondered if she did it on purpose, the skimpy clothes, the hip sway. Just another level of torture to go along with her "banter." *Oh, hello, Kyle, not only am I wild and unpredictable, but look at my perfectly toned ass. I know you'd like to get your hands on it.*

"Kyle, do me a favor." Jacob clamped a hand on his shoulder, scattering Kyle's less-than-honorable thoughts. Jacob squeezed. Hard. "Don't look at my sister's ass."

Heat flashed up Kyle's face as he tried to argue with Jacob's retreating back. "I wasn't—"

But Jacob had already taken to the stairs, and unfortunately, the argument would have been a lie.

Damn it, he had been staring at Grace's ass.

TEN HOURS LATER and Grace was still fuming. Kyle had the nerve, *the nerve,* to call her painting "little." To roll his eyes at what she loved, what she slaved over, her passion. Because he was so much smarter with his business and money and blah, blah, blah.

She'd show him where he could shove his time-is-money speech.

Grace sat on the second-story balcony cross-legged, watching the street below. At first she'd forgotten about the insult, but then Jacob had left and Kyle had informed her he was going for his evening run and he'd set the security alarm.

Being alone in the big house had led to thinking about Barry. Had he gone back to Carvelle? Did he hold a grudge against the woman who'd testified against him?

Grace shuddered. That was when she'd begun to focus on Kyle's insults, on exacting revenge. Because it was way better than thoughts of Barry. Every once in a while a smidgen of conscience would poke through, reminding her Kyle wasn't 100-percent jerk. He'd come to her room after her bad dream to check on her, even offered a weird kind of comfort.

But if she let herself be rational, she started

thinking about Barry. So here she was, waiting for Kyle to come back. He'd already been gone twice as long as the night before. Where the hell was he? She was good and ready to show him just how childish she could be.

Her phone buzzed. She looked down at the text display, relieved it was Jacob, not Mom or Dad. Will you call me around ten and demand I come home? Grace rolled her eyes. Jacob needed to grow a pair when it came to his less-than-charming dictator of a girlfriend.

Balls. Get some. When he only texted back a curse, she smiled. At least there were some ways her little brother still needed her.

Grace checked the time. She'd been waiting for forty-five minutes now, and neither parent had texted. One day and things were already different. Maybe it was a sign she should just let it go. Prove her point in some less silly way, just be happy this little plan of getting out of Carvelle was working. She stood for one more scan of the street and grinned.

There he was, in the distance. She purposefully focused on the two buckets she had on the patio table. Watching him run could be...distracting, and she wasn't going to be distracted.

She picked up one bucket of lemonade, and when he was close enough, she put her plan into action.

"Hey, Kyle?"

Right as he looked up, she upended the contents of the bucket over the balcony. He tried to move out of the way, but surprise allowed most of the contents to hit their target. When he didn't move, instead just stood there holding his arms out as liquid dripped off, she upended the other.

"Damn it, Grace. This is not funny." He shook his fist at her, which made him look even more ridiculous, and she doubled over in laughter.

"By the way," she said, struggling to stop laughing enough to speak, "it's not water."

When he dropped a very loud F-bomb, Grace laughed even harder.

He peeled off the wet shirt, cursing impressively for a repressed suit. But her humor was short-lived when the chorus of *oh, craps* returned. Because she hadn't exactly expected him to take off his shirt and give her a firsthand view of the hard plane of his chest or the slight ridges of his abs.

And his shoulders without a stupid polo or button-up were quite impressive, and that tattoo? Well, that was—

Wait a second.

"You have a tattoo!"

He quickly flung his wet T-shirt over his shoulder, hiding the black mark of ink before she had a chance to make out what it was. "No."

"I saw it!"

"No, you didn't." She opened her mouth to argue,

but he was stomping away. Delighted with herself for finding out Mr. Stuffy had a wild side, Grace scurried into the house, determined to find him before he could put his shirt back on.

Kyle had a tattoo. The very thought made her giggle. She bounded down the stairs, hoping that the design was something hugely embarrassing. A butterfly. Fairy wings. A unicorn. Oh, the possibilities of her imagination were endless.

All the crap he'd given her about her tattoo and he had one. It was too great. She laughed again, unable to stop herself.

She managed to get to the bottom of the stairs just as he stepped into the house. The shirt was still draped over his shoulder.

"You have a tattoo," she repeated, poking a finger at him. "I saw it." She tried to reach for the T-shirt to pull it off his shoulder, but he was too fast and stepped away. "Come on. Let me see it. After all the crap you've given me about mine, I deserve to see what yours is."

"The difference is I don't flaunt mine." He turned his back to her, tried to exit on that line, but she grabbed his shirt in the nick of time, starting a tug-of-war with him. He won, but had to turn in order to do so. When he faced her, his eyes were blazing angry, his scowl wedged so deep, grooves appeared around his mouth.

A smart woman would back off. He was livid.

It was the principle of the thing as much as it was fascination in making Mr. Reserved and Stoic lose his cool. "Don't be such a baby about it." She tried to snatch the shirt again.

His hands clamped around her wrists. "Knock it off," he growled through clenched teeth.

It probably said something wrong about her that his authoritative directive and his big hands around her wrists caused a slow, tingling sensation of awareness to flow over her skin.

"I just want to see it." She blinked up at him as he stepped close enough to her that their knees were touching. She could smell the lemonade on him, feel the sticky sugar of it on his hands. If she leaned just a few centimeters forward, her breasts would brush his wet, sticky chest. The tingling of awareness went deeper now, became more of a longing.

"It was a stupid mistake I made a long time ago. Forget it." His voice was low and strained, as if it was with great effort he spoke at all.

His eyes, that dark, intense blue, held her gaze. She was tempted, so damn tempted, to close the little distance between them. The weirdest thing though was, from the way his eyes held hers, the way his jaw clenched tight as if he was holding back, she had a feeling he was just as tempted.

It was hard to catch a full breath with her heart beating so damn fast, and when she spoke it came out breathless. "Are you thinking about making another stupid mistake?"

He didn't speak or move for a full thirty seconds. She knew, because she was counting. It was the only thing that kept her from imagining what it might be like to let him touch her, press his mouth to hers.

His hands gentled on her wrists, and then he let them go. He exhaled loudly. "I don't make stupid mistakes anymore," he said flatly.

Grace swallowed, all too afraid regret was the feeling washing through her instead of relief. She took a deep breath, determined her parting comment would be flippant. He didn't need to know she would have been more than willing to go at it on the floor with him.

"Too bad." She flashed him a saucy smile and then flounced out of the kitchen. But when she made it to her room, she collapsed onto her bed and let the *oh, crap* chorus take over.

Except, even as the *oh, craps* rattled around in her mind, she found herself smiling. It might be kind of fun to poke at this weird attraction. It would be downright fascinating to see how Kyle responded.

When her phone buzzed, she didn't even care that it was Mom.

KYLE KEPT HIS entire body tense as he walked through the house and up the front staircase. He had to focus on the anger, the fury, or he might be all too tempted to follow Grace up the back staircase.

And then...

Well, he didn't want to think about "and then." He wanted to think about what kind of idiot made two buckets of lemonade and doused some unsuspecting victim with it. He wanted to think about why his best friend's sister was such a royal pain in the ass and why that was suddenly his problem.

He managed to think all of that. At least until he stepped into the shower and the warm spray began to soothe the tense muscles. The smell of lemonade dissipated, but the smell of Grace did not.

Damn it, he didn't want to know what she smelled like. Something sweet and light and intoxicating. Kyle rested his hands on the cool tile of the shower wall, let his head hang. The anger washed away with the lemonade, leaving something that might have been pleasant if it weren't so unnerving.

Calmed and relaxed by the warm water pounding into his back, the moment played over for him. When they'd stood there, so close his breath had fluttered the hair around her face, she'd looked at him as if...as if she felt some inkling of that same jolt. As if he wasn't her brother's stuffy, boring roommate.

He liked that look way too much. Kyle wrenched

the water to cold for a few minutes, then stepped frigid and shivering into the bathroom. Grace was off-limits for a lot of reasons. She was his best friend's sister. She was the antithesis of everything he looked for and respected in a woman. And no matter how often he forgot it when she was poking at him, there was a very serious reason she was here.

A reason he was all too familiar with. How many times had his father been released from jail, leaving Kyle with the sick fear he might show up and ruin this amazing life he'd worked his ass off for? How many times had Dad gotten close to doing just that?

Too many. When a man was constantly getting locked up for petty drug charges, releases were quick and inevitable. The only reassuring part was that dear old Dad always wound up back in jail. It was the one thing Kyle could depend on. It just sucked to be dragged into a knock-down, drag-out fight every damn time.

Kyle stepped out of the bathroom, realizing with a sigh that he'd tracked a mess through the house. So intent on distancing himself from Grace and her melted-chocolate eyes he'd completely forgotten he'd been covered in sugary liquid.

Well, good. It would give him something to concentrate on that wasn't his father or Grace or the strange way life gave him an insight into what she might be feeling.

Kyle began to clean the drips, following a trail from his bathroom, down the hall and stairs. When he reached the kitchen, he stumbled a bit. Grace was already there, mopping up where he'd dripped by the door.

Kyle cleared his throat. "I was going to do that."

She bobbled the mop. "Oh." She turned around, blinked a few times. "Well, I did kind of make the mess."

They stood in awkward silence on opposite sides of the kitchen. Kyle wished he could muster up some of the anger he'd felt earlier. Mainly he just felt tired and confused.

"I'll help."

He washed off the rag he'd been using. Crouched on his heels, he began to wipe the splotches of lemonade off the tile. Somehow, they managed to meet in the middle where there was a rather big puddle. Because that was where they'd stood way too close and talked about mistakes.

Which he wasn't making anymore. Had to remember that.

Grace rested her head on clasped hands at the top of the mop, studying him. "Can't you at least tell me what it is?"

She had a knack for taking a completely benign moment and making it either infuriating or the other thing. The other thing he didn't want to think about. "No."

"Is it that bad? I mean, I'd think if it was something really stupid you could have gotten it removed by now."

"It's not bad. It's just none of your business."

She wrinkled her nose. "I wouldn't be so interested if you weren't being so weird about it."

"I'm not being—" Kyle stopped himself. She wasn't going to let this go, and what did it matter? What did it really matter if Grace knew? Kyle studied the woman in front of him. She represented everything he didn't want. Chaos. Letting her in on his own chaos drew her closer, and the closer she got, the harder she'd be to push away. The harder the chaos would be to control.

But she would be a thorn in his side either way, because she wasn't going to give up on this until she knew. Grace didn't give up on anything, even when she should.

She tapped an index finger against her elbow. Her nails were painted a bright, blinding orange.

"I imagine you got your tattoo to stand out?"

She frowned at his assessment. "If I wanted to stand out I'd get one on my neck or get a sleeve of them. I got mine because— Nope. No way, you're not turning this around on me. You're going to tell me one way or another."

"Has anyone ever told you you're pushy and ob-noxious?"

She grinned, her pretty face brightening with humor. "I live for those kind of compliments."

Kyle let out a breath. "It's a compass."

Grace furrowed her brow. "A compass? Like north, east, west, south?"

"Yes."

"Why a compass?"

He wasn't going into this. Not with her. "I don't know. I was sixteen with a fake ID. I didn't put a lot of thought into it." Liar.

"Of course you did." She shook her head so the tips of her rainbow-colored hair bounced out from under the layer of brown. "If you didn't care what it was, you would have gotten something stupid like barbed wire around your arm or Bugs Bunny on your calf. But you got a compass on your shoulder. It means something."

Kyle leaned back against the countertop, gripped it with his hands. He should walk away. He sure as hell shouldn't tell her why he'd gotten it. Why he kept it. It was none of her business and he was all too afraid it would be another notch in the already too-long "things we have in common" list.

"Let me see it," she demanded, pushing the bucket of water and mop to the edge of the kitchen. She leaned the mop against the wall, ignoring the little puddle she'd made when water sloshed over the side.

When she started walking toward him, he held out a hand. "Stop right there."

"Just let me see it." She batted her eyes. "Pretty please."

It took every ounce of effort not to smile at her. "Go to hell."

She snorted. "I'm beginning to think you're not as stuffy as you pretend."

Any threat of a smile vanished. "Yes, I am."

She cocked her head. "If you don't show it to me, it's going to be my mission to see it. Which means I might have to jump in on you when you're in the shower." She waggled her eyebrows and grinned as though she might even enjoy it.

Either he was going to have to show her or things were going to get strange, and at the moment showing her a small piece of himself seemed much better than delving into that strange.

Doing his best to scowl, Kyle pulled the collar of his shirt over his shoulder so the tattoo was visible. "There. Happy? Can you leave me alone now?"

She most certainly didn't leave him alone. Instead, she touched the tattoo lightly, with just the tip of her index finger, but he felt the force of that touch everywhere. A punch of awareness that had no business being associated with someone like Grace.

"I like it."

"Fantastic." His voice lacked the biting edge of sarcasm he was going for.

She traced the outline of the intersecting lines and he was painfully aware the simplest, most innocent touch from Grace was giving him an erection. Since he was no longer sixteen, it pissed him off. "Do you mind?"

"So why the compass?" She finally withdrew her hand, and his heated skin managed to cool enough that he could think rationally.

"What do you care, Grace?"

Her eyes met his, soulful and honest. "I don't know. I think there's more to you than you let on. You were nice to me last night. I think..." She tilted her head. "I think there might actually be someone I'd like to get to know under all that surface stuff."

He swallowed down the jolt of emotion. It was because she was curious, because it was a mystery, things Grace never let go. It had nothing to do with him. Surface or under the surface. People didn't care about him enough to get to know him. That was how he preferred it. Life wasn't messy that way.

"Just give me one reason why you chose a compass and I'll stop annoying you." She poked him in the stomach, a friendly jab. Certainly not a lover's caress. His dick didn't seem to know the difference. If he told her, she'd go away, and right now he wanted that more than his next breath. "To remind me to follow true north."

She frowned. "What does that mean?"

"You asked for one reason. That was it. Good night, Grace." He turned and walked out of the kitchen, using every ounce of control not to break into a run. Grace was requiring a lot of self-control on his part.

CHAPTER FOUR

GRACE STOOD IN front of her easel, frowning. Some-how the idea of painting the river below on a sunny day had morphed into something dark and violent.

She'd had another nightmare last night. Was it a nightmare when you were replaying an actual moment in your life? When it was just reliving a night that was supposed to be a simple third date but had turned into the culminating moment of the next seven years?

Grace squeezed her eyes shut. Seven years. This wasn't supposed to keep happening. At this rate, she'd have to go back to therapy, and she really didn't want to do that. Therapy had been great for her. It had helped her leave the house again and trust people again. Well, mostly. It had worked.

If she went back, it would be admitting defeat. Barry would win. If she had to have someone help her out of this pit of fear again, seven years were wasted.

She didn't want to remember, but the dream, the actual memory, crept back into her mind, infil-trated all those defenses she worked so hard at.

Even the paintbrush in her hand and desperate pleas of her mind couldn't shake it away.

You think you can break up with me?

She could still remember, dream or no dream, the exact sound of Barry's voice when he'd said those words. Cold. Detached. Creepy because he'd been so absolutely incredulous. As if it were so unheard of. He was in disbelief.

And then he'd gotten angry. Quickly. His expression had gone from wide-eyed incredulity to squinty-eyed fury.

You don't get to break up with me, Grace. I'm in charge here.

The first blow had hit her face before she could even brace for it. It had been so unexpected, so out of the realm of her expectations she couldn't even flinch away. His fist had just plowed into her face.

Pain and shock and fear. So much damn fear. Maybe she'd held up her arms trying to protect herself. Maybe she'd tried to fight back. The rest was really a blur. His fists. Pain. Crying. Yes, she'd definitely started crying because she didn't know what to do, or how to stop it.

Then blackness descended. She couldn't see, she could barely breathe. Every inch of her body was on fire with a sharp, blinding pain. Something connected with her rib cage, sending another shock wave of agony through her body.

Nausea coated her stomach and she could feel

the sickness rising, but she couldn't move her head, couldn't speak, couldn't cry. Both in the memory and in the present, she was paralyzed with the fear and pain.

Suddenly the pain left, replaced by a shocking cold nothing. *You're dead,* her mind said matter-of-factly, and for a moment she was glad. So glad the pain was over. What did it matter if she was dead?

But other people's voices began to silence her own. *Don't leave us, Gracie.* Mom's voice. *We love you, Gracie.* Dad's voice. *Fight. Fight for it. We need you.* Jacob's voice.

The pain rushed back, so quickly she couldn't breathe, but when she did manage a strangled breath the pain was soothed by their words of love. It was what had brought her back, those words. She knew that for sure. And there was a slight comfort in that, but it was a kind of comfort that had her sobbing in the here and now.

She could hear the fear in their voices, and she hated being part of the reason they'd been afraid. Hated that Barry had given them this kind of gut clenching pain that seven years hadn't erased.

Those years between then and now had not dulled the intensity of the dream/memory, only its frequency. It made sense she'd have it again knowing Barry was free. Free to do whatever he liked. But she hated that they were all living with this again.

She wiped at the tears on her cheeks, looking at the painting, now dark and dreary. She wouldn't let him have this, too. He had her dreams, her memories, her fear. But not this.

"Leak into my art all you want," she muttered. "You will not win." Grace carefully cleaned her brushes and put everything away. She'd break for lunch, call Mom for the daily check-in and come back ready to paint something different. Jacob's interior decorator and administrative assistant were adopting a baby soon. She'd paint them something bright and cheerful as a gift.

Grace headed down the stairs to the kitchen, but the ebb and flow of conversation stopped her at the bottom. When she peeked around the corner, Kyle and Jacob and a handful of their employees were sitting at the table.

It was odd to feel so out of place. She'd met everyone at the table many times, but it was rarely during business hours. She'd never walked in on what appeared to be a meeting.

And maybe she was too raw, too beaten down by the things that plagued her to force the kind of confidence she didn't really have.

To face Kyle after he'd been so decent and comforted her. Let her cry on his shoulder. Kyle. Of all people.

Grace looked down at her faded jeans and paint-splattered henley. The group at the table were all dressed in business casual, looking pretty and put together. Leah, the electrician, was wearing jeans and work boots, but even she looked more like a businesswoman than Grace with her hair pulled back into a perfect ponytail and silver hoop earrings.

Grace swallowed down the unwelcome wave of intimidation. Men with big fists and muscles were intimidating. People with college degrees and business savvy and elegant wardrobes were not.

Her feet didn't listen, because they refused to move.

"Gracie, don't be shy. We're just having a working lunch. Come on in and help yourself to whatever."

Grace tried not to wince at Jacob's words or Kyle's brief glance. A glance that seemed to scoff at the idea of *her* being *shy*. Which was right. She wasn't shy in the least.

Forced into action, Grace entered the kitchen. "Just going to grab a sandwich, then I'll go back to my room."

"Don't be silly." Susan, MC's administrative assistant, smiled. "We're just talking."

"Yeah. We only call it a working lunch to lure Kyle out of his office," Leah added, grinning wider when Kyle sent her a disapproving look.

"Yes, well, we were discussing the Martin house, if you forgot. I call that a working lunch."

"We can take a break," Jacob replied, patting

Kyle on the shoulder. Even Grace knew it was a sign for Kyle to lay off.

It didn't make her want to stay as it usually did. In the shadow of all of these people—successful people—Grace didn't feel much like yanking Kyle's chain.

Grace went to the fridge and made quick work of putting together a sandwich. She opened her mouth to excuse herself, but Jacob requested a Coke. When she brought it to him, he nudged her into the chair next to him.

"Sit. Eat. Relax."

Before Grace could retort, Kelly leaned closer. "I love your hair." Kelly touched the ends of a pink strand and Grace gave Kyle a triumphant look. He looked down at his bowl of vegetables.

Was he really sitting there eating a bowl of vegetables for lunch? Of course he was.

"Me, too." Susan patted her short black bob. "I wish I had the guts to do something different. I want to go platinum blond. Or maybe just shave it all off."

"You are not shaving your head. Our baby will not have a mother with a shaved head."

"Speaking of babies, I was thinking about painting something for your nursery, if you like. Have you picked a theme?"

"What a great idea! We haven't picked a theme yet. I want to do unisex and Susan wants to know the gender first." Kelly rolled her eyes.

"I guess if they're talking about hair and babies, that means we have to talk about sports," Jacob interrupted, leaning back in his chair. "How 'bout them Cubbies."

Leah booed and tossed a napkin at Jacob.

Instead of Kyle's joining the conversation, his mouth pressed into a firm line. "I think the business portion of this meal is over," he said stiffly. "I'll be in my office should anyone need me."

Though he didn't look at her, Grace felt admonished. As though somehow the conversation's devolving into something besides business was her fault. She looked helplessly at Jacob. "I'm sorry if I ruined your meeting."

"Don't be crazy," Leah said with the wave of a hand. "That's just Kyle."

"He has this condition. It's very serious." Susan shook her head and clucked her tongue. "The minute anyone starts having fun, his brain starts ticking like a bomb. Too much exposure to normal human interaction will give him an aneurysm."

Jacob patted her shoulder. "You know how he is, Gracie. Don't take it personally."

Right. It wasn't personal.

It sure as hell felt personal.

WHEN SOMEONE KNOCKED on the door frame of his office, the last person Kyle expected to see standing in the opening was Grace. Especially a frowning Grace.

"Are you busy?"

Yes. Very busy. Very busy trying to stop thinking about you. When she kept popping up, it was hard to manage. "Well, I—"

"It'll only take a minute." Since she didn't advance farther into the room, he felt safe enough to be gracious and nod.

"I'm sorry if I interrupted your business lunch. It wasn't my intention."

The formal words and the detached way she spoke shocked him enough to be rendered momentarily speechless. He opened his mouth and no sound came out.

"I only wanted to get some lunch. Next time, I'll be sure to avoid anything that might intrude on business. No matter what you think, I'm not here to interfere. So I'm sorry. I don't want to mess anything up or distract anyone or ruin your—"

"Stop."

"Stop?" Grace walked closer, confusion etched across her face.

"Stop...apologizing." Kyle shoved out of the chair. When he was sitting, she could stand too close. Standing, he could keep some physical distance.

"But I—"

"You didn't do anything wrong." Kyle was at

a loss as to what to do with his hands. He always knew what to do with his hands. They rested stiffly at his sides, but they seemed to have their own mind when Grace was around, so he shoved them into his pockets. "If I gave you the impression you were intruding, I apologize."

She cocked her head. "If I wasn't intruding, why did you get all weird? You were sitting and eating lunch until I came along."

"It's just…" Kyle cleared his throat. He felt oddly panicked. In the midst of panic, truth could escape. He did his best to lock it up.

"It's just what?"

"I just…" *Shut up!* his brain screamed.

"You just what?"

Kyle glared at her. "This is nothing new. We have a working lunch. They start talking about… things. Kelly and Susan talk about the surrogate or the baby. Jacob talks about whomever he's dating at the moment. Leah has something snide to say about Jacob's woman du jour and I…I leave."

"Why?"

Kyle swallowed. "Because that's what I do." It was bad enough he'd explained that much. If he explained she only made it worse, only made it harder to shut down and back away, chaos would break loose. The kind of chaos that always came with emotion and feelings and…life.

"Why?"

Kyle inhaled, trying to find some balance, some clarity. How had something so detached suddenly become about him and his many issues? "No apology is necessary for lunch. Now, if you'll excuse me—"

"If you're trying to make me not want to get to know you, you're really, really failing." She gave him a sympathetic pat on the elbow. "Get back to work, Kyle. We'll talk later." She grinned, and it felt like a threat.

CHAPTER FIVE

A KNOCK SOUNDED at the door, three precise raps. Definitely not Jacob. He usually pounded once and barged right in. Only Kyle would knock as though he was concentrating on the action.

When Grace opened the door, instead of finding Stuffy Kyle, she found Runner Kyle. Man, she really liked the way Runner Kyle looked. It made the man underneath, whoever that might be, even more appealing.

She leaned against the doorjamb and smiled brightly. "Hey. What's up?"

"I thought your mother was coming over this evening."

"Her meeting went late. We rescheduled for later in the week." Which had made the decision to stay with Jacob seem like a genius move on her part. If she'd stayed home, alone, in Carvelle, Mom never would have let a late meeting stop her from hovering. Things were better already. A few more weeks and Grace was sure she could go back home without devolving into a psychotic mess.

"Oh." Kyle frowned. "Well, Jacob is out with Candy."

Grace rolled her eyes. "I know. She practically strong-armed the little wimp into taking her to a movie. I have to say it's nice, though. Hovering is kind of what I moved out here to avoid. Jacob sure as hell isn't hovering."

Kyle looked around her room at the handful of canvases she'd propped against the walls. Usually, Grace was all for people looking at her art, but something about Kyle's scrutiny made her stomach clench. "Is there something you wanted?" she asked, hoping to get him on his way before she felt compelled to ask him what he thought.

"I'm headed to the gym. I'll set the alarm before I go, but I'll be gone longer than I usually am when I just run around the neighborhood."

Grace tried to act nonchalant. This was no different from when he ran in the early evening. Just because it was dark and she'd be alone for a few hours was no reason for this wiggle of fear to work through her chest.

"Grace?"

"Right, yeah. Go. I'll be fine." She tried to smile and failed while the wiggle intensified to a flop. "Can I come?" she blurted. She managed a casual smile instead of a wince of embarrassment. "I've been using Jacob's weights, but he's got sissy ones."

Kyle's mouth actually twitched into an almost smile. "If you'd like."

"Great. Give me ten minutes." She closed the

door before he could change his mind. As she changed, she refused to dwell on the fact that her heart was still racing and her palms were still sweating from the idea of being alone at night. Even after spending seven long years making sure no one could ever hurt her the way Barry had again, even with a loaded gun in her dresser drawer. Barry's being free sucked all the power from the things that once made her feel safe.

She'd deal with that later. When Barry's being free became normal and inconsequential. *Oh, please, God, let that happen.*

Dressed, Grace stood in front of the nightstand drawer, contemplating the gun. Usually she took it with her if she left the house, but with Kyle around she wasn't sure that'd be such a great idea. And she didn't know what kind of lockers his gym had. No, it was best to leave it behind.

And the idea shouldn't make her vaguely nauseous.

Pushing that away with the rest of her worries, Grace hurried downstairs to where Kyle was waiting. He leaned casually against the counter, checking something on his phone.

"You should ditch the khakis more often." Maybe if she goaded him into his typical disdainful eye rolls, she could ditch the panic and the insecurity in one fell swoop.

He gave her that condescendingly patient look. "I'll keep it under advisement. Are you ready?"

Grace nodded, feeling jittery and amped. Her body practically vibrated with it as she followed Kyle out to the car. She couldn't stand the silence. In silence, she could think far too much.

"So what do you do at the gym?"

She watched as he went through a precise routine of buckling his seat belt, turning on the ignition, adjusting the radio to a lower level, checking the street behind him. Was he precise in everything he did?

Grace had to fight back a giggle as her mind immediately jumped to sex. Well, at least her nerves weren't making her a total wreck.

"I swim Wednesday and Friday nights."

Grace took in the broad shoulders and thought of the muscled arms she'd seen when he'd peeled off his shirt the other day. Yes, she could definitely picture him as a swimmer.

"Are you one of those guys who do those run, swim, bike things? What's it called? A triathlon?"

"I have done them in the past, yes."

"Do you have the cute little bike shorts?"

He gave her a disapproving look. "No, I do not."

"Bummer." She grinned when he shook his head, his knuckles going white as he pulled into the lot of the gym. "You're so easy, Kyle."

"Great. Here." He handed her a little piece of paper. "This is a guest pass."

"You sure do think of everything, don't you?" she muttered. Even if she belonged to a gym and got guest passes, she was pretty sure she'd lose them before she ever had a chance to use them. Not Kyle, of course.

Grace followed Kyle into the Bluff City Fitness Center, impressed by the big, bright lobby. She usually worked out at the Carvelle High School weight room or track thanks to Dad's being the baseball coach. This place was twice as clean and smelled ten times better. No doubt the equipment would be superior, as well.

What had been a rash decision to avoid being alone wasn't turning out half-bad. Maybe if she worked out hard enough, she'd manage a dreamless sleep tonight. Kyle gave her the basic layout of the place before disappearing into the men's locker room.

Grace spent the next hour quite happily busting her butt on the weight machines. If after that she wandered over to the big windows overlooking the pool, it was only because the free weights were right there and she needed to check out if they were the brand she liked. If her eyes happened to scan the pool below and pick out Kyle's long, impressive arms slicing through the water, well, who the hell could blame her? Watching him do stuff might be a little on the creepy side, but jeez, it was better than the alternative. Thinking about Barry.

Instinctively, Grace scanned the people around the pool. Her blood turned to ice at the sight of a large man with black hair standing off to the side. Her stomach pitched, fear paralyzing her breath.

And then a little girl ran across the wet concrete with open arms and the man smiled, hoisting her up.

Not Barry.

Grace stumbled back into someone running the track around the weight machines. She mumbled an apology. *Not Barry. Not Barry. Stupid, stupid mistake.*

She closed her eyes, sucked in a breath. Well, seeing Barry where he wasn't hadn't happened since the trial. Grace opened her eyes, squinted at her shoes. She let out her breath, took another, easier this time.

Regression. Plain and simple. Unacceptable.

Grace took to the track and began to run. Hard. Eventually she would exhaust herself enough so the panic and fear and worry that this feeling would always be a part of her life would disappear.

Or at least hide away for a while.

Her lungs burned, her already tired muscles screamed, but Grace kept running. She wasn't going to stop until the pain drowned out everything.

KYLE CRESTED THE STAIRS, hoping Grace would want to stick around at least another thirty minutes so he could get some spinning in. He was toying with the idea of doing a Half Ironman in October, and he'd need to pick up the pace of his training.

Which wouldn't be all that hard with Grace underfoot. Exercise was far more appealing than enduring any more alone time with her. Somehow, it always ended up with him flustered, revealing too much. And worse was when she showed a hint of vulnerability. He didn't like what it brought out in him, this strange need to help and commiserate and smile. Worst of all, smile.

Kyle didn't commiserate and he didn't let people into the dark places of his mind, so it was best to avoid Grace as much as possible.

He scanned the machines, looking for Grace's rainbow-streaked ponytail and that ridiculously yellow, ridiculously tight exercise shirt she'd been wearing. He didn't see her on any of the machines, but he caught a bullet of yellow out of the corner of his eye.

She was running the track. Hard. His stomach did a sickening slow roll when he saw her expression. When he recognized it as panic and fear.

He should know. He saw that expression enough in the mirror. Not knowing what he was going to say, Kyle still found himself taking to the track and running until he caught up with her.

When he fell into step next to her, she actually flinched, stumbling over her feet a little. He reached out to steady her, but she jerked away.

"What are you doing?" she huffed out, not bothering to slow down once she'd regained her footing. Her face was red, her words barely audible through the gusts of breath she was sucking in and letting out.

"Take a break, Grace." Good Lord, how long had she been going at this pace? The breakneck speed was enough to have even a seasoned runner like him exert a lot of effort.

"Nope." But she began to slow. It took a while, another two laps, and then she was down to a normal pace. "What are you doing?" she repeated, breathing heavily. Sweat dripped down her temples, and her chest heaved with the effort to breathe.

"Hoping to keep you from having a heart attack."

"I'm fine," she snapped, a shot of temper so unlike her.

She looked so close to breaking down he was afraid sympathy might lead to the possibility of tears, and he was not at all comfortable with that. So he went for a different reaction instead. "Don't be obnoxious."

She stopped dead in her tracks so quickly he almost toppled over trying to stop with her.

The outrage on her face was short-lived, morphing into eyes filling with tears and a quivering lip.

Crap. Wrong tactic.

"I'm not done yet." She put her hands on her hips and took a deep hitching breath. "I'm not done yet."

He took a step away from her. *Just leave her alone,* his mind instructed. "All right." But his feet didn't listen to his mind, because he didn't take any more steps away.

"I just need..." Her voice hitched, but she shook her head as if to shake it off. "I just need..."

Kyle couldn't stand it any longer. Knowing all too well what it was like to fight those gnawing, oppressive feelings. The way they dug into every wound, making them deeper, more painful. It was too much to bear seeing those feelings on Grace. Gently, he took her arm and led her toward the stairs. "Come on. Let's go home."

He expected her to fight him, but she didn't. Perhaps she was too busy fighting the tears shimmering in her eyes.

He stopped in front of the locker room and she nodded in silent understanding. Forgetting his normal after-workout routine, he grabbed his bag out of the locker. When he returned to Grace, she was slumped against the wall, her eyelashes suspiciously wet.

He took her arm again, not sure why. Crying didn't make her incapable of moving on her own, but he didn't know what to say, so a friendly touch seemed the way to go.

Grace climbed into the car, her body tensed from head to toe. He slid into the driver's seat, and though the rational part of his mind told him not to look, he couldn't help himself. When it came to Grace, the other part of his brain too often took over.

She was curled up in her seat, forehead pressed to her knees. He opened his mouth to tell her to buckle her seat belt, but clamped it shut. He'd just drive with extra caution.

"I'm not going to cry." Her voice was muffled by her knees.

"Praise every available deity."

She laughed. "I like it when you're funny. It's much better than pretentious-asshole Kyle." She turned her face so her temple rested on her knees and she looked at him, just the hint of a smile on her lips.

He looked at the windshield. "I wasn't really trying to be funny."

"Things were fine when he was locked up." Her voice was a whisper. "No, they were good. Great. Why does it have to change?"

"The unknown tends to screw with us a lot more than what we know for fact."

"Yes! Exactly. I don't even know if he'd try to hurt me, you know? I mean, we'd only been on three damn dates, so it's not like I was the love of his life. Maybe he doesn't even care that I testified."

Her vigor faded and she slumped in her seat. "And maybe he does."

"Grace." What could he say? What was there to say? He knew the weight of uncertainty, the oppressive bulk of it. He remembered reading *The Crucible* in high school and thinking it felt a lot like the way being pressed to death must feel. Except lucky Giles had an end. This way, you just felt it all the time, that heavy weight, that struggle to breathe.

He'd done what he could to circumnavigate it, but he knew his way wouldn't fit Grace. She was too bright and vibrant to mold herself into something else, someone else. So he had no advice. Only silence.

"Did your parents beat you?"

The question didn't surprise him, but he never knew how to answer it. Had he been hit? On occasion. But beaten in the after-school–special sense? No. And now, well, it didn't constitute beating if he dished it right back. "Not exactly. What happened to us isn't the same." Not at all. Grace was innocent. He was not. "But I know what it's like to try to beat something and feel like you'll never win."

Grace rested her hand on top of his. Kyle let the feeling of human contact, human comfort, wash over him for a minute. Just a minute. Any longer and he'd take more than he deserved.

"Let's head home." Kyle lifted his hand from Grace's and turned the key in the ignition. Part of him wanted to see what expression he would find on her face, but fear bolstered the rational part of his brain and he kept focus on backing out of the parking spot.

"It's nothing to feel ashamed of."

But that was exactly what he felt, what drove him. Shame. Of everything he'd let happen in that trailer for eighteen years. Of everything his father still could bring out in him.

GRACE WAS SPRAWLED on Jacob's bed, painting her fingernails a bright purple. She was not thinking about Barry. She was not thinking about losing it at the gym. And she definitely wasn't thinking about Kyle being understanding and nice. About how he was more complex, more kind, more fascinating than she'd ever given him credit for.

Instead she was thinking about how she was going to wring Jacob's neck for ditching her again so she'd felt compelled to go to the gym with Kyle. Maybe he'd thought she'd have Mom for company, and maybe at the time she'd been happy he was giving her lots and lots of space, but still. He was a grown-ass man, and would it kill him to stand up to his girlfriend?

So a little payback was in order. Step one: fill his room with nail polish fumes.

Grace studied her purple nails and smiled. Mission accomplished. Step two: wait for him to get home and poke and prod him over being such a wimp when it came to women.

Jacob opened the door and immediately scowled when he saw the nail polish bottle. "Okay, what did I do this time?"

"Oh, I don't know. Ditch me every night this week ring any bells?"

He threw his keys and wallet onto the nightstand. "First, I thought you wanted space. Second, I know." Jacob sighed and kicked off his shoes. "I suck."

Grace frowned. It wasn't like him to give in to her so easily. "What's up with you?"

"You and Kyle will be happy to know that I broke up with Candy." Since she was sprawled across his bed, he took a seat on the floor, leaning his back against the wall.

Part of her did an inward jig, but putting on her big-sister hat, she remained outwardly neutral. "It's not like you to do the breaking up."

He tapped his fingers on his knee, frowned at the floor. "Even I can be forced into breaking up with someone when there's an ultimatum involved."

"What was the ultimatum?"

Jacob closed his eyes, bounced his head against the wall. "Idiotic."

"Ah, so it was about me."

He opened one eye and studied her. "Self-absorbed much?"

Grace only had to lift an eyebrow to have him deflating.

"Okay, maybe partially about you, and me wanting to stick around the house more than take her out."

"I know I should keep my mouth shut—"

"But you're not going to."

"She was awful." Not nearly good enough for her brother. He had a bad habit of being unable to do anything alone. She couldn't remember a time since high school when Jacob had gone more than a few weeks without a girlfriend. "She wasn't even nice."

"You're right." Jacob nodded solemnly. "I don't know. I just…" He shook his head. "It's not fun being alone."

"You're not alone."

"You know what I mean." He gave her a pointed look. "We seem to have opposite fears."

She folded her arms across her chest and flopped back on his bed. "It's not fear. I like being alone."

"You like not taking a risk."

She shrugged and stared hard at the ceiling. "So what?"

"So Barry was one guy."

Grace knew that. Intellectually. But the intellectual part didn't always win. She'd grown up with Barry, had known his family; going out with him should have been safe and easy.

But it hadn't been, and the fear that it could happen again meant even the prospect of a date made her break out in hives. The prospect of something new left her feeling like an insecure teenager.

Knowing it was so damn stupid didn't change how she felt, though.

She wondered how much Kyle dated. His trauma had stemmed from his family, but in all the years she'd known him, she couldn't bring to mind any women in his life. Maybe the mention of a date, but never a girlfriend.

Maybe he was gay. She smiled a little, thinking of the moment in the kitchen when he'd been awfully close, and just as affected as her. No, she didn't think that was it.

And wasn't it interesting that when she thought of that moment and Kyle, she didn't get that sick, nervous feeling over the prospect of something new?

"Do you know what happened to Kyle?" That wasn't what she'd meant to ask, but, well, why not ask?

Jacob pressed his lips together, his tell. Lying had never been his strong suit. "What do you mean?"

"When we were kids. I mean, I guess everyone in Carvelle knew his parents were into drugs and stuff, but what happened to him? What makes him…the way he is? Spill it."

"I don't know much, Grace. Kyle's not big on sharing. Why?"

She shrugged. "I just don't get him." And the fact that she *wanted* to get him wasn't something she wanted to analyze.

"Give it time. He warms up after a while. You get kicked around most your life, being a little stand-offish is how you cope."

"How come nobody ever got him out of there?"

Jacob sighed, got up and then pushed her legs to the side so he could plop onto the bed next to her. "I don't know. Bad stuff happens. You know that better than anyone."

Yeah, she did. Maybe it would be best to leave it at that, but Grace didn't really have that kind of self-control.

"Should I be worried about this weird thing you and Kyle have going on?"

Grace studied her toes. "What weird thing?"

"Give me a break. You're sitting here asking about him. Then there's the staring, the bickering, the very careful not staring. I may be a guy, but I'm not blind."

"You're a *sensitive* guy, though."

Jacob elbowed her calf and she laughed. "You're a catch, little brother. Stop dating anyone who walks by and maybe you won't keep ending up alone."

"She wasn't that bad. All the time."

"I wanted to tell her to go to hell every time she pranced around on those fancy heels wrinkling her nose at me." Grace smiled blandly. "But because I love you, I didn't."

"I wanted to punch Kyle in the nose when I caught him staring at your ass." Jacob smirked. "But because I like both of you, I didn't."

"Kyle was staring at my ass?"

"You're happy about that?" The disgust in his tone delighted her even more.

"It's flattering. Besides, I do have a very nice ass." Grace flashed him a grin.

"Gross." Jacob pushed to his feet. "On that note, I'm going to take a shower and erase this conversation from my mind."

Grace knew she probably should erase it from her mind, too, but she didn't want to. Not even a little bit.

CHAPTER SIX

SQUEAKS, LAUGHTER AND chatter booming from the kitchen could only mean one thing. The whole McKnight clan had descended upon the house.

Kyle sighed. They were a loud, gregarious, demonstrative bunch, and he avoided them as much as possible. Mrs. McKnight always, *always* hugged him. He never knew what to do about it. Mr. McKnight would pat him on the shoulder and tell him the same joke he'd been telling his high school baseball players since the beginning of time. "A man with a wood eye asks a girl with a harelip to dance. She says, 'Would I? Would I!' He replies, 'Harelip! Harelip!'"

Then there was Grace's music teacher aunt who preferred singing to actual speaking, and a cousin who was always sneaking out for smoke breaks, not always of the tobacco kind. Added to all that noise and touching, the cousin's four-year-old daughter always insisted on crawling into Kyle's lap anytime he sat.

Kyle turned in retreat. He would hide away in

his office for a bit longer. His grumbling stomach would just have to wait.

"Where do you think you're going?"

Kyle winced and turned to see an all-too-amused Grace standing in the hall between living room and kitchen. "Well, I…"

She shook her head. "Who knew you were such a coward?" She advanced on him, and he would have backed away, but he wasn't *that* big of a coward. Her hand latched on to his arm. "We're all going out to dinner and you have to come."

"Oh, no, no." Kyle tried to pull his arm away, but her grip was firm. "I have plans."

She narrowed her eyes. "Liar. Come on. A dinner with the McKnights is just what you need to lighten up."

"As I keep telling your brother, I'm plenty light."

She snorted and kept pulling him toward the noisy kitchen.

And that was how Kyle found himself sandwiched between Jacob and Grace in a large booth at the Bluff City Pizza Hut.

Kyle focused on his off-white plate etched with the knife marks of years of use while Grace's aunt belted out an aria from some opera she'd recently attended, the four-year-old demanded money to play games and Jacob and his dad told old baseball war stories. Meanwhile, Grace's cousin kept trying to talk to her about Barry while Grace kept trying to change the subject.

"I saw him at the grocery store yesterday," Paula was saying in a conspiratorial whisper the whole restaurant could no doubt hear. "He had on this black sleeveless shirt and there was this giant tattoo on his arm. He didn't have that before, did he?"

Grace fidgeted next to him and her bare arm brushed his. Luckily it was very hard to fantasize about someone whose leg was pressed against his when his other leg was pressed against her brother's.

"I'm not sure. Do you want me to give Bella some quarters for Pac-Man?"

Paula waved her off. "No, no, no. I'll get it in a second. Anyway, he bought a twenty-four pack of Natty Light and a carton of Kools and—"

"Grace, did Jacob tell you that a client of ours is interested in buying one of your paintings?"

The entire table went silent. Kyle wasn't sure if it was because of what he said or because he was talking at all, but at least Paula stopped yapping about Barry.

"What?"

He kept his attention on his plate, having no desire to see what expression might be on any of their faces. "Jacob hung the painting of the river in the kitchen and a client of ours asked Kelly about it last week. She mentioned you were a local artist and they were very interested." Kyle took a careful bite of pizza, chewed and, okay, damn it, he looked at her because he couldn't not.

Her eyes were wide; her mouth hung open a little. "Jacob, is he serious?" But she didn't look at her brother. Her brown eyes stayed on Kyle's face.

"Well, I wasn't going to mention it until the client made an appointment to see your stuff, but yeah. According to Kelly they were really excited about it."

"Gracie! Isn't that wonderful."

The cacophony of a McKnight dinner returned, but everyone was too busy talking about Grace and painting to bring up Barry again.

Luckily, Kyle wasn't forced to talk after that, but somehow on the drive home he found himself in Jacob's truck. Just him and Jacob. Kyle got the uncomfortable feeling they were about to have a discussion.

"So," Jacob began conversationally. "I saw what you did there."

Kyle shrugged, focused on the passenger window. "What where?"

"The painting thing."

Kyle shrugged again. He had no desire to be called out on this. "It was news. I shared it."

"Yeah, at the picture-perfect time to shut up Paula rambling on and on about Barry. I'm supposed to believe that's just coincidence?"

Kyle didn't know what to say. He wanted to forget about the whole thing and not have this conversation. "She seemed uncomfortable, so I changed the subject. I don't see why this warrants a discussion of any kind."

"I don't know. I think it does. The thing is, we're friends. Have been for a long-ass time. I like you, Kyle."

"Is this where you warn me to keep my hands off your sister?" He was already doing everything in his power.

"Actually, no." Jacob pulled the truck into the drive, stopped the truck. "Whatever weird thing you and Grace have going on is none of my business and, what's more, I don't want it to be. I'm just saying this. I like you, Kyle. That's why we're friends."

Jacob got out of the truck, but it took Kyle a few minutes to follow. He didn't get it. It was more approval than warning, and that was the absolute last thing he wanted.

Another car approached and Grace hopped out, waving and blowing kisses at her parents. Kyle mustered up a smile and waved at the happy McKnights as they drove off again.

Grace approached him, grinning from ear to ear. "Hi."

"Hi."

She didn't offer anything else, and since he was

afraid of anything she might have to say, he walked inside. Of course, Grace followed.

"That was quite the little stunt you pulled at dinner," she finally said.

Kyle shrugged. Apparently that was becoming his default response to her and Jacob. Pretty soon his shoulders would be strong enough to carry bricks from all this damn shrugging. "No stunt."

"You shut Paula up real quick and, God, I needed that. I think you're my knight in shining armor."

"That is the absolute last thing I am, Grace." Just the thought of it had his stomach pitching. He'd barely saved himself; how could he be counted on to save anyone else?

Her smile softened into something sad. "I wish you'd give yourself more credit."

He opened his mouth to argue, but she touched his shoulder. It shut up everything but the beating of his heart.

"I think I get the true north thing now," she said, tracing the spot where his tattoo was under his shirt. "You always try to do the right thing, even when you don't want to." She brushed her lips against his, just as casual as you please, and then grinned. "That's pretty damn attractive." She sauntered away, giving him a little wave. "'Night, Kyle."

Well, shit.

IT WAS STUPID. Idiotic, really. Grace meeting with Kelly to discuss selling some of her artwork wasn't important enough to spend an hour agonizing over what to wear. Kelly was just being nice because Grace was her boss's sister.

Maybe a client did voice some interest in one of Grace's paintings, but this wasn't a thing. It wasn't a thing to get nervous or excited about. It was a blip. A sale. Just as random and inconsequential as any of her Etsy sales.

Grace chewed her lip and surveyed the contents of her suitcase spread across her bed yet again.

"You can keep staring," she muttered to the empty room. "Nothing is magically going to appear." With a curse, Grace shimmied into her only pair of jeans not stained with paint and a bright orange sweater that wasn't worn threadbare.

She might not look überprofessional, but she was an artist, not some financial guru or banking exec.

Grace jumped at the knock on her door. She checked her watch. Still a quarter to. She wasn't running late. Maybe it was Kyle coming to tell her this was all a joke. When Grace opened the door, Kelly, Susan and Leah stood there all smiling. Grace tried to smile back, but there was something about this successful trio of women that always made her normal ease with people she knew disappear.

"I know the meeting isn't for another fifteen

minutes, but I got done with my appointment early. Mind if we come in and take a look at your stuff?"

"Oh." Grace looked back at the clothes strewn everywhere. "I was going to bring a few pieces down. It's a mess in here. Bad lighting."

"Not a problem." Kelly brushed past her. "We can pick a few things to take down to the kitchen, then."

"Trust me. *Messy* is her middle name. Nothing will shock Kelly." Susan smiled, poking her head in the doorway. "Leah and I want to see, too, if that's okay? I looked at your Etsy shop. You have some great stuff."

Grace didn't know what else to do but smile and nod. It wasn't really her room and, hell, what was the worst that could happen? They'd all think she was crazy?

"Susan, look at this."

"Oh, I was going to show you these." Grace pointed to the stack of finished canvases she had stacked against the wall. Rivers and flowers and fruit. Kelly was studying what Grace had labeled her nightmare paintings. Dark, brooding. Some were even abstracts, a real departure for her.

But Susan and Leah oohed and aahed over a stormy river scene. It was slashes of grays and blacks. Muted greens, violent streaks of textured blue.

"This would look fantastic in our living room."

"It is great, but don't we have enough art in our

living room?" Susan offered Grace an apologetic look. "I love it, Grace, but Kelly seriously has an art-buying addiction."

"Please don't...apologize," Grace returned lamely. She was having a hard time breathing normally while they studied her work. It was the same feeling she'd had a few nights ago when Kyle had looked at her paintings.

Uncomfortable. There was no rush of maybe getting a sale. There was only...fear. God, she was so tired of that feeling she'd shoot it if she could.

Kelly started going through the stack Grace had chosen purposefully for the interested client. She held her breath as Kelly made clucking noises with her tongue.

"I wish I had a creative bone in my body," Leah said, looking from the family picture Grace had on the nightstand to a painting of violets. "I love my job, but sometimes it'd be nice to do something not so...mathy."

"I write," Susan added. "But I wish I could do something like this. More visual."

Coming from women who intimidated her, the praise, the envy, it helped put Grace at ease. Maybe they weren't all so different. Maybe she wasn't somehow on a separate plane.

"I think the two river paintings over there will be great for the Martin house. Maybe even the apples. Actually, most of your still-life pieces could be quite usable."

"I—" It was far more than Grace expected, and Kelly seemed shrewd enough about what she wanted for Grace to believe that maybe, just maybe, this was about talent and not her last name.

"Seriously, why didn't Jacob think of this before?" Leah demanded. "I swear he has his head shoved so far up his ass it's a wonder he doesn't walk into walls." Leah winced a smile. "Sorry, Grace."

Grace waved her off. "I love him and he's amazing, but he does occasionally have his head up his ass."

"Regardless of whose head is up whose ass, I'll need prices for these pieces before I can show the options to Mrs. Martin. You'll want to sign them, and then we can make a big deal out of you being a local." Kelly tapped a finger to her chin. "Do you have a business card?"

"Um, yeah. I think. Let me check." Grace remembered she'd put a few business cards in her purse last time she'd gone to Iowa City. She pulled open her purse, began to riffle through the contents.

Leah whistled. "Sweet Glock. Can I see it?"

Grace looked at the gun in her purse. "Um. Okay." She pulled it out of the holster and handed it to Leah. It was almost as personal as letting them look at her art. Even though the gun itself didn't mean anything to her, their knowing she had it opened up a piece of her. The piece she didn't like at all.

"You decorated it," Susan said, joining Leah in the study.

"Well, I…" She had taken some liberties and given it a little paint makeover, just to make it feel less like what it was and more like what she wanted it to be. Painted with the same design as her tattoo, she could pretend it was a symbol, not a shield to hide behind.

"Can you do that to mine?" Leah asked.

"Well, sure."

"You have to join our book club."

Kelly groaned from the other side of the bed.

"Book club?"

"Those two idiots pretend they have a book club and go out to Shades gun range every Thursday night."

Grace looked at Kelly, then back to the two women admiring her gun. She could recognize when she was being invited into a social group. It was rare these days, but she could still recognize it.

Part of her was hesitant. It was still hard to trust people outside of her family. Even the friends she'd known since kindergarten had kind of faded away since Barry. They'd all gotten out of Carvelle, and no one seemed to know how to talk to her after she'd recovered.

Or maybe she'd stopped knowing how to talk to them. Letting those long-distance friendships fade had been easier than trying to bridge the gap of way different lives. Of the elephant in the room of her traumatic event's silencing easy banter.

It was still hard to open up to new experiences because all of that fear ruled her. Grace's hands clenched into fists. "That sounds great. Count me in."

Kelly groaned again. "Well, I'm going to go back to work. Get me a list of prices you want for those pieces. Even better, an email with prices and pictures of each that I can forward on to Mrs. Martin. She'll still want to see them in person, but we can maybe whittle it down, determine how many, et cetera."

"O-okay."

"Yeah, I need to get back, too," Leah said. "I'm supposed to meet with Jacob at one about this new place in Council Bluffs."

"Yes, I'm a part of that meeting, too."

"You are?"

"Kyle's sending me to act as referee. Or, as he put it, so you and Jacob don't kill each other."

The women offered waves and a chorus of byes and Grace was left in the wake, shell-shocked and not at all able to process everything. She might be selling a bunch of paintings. She might be making friends.

Grace smiled. And then she flopped back onto her bed and laughed. Fear could take that and shove it down its throat.

CHAPTER SEVEN

GRACE SAT IN the middle of her room, paintings sprawled around her, trying to make some selections and come up with a price list. To send to a customer. Who might want to buy more than one painting.

She was giddy and terrified and it twisted up into a ball of complete and utter inability to do anything except alternate between staring at the paintings and staring at the notepad balanced on her knee.

She wasn't sure why this was different from putting her paintings up on Etsy, she only knew it *was*.

The knock at her door made her jump; the three precise raps made her grin. "Come in," she called, pushing herself into a standing position and starting to pile up the canvases so there was at least a path on the floor.

When the door opened, Kyle stood there, as expected, but Jacob was right behind him. Not quite what she'd had in mind.

"Uh, what is this? Some kind of intervention?"

"We need to talk."

They looked so grim and serious, her stomach

dropped. Whatever it was wouldn't be pleasant. Were they kicking her out? She couldn't imagine why they would, but if they were... Crap.

"I have to go on a business trip," Jacob said, sounding as though he were announcing a death in the family.

Grace waited for the serious thing, but they both looked at her expectantly as if she was supposed to have some kind of response. "Um, okay?"

"We've been working toward this deal for six months now. We can't put it off. Now, I'd go myself, but they need the contractor."

Grace blinked at Kyle. She was missing some important key to this conversation, but they seemed to think she should understand what any of this meant. She didn't. "Okay?"

"With Jacob gone for a few business days, the likelihood of you being in the house alone increases. I have meetings off-site occasionally, and while some of them can be rescheduled, some of them are pretty well set in stone."

"Do you think the Abesso guys could come here?" Jacob said, turning to Kyle.

Kyle frowned, now facing Jacob as though she weren't in the room or part of this bizarre conversation at all. "But I wouldn't be able to see the stock."

"Good point. Maybe—"

"Okay, what the hell are you two chattering about and what does any of this have to do with me?"

They shared a quizzical look.

"I won't be here. So we need to figure out what to do with you. Who will take care of you."

What to *do* with her? Take *care* of her. She could damn well take care of herself. She'd made sure of that. It might still scare the hell out of her, but she wasn't a child to be looked after. Maybe she had little setbacks like the stupid incident at the gym, but she'd dealt.

With Kyle's help.

Grace squeezed her eyes shut. Okay, maybe she didn't have it as together as she wanted, but she was working on it. Regardless, it was her problem and her burden to bear. Not Jacob's, not her family's and most certainly not Kyle's.

"It's important that someone's looking after you," Kyle added, as if that helped the situation.

It didn't. She hadn't spent the past seven years working on herself so her baby brother had to look after her. She hadn't taken up temporary residence here to make anyone's life more complicated. She might not feel comfortable being alone yet knowing Barry was free, but being babysat? That was what she was trying to get away from.

"I do not need looking after," Grace said, trying to remain calm. Trying to keep her emotions under control. She took a deep breath and forced a smile. "I appreciate the concern."

Kyle and Jacob exchanged frowns.

"Go on your business trip, Jacob. I don't know why we're even discussing this. It's not different from when you were dating Candy and weren't ever here."

"But that was different, and the reason I broke up with Candy was so I could..." He clamped his mouth shut.

Right. Apparently it was because of her. Fantastic.

Kyle took a step forward as if to stand between her and Jacob, but when he spoke, it was to Jacob, not to her. "Your parents have backed off. Perhaps..."

"I think they need more time. They're backing off because *I'm* here. If she was alone, they'd harp all over again."

Grace's stomach cramped. In other words, nothing would ever be normal. A hard realization she didn't have the stomach for right now.

"Don't you have an aunt who lives in Ohio or something? Maybe she could visit."

Grace could honestly not believe what she was hearing. "Uh, hello?"

Two clueless pairs of eyes blinked at her.

"You know I'm right here, right? I didn't suddenly become invisible. I'm here. Older than both of you, or do I not have the equipment required for your little 'what to do with Grace' club?"

"Grace, come on. We're trying to figure out what to do, to keep you safe."

"I'm not your problem to solve. Not the crazy wife in the attic you worry over what to do with or who to ship me off to. I'm a person, and I can take care of myself and keep myself safe. Coming here was not about having a bodyguard, it was about getting Mom and Dad to ease up on the worry and because you have a security alarm. I can absolutely take care of myself." Couldn't she? She wasn't even sure, but letting them know that was even worse than being unsure.

"You're not a problem, Gracie. I just—"

She held up a hand. "Enough. You go do whatever business you have to do. And don't you dare ask anyone to watch over me like I'm some kind of incapacitated loser. I'll handle it."

"You're overreacting." Kyle said, his calm, detached way of talking irritating the crap out of her. "This isn't about you being 'incapacitated.' I want…" He stopped himself, cleared his throat. "*We* want you to be safe."

She blinked at him, but he looked away. He hadn't said *we*. He'd said *I*. Jacob was giving Kyle a weird look, too, so Grace knew it hadn't been her imagination. He'd said *he* wanted her to be safe.

And what did that mean?

Jacob shook his head. "Kyle's right. We want you to be safe."

"My safety isn't dependent on you being here or not being here." It was dependent on the guy who'd beaten her into a coma and who was recently released from prison.

She turned away from them. "I'll be fine here. You go on your trip. Kyle will go to his meetings. When no one's here to watch out for the incapacitated loser, the alarm will be on and all will be fine."

"She's right," Kyle said. "Um, not the loser part. The 'all will be fine' part."

"Yeah, and it wouldn't be hard to schedule it so someone is always here. If you're at your meeting, Leah or Kelly or Susan or—"

Grace groaned as loud as she could and pointed at the door. "Get out."

"What?"

"You don't get it! You just… You're infuriating. Both of you. Get out. Go plan your little 'keep Grace on lockdown' schedule elsewhere."

Jacob's phone buzzed in his pocket. He pulled it halfway out, glanced at the screen and cursed. "It's Jeff Stein from Council Bluffs." He pulled the phone completely into his palm, then frowned at Grace. "We'll discuss this later."

"Will we, Dad?"

He opened his mouth, then shut it with a scowl. Swiping his finger across the phone screen, he stepped out of the room.

So she was left with Kyle. He stared at some spot on the wall, hands shoved deep into his pockets. "I apologize if you feel that we were being... insensitive. It wasn't our intention to make you feel like you didn't have a say. That's why we came to you."

"And discussed it as if I weren't even there."

"That wasn't our intent. I'm sorry if it was our execution."

Grace rolled her eyes. "Can't you just say you're sorry like a normal person?"

"Probably not."

"I should go home. Coming here was supposed to be..." What? Supposed to be what? Easy? She wanted to laugh. Easy died a long time ago.

She liked it here. Beyond having people around, she liked the old house and the river views and spending her days painting instead of fending off drunk passes from Cabby's regulars who stopped in to buy their dinner of a twelve pack. She was making friends. She was building this new life, bigger than the insular world she'd been living in for the past seven years.

She looked at her paintings. More than she'd done in the past six months at home. Everything was more here.

It was still scary. It was still hard. But she wouldn't allow Jacob to make her into his or Kyle's burden, and she wouldn't let someone else think it was his responsibility to watch out for her. If Jacob felt that he had to control her life behind the scenes, it was time to get out. Go somewhere else.

Yeah, just keep running, Grace.

Tears threatened because, *God,* she was so tired of this fear she tried desperately to ignore.

"You have a very tight-knit family that cares for one another," Kyle said in a quiet, even voice, apparently not taking her turned back as a cue to leave.

"Yeah, so?" Since he couldn't see her face, she quickly brushed away the tears on her eyelashes.

"So perhaps you could give Jacob a break."

She didn't understand how he could make it sound so ambivalent, not recriminating or disdainful, simply a suggestion. Like what to eat for dinner. "You do realize I am older than both of you. That penis between your legs doesn't magically make you the protector of all female kind."

"No, but perhaps it gives us an illusion of such."

She turned and blinked at him. "Was that a joke?"

"Perhaps." He was even almost kind of smiling. Just a hint of what a full-blown smile might look like on Kyle.

She laughed. What else was there to do? Kyle was joking with her. Kyle. Joking. With her. Almost smiling. Had anything more bizarre happened than this?

"As much as you want to pretend you're here to give your parents a break, I think we both know that's not altogether true." His tone was level, grave and very quiet. No one could have heard him if they weren't inside her room. The words made something in her chest hitch, so she looked out the window to the river below.

But Kyle did something she hadn't expected at all. He stepped next to her. So close their shoulders were almost touching. "If you were well and truly in control of this, you wouldn't be afraid to be alone. No one could possibly blame you for being afraid."

"It's not about...that." Sad, but admitting it in words she was afraid she felt like a failure, and even if Kyle knew the truth, she didn't want to vocalize it. "I could be alone if I had to."

Kyle's silence egged her on. "I could. I'll have to be eventually, you know." She swallowed at the thump of fear in her throat. "It's not about being afraid or not being afraid. It's about being treated like a child. Like I'm not smart enough or strong enough or—"

"No one thinks that." His eyes met hers for the first time. A serious, determined blue. Her heart shivered in response.

"Deciding what to do with me without even asking while I'm standing *right there* says otherwise."

"Point taken." Something she couldn't read

flashed in his expression and he looked down at his hands. "Jacob wants to protect you because he cares about you. That need to protect isn't trying to diminish your intelligence or strength."

"What about you?"

"What about me?"

"You care about me? You want to protect me?"

He straightened, stepped away from the window and her, and completely ignored the question. "Do I need to apologize further? Because I'd really like to get back to work."

Grace turned and studied Kyle's impassive face. He'd said it, hadn't he? *I want you to be safe.* He'd fixed it, but too late for it not to mean something. "I'm beginning to think you like having me around."

His expression went dark, tense. "If I had my way, you would have never been here in the first place."

Grace lifted her chin. If he wanted to take a shot at her, so be it. "And why didn't you want me here, Kyle? Because I ruin your perfect life of order with all my silly questions and poor wardrobe?"

"It's not about you. Per se."

Grace laughed bitterly. "Per se." She should go. Open her mouth and say she'd be back in Carvelle by bedtime, but she didn't want to. Damn it. And Kyle did have a point. No matter how threatened she felt by their machinations, Jacob didn't mean to belittle her in the process. It was just the dumb way men's minds worked.

Except Jacob was her brother. The protecting made sense. Half the time Kyle acted as though he couldn't even tolerate her. "Can I ask you something?"

"I have a feeling I'm not going to like the question."

"Probably not." Grace studied him, standing near the far wall, as separate from her as he could get and still be in the room. He was all pressed and polished in khakis and a button-down shirt. Spick-and-span Kyle. Mr. Businessman. Only Mr. Businessman looked a little scared and a lot wary.

"You know I like you. I've made it pretty clear I'm attracted to you, and sometimes I think we're on the same page. But you're hard to figure, and maybe I'm reading into things. So what's the deal?"

He swallowed, visibly, audibly, but his gaze met hers, very seriously. "Grace, we shouldn't."

Grace took a few test steps toward him and he very subtly backed away. She might not be totally sure and strong when it came to being alone and independent. Yet. But she wasn't going to be shy and retiring and wait around for an answer to magically appear when it came to her and Kyle.

There was something there. Something that didn't scare her. *He* wanted her to be safe. Hell if she wasn't going to take that opportunity when it was given to her. "We shouldn't what? Be honest?"

"Shouldn't...discuss this."

"Why not? I'm a little over the whole 'tiptoeing around it' thing, and I think we've established I'd like to be part of the decision-making when it comes to my life."

His chest expanded and he let out a loud breath. "It doesn't matter what I feel. It can't."

Wasn't that interesting. Not that he wasn't interested, but that it didn't—couldn't—matter if he was. Grace smiled. She liked that.

She crossed the room, keeping her eyes on his. It was so obvious he wanted to back away, but the challenge in her eyes kept him in place. He even tilted his chin up, challenging her back.

Some of that challenge died away when she got close enough to touch, and she would have kept on going until they were touching, but his hands clamped on her shoulders. He held her there, at arm's length, but he didn't put her back a step.

Since Grace couldn't think of anything pithy to say, she didn't say anything. She kept her gaze level on his, but when his eyes drifted to her mouth, her whole stomach flipped. A shiver of excitement skittered over her skin.

"I wish you wouldn't push this."

But she wanted to push. It was something far more appealing than dealing with the fact that she hadn't gotten over all her fears in seven long-ass years. Far more appealing than dealing with her brother thinking he had the right to play puppeteer in her life just because she hadn't totally recovered from her trauma.

"I'm not pushing anything. If you don't feel anything for me, walk away."

He didn't. Indecision played all over his face. From what she knew about Kyle, she imagined there was quite the internal war going on inside that all-too-active brain of his, but she could wait it out.

She knew what his lips would feel like on hers, but just the faintest of touches. She had a vague sense of what he would taste like, but their kiss from a few days ago had been so brief, so totally on her that it had really just been a teaser, an appetizer.

And now she was really interested in the main course.

His hands smoothed down her arms and she thought he was going to let her go, walk away as she'd suggested, but his hands stayed on her elbows, his eyes still on her mouth.

She took the final step to him so they were standing hip to hip, chest to chest. She could hear and see him swallow, but when she tilted her head up, he brushed his mouth across hers. Tentative at first, much like the other night, but when she put her hands on his hips, inching just a bit closer, his mouth pressed to hers firmly.

Everything in her brain fizzled to a stop. When his hands traveled back up her arms, stopped at her neck and pulled closer, her stomach flipped again. And again. The skin on her neck, under the heat of his palms, tightened into goose bumps.

A jittering heat Grace hadn't felt in a long time began to center itself, and when Kyle's tongue traced her bottom lip, she opened her mouth eagerly, deepening the kiss, deepening the shivery feeling along every place their bodies came into contact.

She'd wanted more than the little playful brush of mouths from a few nights back, and boy, oh, boy was she getting it. She nipped at his lip, arched against him. Oh, yeah, this was definitely more.

She wasn't sure what had changed, what had made Kyle inevitably come to his annoying senses, but he pulled away. Grace sighed at the look of utter horror on his face. Way to ruin a moment.

He cleared his throat, dropped his hands as if she were suddenly too hot to touch. Hell, by the heated response of her body, maybe she was.

"Grace." He shook his head, raked an unsteady hand over his short hair. "This is more complicated than just…"

She had no interest in hearing his excuses or his

apologies right now, so she sidestepped him and gave him a friendly pat on the shoulder.

"This whole 'Jacob being gone for three days' thing might have its advantages." She grinned, but because she wasn't feeling as flirty and light as she wanted to, she sauntered past him, not waiting for his response. She needed space, and she wouldn't get it in the place she'd just kissed him.

Been kissed *by* him.

Despite the state of everything, when she heard Kyle mutter an oath behind her, she chuckled. Oh, she was getting in over her head, but it was awfully fun.

KYLE STOOD FROZEN in Grace's room. His gaze was trained on one of her paintings, but he didn't really see it.

He saw Grace.

He'd kissed her. Really kissed her. That had to rank pretty high in the list of mistakes he'd made in his life.

He could try to convince himself she'd goaded him into it, and in a way, she had. But she hadn't kissed him first and she hadn't forced his hand. He'd simply kissed her. Of his own accord.

He forced himself to move out of her room, away from the smell of paint and sunshine. In his office, he tried to focus on his computer, but he thought about the kiss.

The kind of kiss one didn't just forget. The kind of kiss that kept a man up at night wondering what was next.

"Nothing is next. Nothing."

"Who are you talking to?"

Kyle jumped what felt like a foot. "Uh, just… thinking aloud." He cleared his throat, swiveled away from Jacob so he could avoid eye contact.

"Where's Grace?"

"She, uh, went downstairs. I think. I mean, I assume."

"You smooth things over with her?"

Kyle swallowed. "Um. Yes." He kept staring at his computer and could only hope Jacob wasn't reading him like a pathetic open book.

"Maybe we can postpone the trip?"

Yes. That was exactly what they should do. Postpone it until Grace was no longer a houseguest and there was no possibility that he'd be alone in a house with her.

Coward. To postpone the trip would be to risk the job. If they wanted to expand, risking wasn't an option. "No. No, you should go. I'm sure Grace will be fine. We'll keep an eye on her." Which she'd hate to hear him say, but he couldn't help it.

He did want her to be safe. Him. Alone. Regardless of his relationship to Jacob. He cared about Grace. *Damn it.*

Jacob sighed loudly. "Yeah. All right. Thanks for taking care of things, man."

Kyle nodded, hoping Jacob never had any idea just how he had taken care of things. Or the things he was imagining taking care of.

In one breath he'd promised to take care of her, and in the next he'd thought of what she might feel like underneath him.

He'd kissed her. Touched her. Had tasted her and felt her. Soft. Light. He'd allowed himself a taste of something he could never, ever have.

That kiss was Pandora's box, only instead of unleashing evil, it unleashed good. An irresistible goodness that someone like him could not be allowed to have. He'd ruin it. Or ruin himself believing he could have it.

Possibly worse, by kissing her, he'd given her a piece of himself, and it couldn't be taken back. She knew. She saw his weakness, her, and she would push because she was Grace. And it had the potential to unravel everything. *She* had the potential to unravel him.

Not good. Not good at all.

CHAPTER EIGHT

"You could go stay with Mom and Dad. It's not too late."

Kyle fervently wished Grace would go along with Jacob's last-ditch suggestion, but the grimace on her face dashed that hope.

"The last day I was at my house, I woke up and Mom was sitting at the end of my bed. I know they love me and I know they care, but I also know I, and more important they, need this breathing room." Grace gave Jacob a little shove to the door. "Go. I'll take my chances with Kyle."

Kyle tried not to outwardly react, but his mouth turned into a frown anyway. He had no interest in taking his chances with Grace. He didn't trust himself here anymore, and distance was the only surefire way to keep from thinking about her.

About that kiss. About the way she tasted, felt. The smell of her shampoo, the flutter of her breath against his mouth, her tongue on his. Kyle scrubbed a hand over his face.

Get a grip.

Jacob cleared his throat, and it was only then

Kyle realized Grace and Jacob were staring at him expectantly. Since he'd obviously missed a beat in the conversation while he was busy taking a trip to Crazyville, he managed his best bland smile. "Sorry, I was thinking about an email I have to send to the window company. What did I miss?"

Jacob gave him a weird look. Grace gave him a knowing smile. Kyle tried not to run in retreat.

"I was just saying I'll be back Friday night. Call if you need anything. Don't do anything—" he glanced at Grace, then back at Kyle "—stupid." He grimaced. "I gotta go." He kissed Grace on the cheek, whispered something in her ear that made her laugh.

And then Kyle and Grace were alone.

Such a bad idea. Kyle gave half a thought to running after Jacob. They could cancel the trip. MC Restorations was doing all right. They didn't need to expand to the western part of the state.

Kyle sighed. Didn't need to expand, but damn he wanted to. He gave Grace a wary glance. "Would you be opposed to a trip to the gym?" Who cared what happened last time? Physical release was the only thing he'd found that effectively kept his mind off Grace.

She smiled. The kind of smile someone flashes before they upend your life entirely. Which she was doing a hell of a job at anyway. "I have a better idea."

"That is highly, highly doubtful."

Her low, sultry laugh made him want to smile and flee at the same time. But he stood his ground because he was not afraid of Grace.

She took a step toward him. He took a step back.

Okay, yes, he was definitely scared of Grace.

"Let's go for a hike."

She blinked up at him innocently. Except he had a hard time believing anything she suggested was innocent. "A hike?"

"Yeah. I've been wanting to check out Langly Falls Park for ages, but I haven't made it over there yet. We can stop and get some sandwiches and eat dinner out there. I've spent too much time inside lately. I want to picnic in the middle of a bunch of trees, listen to a creek and pretend the rest of it doesn't exist." Her expression dulled momentarily, and then she brightened like the flip of a switch. "I'll keep my hands to myself," she said, waggling her fingers at him. "Promise."

Yes, he could understand that. In the middle of a forest, it was easy to feel like the outside world couldn't get you. The problem was, while she might keep her promise to keep her hands to herself, he was a little worried about his own resolve.

"All right," Kyle muttered. What choice did he have anyway? For the next three days, he was in charge of her. She wouldn't like him thinking of it like that, but if he reminded himself he was responsible for her safety and well-being, maybe he could remember that touching her in any way, shape or form was 100 percent off-limits.

Kyle had spent the past ten years denying himself many an impulse. Grace was a larger challenge than avoiding an argument or indulging in too much to drink, but that didn't mean he was going to crack. Kyle was very used to not getting what the impulsive part of his brain wanted.

And let's face it, this wasn't so much about what his brain wanted.

"We can even go skinny-dipping if you want."

"Grace."

She laughed and patted him on the shoulder as she passed. "What? I was only suggesting it for exercise. Go change. We've only got a couple hours before it's dark."

Kyle did as he was instructed because it was easier. If he went along with things, was his usual bland self, everything would be fine. Grace was too colorful to find him interesting, especially if he amped up the boring businessman routine instead of that of the guy who'd experienced a similar trauma. The guy who understood, who felt compelled to commiserate, comfort, protect.

If he shut that guy up, everything would be fine. He could talk about the cost efficiency versus aesthetic appeal when it came to restoring houses, or he could discuss profit margins and growth plans, or even the anniversary party MC was planning for next week.

If he talked about all the little details that made even Jacob's eyes glaze over, everything would be fine.

He could handle being alone with Grace McKnight for three days. Sure he could.

GRACE'S THIGHS SCREAMED in protest as they reached the summit of the bluff. She wanted to whine and beg Kyle to stop so they could eat, but she'd let him pick the trail and she'd be damned if she was going to look like some weakling.

She was in shape. Just not nearly as good of shape as she thought, or as good of shape as Kyle.

Speaking of Kyle's shape…

He was a few yards ahead of her, wearing cargo shorts and a plain blue T-shirt. Casual Kyle. Woodsy Kyle.

She was beginning to realize all versions of Kyle were pretty hot. Especially now that she'd been pressed against him. Now even Mr. Businessman Kyle was mouthwatering because she knew what it was like to be kissed by him.

She huffed out another breath. The exertion of the hike up the bluff had worked in keeping her from thinking about that kiss for a good twenty minutes.

Hallelujah. Because hot and bothered really

wasn't working for her. She'd been very, very careful about dating since Barry. Okay, she pretty much hadn't dated since Barry. Nothing more than a cup of coffee. But in the tiny town of Carvelle, there hadn't been any men to lust after, so she hadn't really missed being with someone.

Flirting with someone.

Kissing someone.

For basic self-preservation, she was not going to let herself go any further with that train of thought.

Finally, about five minutes after Kyle did, she reached the summit. In a few weeks, the river below would be hard to see through the leafy trees, but right now with just the buds of green decorating each branch, she could see the churning brown water.

One hundred percent worth the climb. A barge moved its slow pace through the murky water. Across the way, bluffs lined the river. An old fishing boat bobbed on the shore opposite them.

"A bit of a haul, but all in all worth it," Kyle said.

Grace was just a pinch comforted to note his breathing wasn't totally even. The hike hadn't been a piece of cake for him, either.

"Ready to eat?"

Grace nodded, not wanting to show him just how out of breath she was. He dropped the backpack he'd worn and pulled out the blanket she'd packed, the food. Kyle being Kyle, he set up everything with meticulous precision while Grace did her best to even out her breathing.

She took a seat on the blanket, cross-legged, facing the river. A slight breeze worked its way through the budding foliage. It smelled like spring and cooled the sweat at her temples.

White clouds puffed overhead, birds sang to each other, squirrels and other little animals scurried in the trees she and Kyle had just hiked through.

It was exactly what she needed. The perfect moment. Kyle handed her the wrapped sandwich and Grace smiled. Even the almost-perfect companion. Who would have thought that spending time with Kyle was actually kind of enjoyable?

She was comfortable around him. She liked goading him. She really liked kissing him. This was what normal people did when they were attracted to someone. It was practically a date. Maybe it was time to dig a little deeper into Kyle.

Grace unwrapped her sandwich, bit into it and studied Kyle's profile as he carefully chewed a bite. "Can I ask you a question?"

"It's doubtful I'll answer it."

She smiled at that. "Why didn't you leave?" Grace thought of her old friends. They'd been smart and ambitious, like Kyle. But they came home to visit at Christmas with their new families. Kyle never stepped foot into Carvelle despite being twenty minutes away.

"Leave?"

"You never go back to Carvelle, not even for Jacob's birthday dinner or the Fourth of July, but you live twenty minutes away. Why not leave altogether? I mean, there are probably a million towns you could have started a business in. Away from Carvelle. Outside of Iowa."

Kyle stared at her for a very long time. She was learning that waiting him out usually yielded results of some kind. If she pushed, he shut down. Withdrew behind that impassive, robot-like exterior. But sometimes, she supposed when he thought the topic was safe enough to discuss, he'd humor her. After a long, smoldering stare anyway.

The smoldering stare was growing on her.

"Did your brother ever tell you how we got to be friends?"

Grace shook her head and chewed her sandwich. She'd never spent too much time thinking about how easygoing, cheerful Jacob had begun a friendship with taciturn, stuffy Kyle. Jacob got along with everyone, but now it did strike her odd that Kyle had let someone in. To be friends. Partners.

Kyle leaned back on his elbows, looked out at the river. "Freshman year we were in this business elective together and our teacher had us do a project where you had to develop your own business. Marketing, accounting, advertising, the whole bit. She assigned us partners and Jacob was mine."

Grace chewed her sandwich and watched as Kyle's usually bland expression lightened into a smile. Since he never spoke about his past, it was interesting to see him relive what seemed like a pleasant memory.

"He never treated me differently, you know. A lot of kids did. The kids from town versus the trailer park kids. Jacob didn't care. He didn't roll his eyes at his friends when he was partnered with me. He just started talking a mile a minute about an idea he had. For a renovation business."

Grace grinned. "He started talking about it when he was, like, ten and they had to tear down Grandpa and Grandma Davenport's house. He's been obsessed ever since, I guess."

Kyle nodded, squinting into the setting sun. "He made it seem real, this stupid high school project. Plausible. For the first time in my life I entertained the thought of escaping Carvelle. Of being...something."

Grace held her breath. It was the most Kyle had ever willingly revealed to her about himself and she wanted him to keep going. She wanted to see all the climbs and falls he'd made to become this puzzle of a man before her.

"He invited me places. I went. He kept talking about this idea, about how we could be partners. I'd never dreamed of trusting anyone enough to be partners, but Jacob is..."

"Infinitely trustworthy."

"Exactly. He was my way out. So when he decided to go to U of I, and I got a scholarship, I went, too. I promised myself I'd never set foot in Carvelle again, and I won't. But when he wanted to stay close to your parents, I stayed, too. Would I prefer to be elsewhere? Sure. But Bluff City's grown on me, and it's a better option than going it on my own."

Grace inched a little closer. Just enough so he wouldn't notice. She wanted to touch him, something innocent. A connection of skin to cement the connection of sharing, but he'd back away.

So instead, she went with what would throw him off rather than with what might shut him down. "Are you leading up to telling me you're in love with my brother?"

He let out a surprised laugh, tried to frown over at her and failed. "Are you really operating under the assumption I'm gay? I'm pretty sure gay men don't kiss women the way I kissed you."

Grace raised an eyebrow, grinned. "Oh, are we going to talk about that?"

Shut down in three…two…one… "No."

"Too bad."

"While we're asking questions…" He purposefully put more space between them. The big coward. "Why didn't you go to art school or college or something?"

Because the question poked at an old insecurity and because the boy from the trailer park had a college degree and she didn't, Grace bristled. "Too good to share a kiss with someone who didn't go to college?"

Kyle shook his head. "Fine. I won't ask questions."

Grace poked at the rocky ground next to her. Mainly, Grace had rolled with the punches life was wont to throw. She'd dealt pretty well, she thought, but sometimes remembering made her bitter. It was the number-one thing she didn't want to be. Bitterness made you give up.

But was what she was doing—living in neutral—any better?

Grace sighed. "I was supposed to go to Lake Forest. I had a partial scholarship, more than enough loans but…" She squinted over the river. "Mom got sick. She, uh, had breast cancer."

Grace didn't bother to look a Kyle. She knew what she would see on his face. Shock. Because the only three people who knew that little tidbit were Mom, Dad and her.

"Jacob doesn't know. He was sixteen and Mom didn't want to upset him. Us, actually. I wasn't supposed to know. She was determined to beat it, didn't want her students to know… So it was this big cover-up thing."

Grace rubbed her forehead. Was she making

sense? It didn't feel like it. Those four years still didn't make sense to her.

"I overheard her and Dad talking about not telling, and then I decided I would put off going to school for a year. I'd stay home and help out. Mom was pissed, but I just told her I'd tell everyone if she made a fuss."

"Grace."

"What? She beat it." Hadn't made it less scary at the time, but Mom had been determined and Dad had been a rock and Jacob had only been moderately suspicious. "Anyway, Jacob went off to school and they were paying Mom's medical bills. You know there's stuff her insurance wouldn't cover? So stupid. But anyway, everything felt too late and then Barry and...I don't know. It all seemed pointless."

Grace pushed to her feet. "The sun is setting. We should go."

"Grace."

She didn't like the pity in his tone so she started collecting her trash and doing what she could to avoid eye contact. It was pointless. Pointless to bring this up or rehash that a couple of years had derailed her life completely.

She liked her life, derails and all. Well enough anyway. No use having regrets about things that couldn't be changed.

His hand rested on her shoulder, but she brushed

it off, feeling a little too raw to deal with sympathetic Kyle. "It's not a big deal. I like my life."

"But you could have more."

"Maybe I don't want more. Is that so wrong?"

His hand slid down her sleeve until his fingertips brushed her bare forearm. "No. Not for some people, but you're…"

"I'm what, Kyle?" She prepared for him to say something negative. All the things he really thought about her even if he found her attractive. She was too wild, too loud, too honest, too inappropriate.

"You're smart. Lively. Bright. Fun. And a very good artist. You could do…anything."

She stared up at him, so shocked by his nice words she didn't know what to say at first. His fingertips hovered on her arm, as if he was caught between the desire to touch her and the need to run away.

"I like my life. I sell paintings online enough to pay for more supplies, and I have a job and a house and a great family. If Barry would stay in jail, I'd love my life. But I don't need more." It made her smile a little that it was true. She had pangs of what she'd missed, but going to college didn't appeal to her now. "I like living in Bluff City and painting. I admit, I could do without going back to Cabby's, and my parents' compulsive worrying, but otherwise I do what I like to do."

"Then that's what you should do."

Grace let out a sigh and sank back onto the blanket. Her parents were always hinting that she should do more. Not necessarily go to college, but something more than work at a gas station.

Then Kyle, *Kyle,* of all damn people just stood there being supportive. She rubbed her forehead. "You're giving me a headache."

"I apologize."

He stayed standing and she stayed sitting. She knew they should head back, but she didn't want to move. She didn't want to think. She just wanted to go back to an uncomplicated life.

Except when was that?

"Kelly hasn't stopped talking about your paintings. You know, you could probably make some money off it. Targeting our clients. Working with Kelly. She likes your stuff. It's something to think about, instead of going back to Cabby's. I mean, I'd think you could probably make minimum wage off your paintings. That's all you make there, isn't it?"

It was baffling that he was standing there giving her career advice in the middle of a bluff. That he wouldn't talk about kissing her, but the course of her life? Sure. Why not? "Who are you?"

He rubbed his hand over the back of his neck. "I wish I knew." Kyle sank next to her. Not touching, but closer than he had been.

She wished she knew how to soothe him. He seemed so troubled, but only he could find his way out of trouble. She'd learned that lesson herself. Only she could choose not to be bitter. Only she could choose to keep moving forward. And one of these days she'd figure out how to choose not to be afraid anymore.

She put her hand over his, and when he didn't withdraw, her lips curved into a small smile. They sat there holding hands in the fading day as if this was normal, as if this could be normal. Even knowing it couldn't, Grace wanted to lean over and kiss him and pretend. Just for a little while.

But…

"Kyle, I'm not going to throw myself at you again."

He let out a breath, withdrew his hand. "Okay."

"So if you could throw yourself at me, that'd be great."

A stilted chuckle expelled from his mouth. "I…I can't do that. This has already gone too far. Whatever it is. I can't. It would be a mistake."

"Because of Jacob?"

"Because of me."

"Because I'm unsuitable." That wasn't a question because she knew that's what he thought. She didn't fit his ordered, mannered, businessy life.

"Because I can't possibly be what you'd deserve to have." He stood and began to fold up the blanket despite the fact that she was still sitting on it.

"We really need to go or it will be dark before we finish the hike back."

Finally, she rolled off, got to her feet. She had no idea how to respond. In one way it was a pity that he'd think so little of himself. But it was also super irritating. If she was honest with herself, though, she wanted to scoop him up and fix all those broken pieces inside him.

She knew she couldn't, but that didn't change the fact that she wanted to.

CHAPTER NINE

BREATHING THE SAME air as Grace McKnight was like being shot with truth serum. Kyle didn't like it one bit.

Telling her about his friendship with Jacob had seemed innocuous at the time, but hell if it was. Now he felt raw. Exposed. As though she'd taken that little tidbit and crawled inside him, seeing all the other tidbits of his life. Things he didn't want anyone to see, let alone her.

He wasn't right for her. He didn't get why she didn't see that, but more so, he didn't get why he'd *told* her that. He shouldn't be telling her anything or talking about their attraction or that kiss or who was throwing who at whom.

Kyle paced his small office. Three long strides one way, three back. He was supposed to feel centered here, but he didn't. He couldn't focus on anything other than Grace's being just down the hall. Wanting some part of him. *Him.*

She made him want to talk, to rehash, to share, and if he gave in, he'd never be able to look at her without seeing pity in her eyes, maybe even fear. As much as he'd been a victim, he'd also been a participant. He wasn't an innocent bystander like Grace.

He'd held a gun to his father's head. Every time he'd seen his father since, the incident had ended in a fistfight. Kyle knew his father was the only one who could bring out that lack of control in him, but he'd never want Grace to witness that, to see that in him.

They might have both dealt with violence, but they were not the same. He could not let himself believe they were the same.

But the pull grew stronger. He could hear music drifting from her room, the smell of paint melding with it.

What would be the harm?

He'd fought to be honorable. What made him different from his parents, his upbringing, was this code of ethics he'd honed ruthlessly for himself. That code did not allow for dragging Grace into the bleak recesses of his memory. Into the pieces of himself that could still be manipulated into being someone he hated.

And if he kept this up, he'd show everything to her. Then what? She wouldn't want to be under the same roof with him. She'd be frightened of what he was capable of considering her own violent past. Or worse, she'd want to help, to fix, to shed her light on his dark. It was such an irresistible idea, except for one little problem.

It was fiction.

Light never conquered dark.

A sudden banging interrupted his depressing inner monologue. It was too close to be someone at the door, so Kyle moved down the hall toward the sound. Toward Grace's room.

She had her door open, so he peeked inside. She was standing on a mishmashed stack of things. Books, boxes, her suitcase. Of course she was. Grace was Grace and therefore couldn't be bothered to get a ladder like a normal person.

She was pounding a nail into the wall. Once she was satisfied with that, she pulled a canvas off the dresser next to her and balanced it on the nail.

Go, his mind instructed. But he was too busy studying the painting she'd hung. It wasn't her usual. The two paintings Jacob had hung around the house were bright and cheerful. A river on a spring day; a tulip just a few days from full bloom. Pretty pastels. This painting didn't match. Though there was a field dotted with purple blooms, the sky was gray and bleak. Clouds slashed across the top of the canvas, and the purple of the flowers was muted.

"Let me guess. Usually you measure the exact dimensions of the room and work up some sort of geometric equation to determine the best possible placement." Grace turned to face him. Though her words spoke of irritation, she was smiling at him.

He would not smile in return. "No." Although measuring didn't sound as crazy as she seemed to think. "Kelly handles the decorations around here. I defer to her judgment."

Grace rolled her eyes.

He looked back at the painting. It was very well done and it suited the room, but something about it coming from Grace made him feel...

Well, that was the problem, wasn't it? She was always making him feel. So why on earth had he walked down that stupid hallway?

"I know it's kind of dark. Moody. But the rest of the room is so cheerful I thought this would be a good contrast. I tied in the decor with the field of violets, but I thought people might be more inclined to study it if the sky was stormy, you know? Something you wouldn't expect. I can take it down if you don't like it. It's just, Jacob said I could hang my stuff here and—"

"It's perfect."

She blinked at him. "Really?"

"It suits the room. Like you said, a layer of interest. You're very good, you know. It'll need a frame, I think."

She opened her mouth, but no sound came out.

He didn't like that she was shocked into silence just because he'd said something nice. He didn't want to be a bad person. He just wanted to fade into the background. "I can give compliments, you know. When they're warranted."

She smiled up at him, too close. The rational, closed-off part of his mind told him to step away, make a polite excuse and go find some work to bury himself in. Unfortunately, there was this new side of his brain. One that hopped the walls he'd spent years erecting and told him to touch her. Just one little touch couldn't hurt.

He could touch and take and be and not show her the bad parts. There could be two Kyles, and she only had to see the one who followed the code. The one who was good and decent because everything depended on it.

Ten years he'd spent building this person, making himself into someone good. Maybe not full of personality or charm, but good. He followed all the rules. Didn't he deserve a reward? Something that made it all worth it?

Kyle cleared his throat, hoping to dislodge the voice that lied. "I didn't come here to…"

Her smile widened. Something unbidden worked its way through his chest. It wasn't all sexual, either. That was where Grace was dangerous. He wasn't just attracted to her—he liked her. Liked the way he felt when he was with her, even when she was driving him up the wall.

"Didn't come here to what?"

"Well." Not an easy or safe way to answer that

one. So he should make his excuses and leave. Any minute now.

"You know, you'd make a great subject to paint." She stepped closer. The part of his brain that usually told him to back away was eerily silent.

"I would?"

"I don't do a lot of living subjects, but let me see." She reached out and grasped his chin, turned his head to the right then left. "Hmm." She was close. Closer than need be. The protests of his rational brain so quiet he could barely hear them.

"You're doing this on purpose." God help him, it wasn't consternation so much as hope in his tone.

She grinned, trailed one fingertip over the line of his chin. "And what purpose do you think I'm aiming for?"

The smile. The challenge. Synapses in his brain stopped firing. Instead of moving away, he stepped closer. The voice inside his head that had kept him from getting entangled in anything he couldn't control for ten years grew quieter and quieter, until there was only silence.

The silence was amazing.

So he brushed the tips of his fingers across the curve of her jaw. That was amazing, too. "Grace." He wasn't sure what it was he was trying to tell her. That this couldn't possibly be a good idea. That he didn't care if it wasn't.

"Mmm?"

His movements were bolder and more confident than he felt, fingers brushing the hair off her shoulder, cupping the soft curve of her neck, slowly pulling her closer until their bodies touched. Until their mouths touched.

He wasn't sure he'd ever kissed someone who was smiling before. The upward curve of her mouth felt foreign and light. Something fragile and special. He sank into it. The new, light feeling. A bright warmth unique to Grace. Her arms moved around his neck and he flattened his hands against her back, holding her close. Her tongue dipped into the corner of his mouth, the soft skin of her palms anchored on the back of his neck.

Her lips brushed lightly across his, and then she laughed, a quiet, comforting sound.

"Is something funny?"

Her fingertips danced across the sides of his neck, sending goose bumps down his spine. "*Funny* isn't the right word." She nipped at his jaw, pressing herself against him so that it was hard to concentrate on anything beyond her warmth and soft body against his. "It's just…" She sighed, her hands traveling down to rest on his chest. "You try to pretend that you're boring and standoffish and cold, but every time you kiss me, well, it's anything but."

"I see." He didn't. At all, but his hands were still on her back, and he lowered his mouth to the spot behind her ear. She shivered against him. It didn't matter if he understood. Only this mattered.

She laughed again. "You're not going to change your mind, then?"

"No." The word escaped before he had a chance to weigh it, to contort it into something bland and controlled.

"Good." She entwined a hand with one of his and led him toward the bed.

He swallowed as his stomach jumped. As he followed. A whisper of the voice of reason managed to break through. *Wrong,* it hissed. *Not for you.* Grace pulled him onto her bed so they knelt knee to knee on the twisted comforter.

A new, louder voice echoed in his brain, drowning out the chorus of wrong. This voice shouted *right.* Everything felt right. He smoothed his hands down her sides, then under her shirt, feeling the soft, smooth skin of her abdomen.

She made a quiet moaning sound, digging her fingers into his shoulders, pulling him closer. He began to lift her shirt, but the jarring sound of a phone stopped him midmovement.

Grace kissed his chin. "I'm going to ignore it."

Kyle slowly let go of the bottom of her shirt, moved his hands to her hips, studied her flushed face. "You should get it. It's late. It might be an emergency."

"It's not that late." The ringing stopped. Nothing

else stood between this moment and the next. But when he leaned down to kiss her again, the phone on the nightstand trilled once again.

Grace caught her lip between her teeth.

"Get it. I'll…wait." There would be no turning back now. No running away. Wrong or right didn't really matter; everything felt inevitable.

Grace moved out of his grasp and reached over to the nightstand. She frowned at the display. "It is a little late for Mom to be calling, but it's probably nothing." She hit a button. "Mom? Is everything—"

The frown deepened, her face paled and any inevitability of him and Grace vanished. Here was the sign from the universe.

"I'm coming. No. I am. Just… I'll be there. It's my house. I'll be there." She pulled the phone away from her ear, and though her eyes moved to him he didn't think she actually saw him. "I need to borrow your car, I think. Yes. That's what I need to do."

There were a lot of terrible things he was capable of, but ignoring her obvious emergency when she was so pale and shaken was not one of them. "What's wrong?"

She swallowed, holding the phone in her hands. Shock and horror and confusion all wrapped up on her pretty face. "My house is on fire."

Kyle stepped away. The voice of reason back,

hissing at him. He'd let down his walls, and this was what happened. Destruction.

Kyle shook his head. Stupid. Foolish thought. He was separate from this. Inconsequential to it. Something in his dark, beleaguered soul laughed, but he ignored it. He wasn't important. What was important was Grace. She moved without ever completing an action. Her hands shook. He had to find the control he'd lost somewhere on the walk from his office to her room.

"Is everyone all right?"

"As far as I know. The house is empty. I'm not sure about the neighbors. Mom didn't mention it. I have to get there. I have to..." She took some halting steps, turned around.

Kyle swallowed down the fear and traded it in for the ruthless, cold control he had to employ to do what needed to be done. Ten years later and he was going to have to return to Carvelle.

"I HAVE TO GO. My house. All of my things." The idea that she was losing everything and she wasn't even there was too painful to wrap her mind around. She moved to grab her purse. Stopped halfway, turned to find her shoes. Nothing made sense.

"I'll drive you." Kyle picked her purse off the nightstand, handed it to her in quick slashing movements.

She blinked up at him. "But Carvelle." Even with

her brain not functioning, she knew Kyle didn't go to Carvelle. He couldn't take her.

"You're in no condition to drive." His eyes were flat, his words terse. "I'll drop you off with your parents."

"Kyle, you don't have to—"

"Get your shoes." He stiffly walked past her. Kyle from two minutes ago was gone. And who would she be in twenty minutes in the face of her house? On fire. Everything she held dear that had been too big or silly to bring. Gone.

Her life. Family heirlooms. Her work. Every piece of art she'd never sold or given away. The perfect kindle for a blaze that had her always composed mother sobbing on the phone.

Grace squeezed her eyes shut, braced her body against the shaking wanting to spread. She pulled shoes from the closet, not even bothering to check if they matched. Walking downstairs was a Herculean effort.

Kyle was waiting, and when she finally reached the bottom of the stairs, he wordlessly stepped out the door. She followed, not sure how her muscles were moving when she could barely form a rational thought.

But somehow she was in Kyle's car, and it was driving down the highway, the night growing darker the farther they got from Bluff City.

He turned the car into Carvelle. She looked out

over her hometown. Too many lights on for this late in the tiny town. Too many people walking the sidewalks at dark. This wasn't right. Maybe it was a dream.

"Where's your house?"

His voice seemed as foreign as the man who'd been kissing her not all that long ago, but that moment was lost. Maybe that was the real dream.

"Elm Street."

He nodded, made the appropriate turns, but as they approached, there was nowhere to go. Elm was blocked off. People in pajamas crowding around, and in the distance bright, flashing lights.

Her house. Or what had been a house. Orange flames fluttered high in the sky, black smoke billowing, water spouting in big arcs in the night. Hers. Enveloped in flame.

Tears formed, and despite her not blinking, they fell onto her cheeks.

Everything gone. The pillowcases her grandmother had embroidered. The painting that had won her a scholarship she'd never been able to use. Her collection of unicorns from when she'd been a little girl. Everything was in this mess of fire, water and smoke.

Everything was gone.

The sob that escaped her lips felt as if it came from someone else. Distant, just as Kyle's warm hand covering hers felt far away as if there was some layer of chill between his skin and hers.

"Let me take you to your parents'. We can find out what needs to be done there."

Grace pulled away and pushed the door open instead. She couldn't leave yet. She couldn't just walk away while her life burned to the ground. No, she had to…

She didn't know what she had to do, but she walked through the crowds of people, ignoring the neighbors who said her name or Kyle calling for her. She moved as though she was in some movie slow-motion sequence until she reached where the fire department had blocked everything off.

"Gracie! Oh, my God, I can't believe it." Mrs. Melvin's hand clamped onto her elbow. "I went outside to let Peanut in because she was barking her fool head off and I saw it. Oh, it's just awful. We called the fire department right away, but I swear it took forever. Carl was out trying to get the garden hose to reach and—"

"Oh, Grace, it's just awful. Just awful. You shouldn't be watching this. Where are your parents? They were here earlier. Do you think—"

Neighbors' voices began to meld together, a cacophony of speculation, horror and commiseration. Grace knew she should thank them. She should be glad they cared, but she couldn't take it. She couldn't breathe as they circled around her in the dark night illuminated by fire and fire truck lights.

Grace opened her mouth to speak, but everyone around her was too busy chattering over one another. She had to get out of here. Before she threw up. Before the entire crowd suffocated her. But they blocked her in, talking at once, over each other, stealing all the air.

Grace closed her eyes, thought about sinking to the ground and sitting with her hands over her ears when a hand grasped her elbow firmly.

"Grace, your parents keep calling your cell." Kyle gently pulled her out of the crowd. "I'll drive you over there and drop you off."

The voices continued to chatter at her, but she couldn't make anything out. She nodded at Kyle and let him lead her back to the car.

IN THE DARK, with Grace pale and shaken in the passenger seat, it was easy to forget where he was and pretend this wasn't Carvelle. There was too much happening around him to pay much attention to the sick feeling in his stomach, to picture the trailer park on the other side of town.

Grace sniffled, leaned forward in her seat and wrapped her arms around herself as he pulled into the McKnight driveway. Mrs. McKnight was pacing the yard with a phone to her ear; Mr. McKnight was seated on the concrete stoop until he saw them pull up.

Mrs. McKnight pulled the phone away, and both she and her husband rushed to the car. Kyle heard Grace's sharp intake of breath right before she pushed open the car door.

"Good. You didn't go. Tell me you didn't go."

The door shut, silencing the rest of Mrs. McKnight's words and any reply Grace offered. Kyle watched them in the pale glow of the streetlight and the motion-sensitive light on top of the garage. Mrs. McKnight's mouth kept moving, just like the neighbors' of Grace's. Why wasn't anyone giving her a chance to breathe?

Kyle shook his head. Not his problem. He'd brought her here because he'd had no other choice. Now he'd dropped her off where she'd be safe and taken care of. He should go. Just back out of the drive and head back to Bluff City. He had nothing to do with this. Grace was fine now. Safe with her parents. What did he have to offer?

He stepped out of the car.

"Oh, I'm so glad you drove her, Kyle," Mrs. McKnight said with a sniffle, her arm entwining with his and pulling him toward the house as Mr. McKnight led Grace ahead of him. Panic began to infiltrate the idiocy of getting out of the car and Kyle struggled to keep calm, focused. Darting away from Mrs. McKnight's overpowering grasp wouldn't help anyone.

"I should—"

"I know you don't like to come to Carvelle. It just makes me all the more grateful you helped her. All the more grateful you and Jacob have been watching out for her." She sniffled again. Kyle tugged on his arm, lightly. Her hold didn't loosen.

"Mrs. McKnight—"

"Can you imagine if she'd been there?" Mrs. McKnight's voice squeaked and she pulled a tissue out of her robe pocket with her free hand. "If she was *supposed* to be there. No one in that house. No reason for this." Mrs. McKnight blew into the tissue. "I'm sorry. I'm blubbering. I'm a mess. I can't stop thinking about all the possibilities. Horrible what a man can do."

Kyle didn't know what to say. What was there to say? He knew what a man could do, and it was worse than set a fire.

But what if Grace had been home in Carvelle? As Mrs. McKnight said. What if she was *supposed* to be home? "So it wasn't an accident then, the fire? It was set?"

"Too early to tell, but... Everything was shut off. What could have started a fire?" Mrs. McKnight shook her head. "Colin says I'm getting ahead of myself, but it had to have been Barry. It just had to have been."

Kyle let out a slow breath. If he didn't concentrate on his breathing, he'd concentrate on the type of person who knocked around women. Who would leave someone innocent and sweet like Grace to die.

If he thought about that, the feelings of rage and retribution returned and he was back in a trailer with a gun to his father's head.

"I should get back," Kyle said as they reached the door. He couldn't set foot inside the McKnights' cozy little house. He didn't belong. No amount of money, nice clothes or kissing Grace could make him belong. "If there's anything I can do..."

Mrs. McKnight patted his arm and finally, finally released him. "You're a good boy, Kyle. A good man, I guess. I'd appreciate it if you wouldn't call Jacob. He'd rush home and I don't want him driving late at night all worked up. Lord knows he never knows what to do when he's angry, and this will send him through the roof. Colin and I will call him in the morning."

Kyle nodded, swallowed down the arguments against her labeling him good. If he was a good man, things would be different. "Please, call my cell if you need anything else." He turned to leave, made it all the way to his car, but when he slid inside, he noticed Grace's purse was still in the passenger seat.

He couldn't just leave with it. She might need

something. In fact, she probably wanted something of her own. Something she hadn't lost.

He picked it up, let his fingers trail across the canvas. The image of her face watching her house be devoured by flame and water would be etched in his mind forever. Everyone had been talking to her, crowding her, but she'd just looked at the house in pain.

She didn't deserve this hand. Not her. Kyle's fingers dug into the heavy purse.

He was not a good man. Not even close. But he could do something. He could give her something. Be there for her somehow.

Kyle placed the purse back on the passenger seat and backed out of the driveway. She needed more than a heavy purse she'd grabbed in haste. He could make one more trip. Get her some of her clothes so she could feel normal tomorrow. Herself.

Get a few things. One last trip to Carvelle. Then, when it was over, and he was back in Bluff City for good, he'd extricate himself from the whole thing so something like what happened in her bedroom never happened again. If he had to move out of the damn house on the bluff to accomplish it.

CHAPTER TEN

GRACE TOOK A deep breath. In the hall bathroom of her parents' house she finally had a moment to herself, to breathe. Just her. No police and questions. No crowding and worrying. No overpowering need to smooth things over, to tell her parents everything was fine.

Nothing was fine.

Grace studied her own face. What had she done to deserve this? Whether it was an accident or Barry, what wrong had she done in her life to warrant another hit, another blow?

Grace sighed and gripped the sink, letting her head fall forward. It didn't matter. Good or bad didn't matter. The world wasn't one big scorecard. Hadn't she learned a long time ago that people didn't get what they deserved?

Grace took another deep breath, splashed some water on her face. She was getting to the numb portion of the whole ordeal. She would go to her old room and sleep. Sleep for a very long time. Her parents could handle the phone calls from concerned neighbors for one night. The police were looking for Barry, keeping an eye on her parents' house.

She'd take over everything tomorrow once she had some energy. Once fight replaced numb.

God, *God,* she hoped it would.

She stepped out of the bathroom. The living room was empty. Everything quiet. She hoped that meant Mom and Dad had gone to bed.

A knock sounded on the door. Grace's heart leaped to her throat, panic seizing her. Oh, God, it was happening again. The irrational fear at every little thing.

Bad guys don't knock on the door, Grace. Tell that to her shaking hands. Bracing herself against those shakes, Grace moved toward the door with hesitant steps. She peered out the peephole and her heart did a different kind of flop.

She opened the door to Kyle. "What are you doing here? I thought you left."

He seemed startled to see her. "I…I thought your parents would answer. Um." He shoved her purse into her arms. "You forgot this in my car," he said stiffly.

"Thank you."

"I brought you a few of your things." The stiffness eased into something closer to discomfort and embarrassment. He slipped a large canvas bag off his shoulder and handed it to her. "I hope you don't mind me poking through your stuff, but

I thought you might like...you know, your own things right now."

Grace swallowed. When the lump in her throat didn't dislodge, she swallowed again. "Thank you," she croaked. "I..." She took the bag, peeked at the contents. Visible from the top was a sweater, the family picture that had been on her nightstand at MC, her toothbrush.

Grace set the bag down, hoping if she moved she wouldn't be inclined to cry again. Hadn't Kyle seen her cry enough? But this... God, this sweet gesture coming from him. It really was too much.

"That means a lot."

"It was nothing." He seemed desperate that it be true, but his returning to Carvelle a second time after spending ten years away wasn't nothing. Grace could never see it as nothing.

She met his gaze for the first time. "Kyle." She didn't know what to say. Didn't know what to do. She tried to blink back tears, tried to be stronger and braver than she was. But it didn't work. This was all too much.

"Don't cry." He reached out, touched her elbow, almost desperately. "Everything..." He trailed off, looking pained.

"You can't say it, can you? Good for you." It was refreshing that someone didn't feel the need to lie to her. To try to smooth over the pain and hurt. This sucked, and it wasn't okay. The pain and hurt were there. End of story. Her things and memories were gone forever. Things that could never, ever be replaced. "Everyone keeps saying it'll be okay, but it won't be. You know it won't. I know it won't."

He stared at her with those piercing blue eyes. His hands clamped onto her shoulders. "Grace."

She shook her head. "Don't lie to me, Kyle. I've been here before. It won't be okay. Losing my house will never be okay. What happened before will never be okay." Her voice broke. The tears she wanted so desperately to be in control of trickled onto her cheeks.

"You're right. It'll never be okay. But that's life. Things aren't always going to work out. We both learned that the hard way, right?"

She sniffled, nodded. Foolishly wished he'd pull her into a hug and soothe her and tell her everything would work out even if it was a lie.

"But you are the strongest woman I've ever met. You are…" He swallowed. "Something bad happened and you made the best of it. You survived and you didn't shut yourself away. You'll do the same here. It won't be easy, but you'll do it because that's who you are. You are strong and brave and better than what anyone can do to you." He brushed haphazardly at the tears on her face. "Okay?"

Grace wanted to sit down. Wanted to sink right onto the floor, because his words did just that. They floored her. Did he really think all that of her? It didn't compute. No matter how close they'd gotten, it was more credit than, well, than she thought she deserved. She tried so hard to be strong, but all she could think of were the times she'd failed. When fear had won.

"It might not be okay." His thumb brushed across her jaw. "But you will be."

It just about did her in, so she stepped into him, and he finally offered what she'd foolishly wanted. A hug.

"You're exhausted. You should go to bed." But he squeezed her to him instead of pushing her away as she might have expected under different circumstances.

Yes, she was tired. Yes, she should go to bed. Instead she tilted her head back and pressed her lips to his. Nothing hot and heavy. Just a kiss. A little physical comfort from a man who'd given her more than anyone else had tonight. The bag of things, his words. He'd handed her a piece of herself when she'd felt like nothing more than an empty vessel.

A throat clearing interrupted the otherwise quiet room, the otherwise comfort of the kiss. Kyle practically tripped over himself stepping away from her.

Grace turned to see her father standing there with an uncharacteristic scowl on his face. "Well," he said. When he didn't say anything beyond that, Grace almost laughed.

"Thanks for bringing my stuff," Grace said,

returning her gaze to Kyle. He had his hands shoved in his pockets. This would all be cute and kind of funny if not for the reason she was here, or the fact that she was thirty, not sixteen.

"It was no problem. I'll see you later." He hesitated, and then backed into the night.

On a sigh, Grace closed the door. When she turned to face her father, he was still scowling.

"Gracie, you know I like Kyle well enough, but—"

"Not tonight, Dad. Not tonight." She picked up the bag Kyle had dropped off, wanted the goodness of that act to blind the bleakness of this night. It didn't, but it tried.

Dad grunted, but when she passed him he put his arm around her shoulders and walked with her into the kitchen. "Go to bed. There won't be any more news until morning."

News. Grace didn't want any news.

"It'll be okay, kiddo." Dad squeezed, then released her. He managed a smile, the wrinkles creasing into his skin. He looked tired and old. It hurt her heart, if it was even possible for it to hurt more.

"You and Mom need sleep, too. Where is she?"

"I wrangled her into bed. God knows she's not sleeping, but at least she's horizontal."

"I don't want her to—"

"We're your parents. We'll worry. End of story." It was his best no-nonsense teacher voice. "Now go to bed. Maybe with a little rest under our belts we'll all be a little clearer in the morning. They'll know what caused the fire. The police will talk to Barry and take him in if he did it. Nothing else to do but sleep."

Grace forced a smile and headed down the hall to her old room. Dad was wrong. There were plenty of things to do besides sleep. Worry. Feel sorry for herself. Curse Barry to hell and back. Wish he was dead, whether this was his doing or not.

Grace stepped back in time. The wood paneling of her room, the dark purple curtains. Old photographs and books. A comforter as old as her high school diploma. It was hers and not hers at the same time.

Grace pulled the sweater out of the bag Kyle had brought. The picture. Her toothbrush. Underneath were a pair of sweatpants, a T-shirt, deodorant. A strange mix of things, but they were hers. That was good enough.

Grace sank onto the bed, and as she pulled the shirt out of the bag a folded-up piece of paper fluttered to the ground. She picked it up, unfolded it.

It was the caricature she'd drawn of Kyle. A week or so ago, but it felt like years. He'd kept it. Anal, pragmatic Kyle had kept her silly little scribble.

When she laid her head down on the pillow, she began to feel the numb and hurt wear away into the fight she desperately wanted. Maybe Kyle was right. This wouldn't be okay, but hell if she let something make her not okay again.

KYLE TURNED THE CURVE, hard-edged ice shifting in his chest. The kind of feeling he hadn't let in for a long, long time. It was different from what Grace brought out in him. Not uncomfortable, not sweet and light and good. Hard, sharp, shaving away all that goodness.

Ten years had changed Carvelle. It had expanded slightly, updated in places, but this little section of it looked the same. Even in the pitch-black of the small-town night, with the fire on the other side of town dying down, Kyle knew the trailer park was the same.

He stopped his car at the entrance. *Don't do it. Turn around. Go home. Don't do it.* Though his mind chanted reason, it barely registered. Just a faint dread, a vague sense of wrongness.

Kyle slowly pushed the car door open and stepped onto the gravel. Might as well end this day of chaos with a trip to its beginning.

It smelled the same. The sweet, earthy scent of a spring night not strong enough to cover up the smell of trailer. A metallic, dirty smell. Somewhere there might be trailer parks full of cheerful hanging pots; children's toys not covered in rust; and decent, hardworking people.

Not in Carvelle.

Kyle took a halting step on the gravel road that ran down the center. Actually, calling it gravel was generous. Most of the rock had been pounded into the dusty ground or washed away so that this was really only a path.

Much like the trailers that lined it on either side. Worn down and out. He could only make out the edges of each mobile home in the faint lights, in the inky black of night, but he could still see it vividly, as if he'd only left yesterday.

Kyle's hands clenched into fists as he slowly, painfully walked to the last trailer on the left. All he could see was the shape, but it didn't matter. The ice in his chest dug deeper, the pain slashing harder.

Avoidance had worked for so long. What the hell was he doing here? Facing this. It was stupid. Pointless. So he'd grown up here, in this hell? So what?

Barry had grown up here, too. A double-wide. His dad had been an alcoholic, but his parents hadn't been junkies. They might have been abusive; that Kyle didn't know. What he did know was that Barry and he came from the same place.

But Kyle had gotten out and stayed out. This beginning might live deep inside of him, but didn't he get to control what that made him? So Barry had chosen to beat up women and possibly set fire to houses. Kyle had chosen something else.

And it didn't include coming back here. And it didn't include feeling all the violence he was capable of. He'd developed a control only his father could still unravel. He'd grown that control so big it was an entity of its own. If he could control his fate enough to get him out of here, who said he couldn't control the bad enough that he could have a little good?

"I won't be like you," he whispered. If anyone came upon him they'd think he was crazy. Maybe they wouldn't be wrong. "I won't let you win."

Maybe there was the potential for evil inside of him, but he would bury it so deep it could never make its way out. He wouldn't belong here. Not now. Not ever.

GRACE LAY ON the bed, staring at the ceiling. She should get up. She knew she should get up. She just wasn't ready to face everything yet. She needed a few more minutes to find strength. Fight. Somewhere between two o'clock in the morning and now, exhaustion had carved any fight out of her.

Being gritty eyed from lack of sleep and having a headache the size of Texas brewing behind her eyes didn't really help.

When the door creaked open, Grace lifted herself up onto her elbows. Jacob slid in. Grace let out a long sigh.

His hair was a mess; stubble dotted his jaw. He'd obviously come home in a hurry. His guilt-ridden expression tied her stomach into a knot.

"I'm sorry."

"Jacob, you didn't set that fire."

He shook his head, moving to the end of her bed and taking a seat. "I should have been there. I should have been at home so I could drive you here. I mean, what if Kyle hadn't driven you back to Carvelle? What if he'd been out running or at the gym? What if he'd flat-out refused?"

Grace wanted to laugh because what Kyle had been doing was pretty far removed from running or being at the gym or refusing *anything*. "He was there. He did drive me. It doesn't matter."

Jacob shot to his feet. "It does matter! I should have been there. Leah's right. I'm a self-absorbed asshole. I was so busy thinking about me—"

And then Grace did start to laugh.

"What?" he demanded, raking fingers through his already crazy hair.

"You're kind of making this all about you right now, you know?"

His jaw dropped and he sank back onto the bed. Then he cursed. "You're right. Christ, you're right. I…" He shook his head. "Here's the deal. I haven't been taking care of you like I should, and that stops now. You're going to come home with me, and I'm going to be with you 24/7."

It was Grace's turn to push off the bed. "I don't want that."

"Too bad."

She glared at him. "I am not going to be a prisoner. I don't care if he did this. I don't care if he's after me. I'm not going to…" She couldn't finish, because it was laughable. Of course she was going to be afraid. She'd been afraid before he'd done anything.

And she didn't even know for sure he *had* done anything.

Except the police had informed her Barry was nowhere to be found. He'd broken parole, and, well, that couldn't bode well.

Grace squeezed her eyes shut. "I don't want a shadow. I don't want this." But here it was. "The police are taking care of it."

Jacob snorted. "Pardon me if I don't put a lot of faith in Garret Simmons. Maybe twenty years and a hundred pounds ago, but now?"

"What are you going to do if Barry comes after me?"

Jacob stood up. "Protect you."

Grace laughed bitterly. "You and what army? He's twice your size. I have just as much a chance of fighting him off as you."

"Listen—"

"No. No, you listen. You want to stop being a self-absorbed asshole, listen to me. This sucks, and it's scary. But I'm not going to hide behind you or Mom and Dad. I can't keep hiding." Her voice threatened to give out, the fear threatened to strangle her, but she had to fight it. She had to fight for herself and her life this time. She wouldn't go back to being so scared she couldn't leave her parents' house. She wouldn't go back to needing therapy just to smile at a stranger.

"Grace. We want you to be safe."

"Of course you do. I want to be safe, too, but I need...I need to know I can be alone and stand on my own two feet, too. I wasn't there before, but you know what, if this was Barry? Well, he pissed me off enough to be more angry than scared." At least, she hoped she'd still feel that way the next time she was alone.

Well, even if she didn't, she'd try. No more cowering. No more living life on the fringes without even really realizing it. She was going to take risks. She was going to stand up for herself. And she was damn well going to keep her gun within reach at all times.

Grace looked at the caricature of Kyle she'd placed on her nightstand. There were things she wanted, things she'd been afraid of, and she wasn't going to do it anymore. If it took every ounce of strength and bravery Kyle seemed to think she had.

"Look, I'll go home with you because I want Mom and Dad to go to work. I want them to have some semblance of normal." And maybe, just a little bit because Kyle was there, because she didn't want to give up or forget whatever was growing between them. "I'll go with you because your house has an alarm system, but you won't be by my side all the time, okay? You'll do your job and I won't be scared into hiding behind my baby brother until Barry comes after me. I won't trade one prison of worry and suffocation for another. Okay?"

"Grace."

"Otherwise I won't go. I won't go just to have you hovering over me like Mom and Dad. Someone's got to give me credit for being strong and smart enough to do this." Starting with herself.

"It's not about you. It's about him."

"That's not fair. Something has to be about me." For once in her life. This was going to be about her. About what she wanted and how she wanted to live. "Things are going to be different. I want to live knowing I can be happy even if Barry is out there. He broke parole. He's going back to jail, but I want to know I can live knowing he's out there because even if he goes back to prison, he'll be out again someday."

Jacob rubbed a hand over his face. "I—"

"Not about you, remember?"

He laughed without much mirth. "We're all going to worry until he's back in jail. We're all going to want to protect you."

"Of course you are. Situation reversed I'd worry

and want to protect you, too, but I'd also give you enough credit for being smart enough to protect yourself."

Jacob snorted. "Easy for you to say. This is about a man who's hurt you, not how smart or brave or strong you are. It's about a threat to you."

"But—"

"No buts. That's what it is."

"All right, all right."

"Now, Mom made a crazy big breakfast. We're going to go eat, convince them you'll be safer with me and then we're going to head to Bluff City."

Grace had to bite her tongue. She hated that bossy, ordering tone he used. Hated that, despite what he said, he was still treating her like an incapacitated idiot. Hated mostly that a tiny part of her wanted to let him and her parents take over while she hid until Barry was in jail again.

But there was no point in admitting that or arguing with him. He couldn't understand. Neither could her parents. No one understood. She looked at the caricature again. Well, maybe Kyle understood, at least enough to give her what she needed.

Imagine that.

So Grace would let her family fuss over her and think they were doing something.

The truth was, if Barry really wanted to hurt her,

he would. It didn't matter what Jacob or Mom or Dad did. He'd find a way.

Instead of fearing it, of letting it ruin her, she had to accept it. And live anyway.

CHAPTER ELEVEN

"You still haven't told us why Jacob can't make the meeting."

Kyle frowned at Leah. "You'll need to be at the Martins' by one. Take notes on everything and email them to me."

"I need a reason the contractor isn't there, Kyle. Even if most of what we're dealing with is electrical and plumbing, there needs to be a reason Jacob isn't there."

"Something came up."

"Kyle."

He let out a breath. "Tell them Jacob has had a family emergency. They can reschedule for later in the week if they'd like, but you and Henry can go over most of the meeting today."

Leah chewed on her bottom lip. "Family emergency? Is everything okay?"

"Everything will be fine." The lie he hadn't been able to vocalize to Grace last night seemed imperative right now.

"Is that why Grace isn't around? And why we suddenly have the security system on 24/7?"

"Yes. Now, do you have any questions about the meeting?"

"No, I have questions about Jacob. About Grace."

A door downstairs closed loudly. Perfect excuse to escape Leah's inquisition. As far as Kyle was concerned, what happened last night wasn't his business to spread. Maybe Grace wanted to keep it quiet. Everyone in Carvelle knew about it; that was how small towns worked. She deserved a place to come where everyone wouldn't be harassing her about how she was holding up.

God, he wondered how she was holding up. And hoped, however foolishly, she would come back here instead of staying at her parents' house.

Kyle grabbed his file on the Martins and stalked into the hallway. "I'll give the papers to Henry, since who knows where they'll end up if I let you take them into your disaster area of a truck."

"I'm not letting this go, Kyle."

"Of course not," Kyle grumbled. As he got closer to the stairs, he could hear someone's footsteps. Now that he'd mandated that the alarm be in place, only those with a code would be able to enter. Since Susan, Leah, Kelly and Henry, MC's plumber, were all inside, only Jacob was left.

But it wasn't Jacob who stepped into the hallway. Kyle fumbled with the file in his hands, managed to squeeze them closed before the papers spilled onto the floor. "Grace. Hello."

It hadn't even been twenty-four hours since he'd seen her last, but she looked different. Still pale, still withdrawn, but less like a breeze would shatter her or bring her to tears.

"Hi."

"Y-you're back."

She stuck her hands in the pockets of her baggy jeans. Baggy enough he wondered if they were even hers. "Yup. That's okay, right?"

"Of course it is." His voice cracked. Christ, his voice had actually cracked like he was prepubescent.

"Well, isn't *that* interesting."

Kyle glared at Leah, who was studying Grace. "Don't you have work to do?" he said, holding out the file to her.

Leah took it from him but didn't leave. Instead she crossed to Grace. "Is everything okay? Kyle said you guys had a family emergency but is being obnoxiously tight-lipped. Is Jacob okay? Are you okay?"

"Yeah. We're fine. Everyone's fine. Jacob's downstairs."

"The meeting, Leah?" Kyle knew he was being pushy, but Grace wasn't offering details and he didn't want Leah pressing for them.

Leah considered Kyle, then Grace. "All right," she said. "Do you still want to come to book club tomorrow? We won't be offended if you want to skip. There's always next week."

Grace pulled her bottom lip between her teeth and then straightened her shoulders. "No. No, I'd really like to come. If that's all right?"

"Of course it is. I'll pick you up at six." Then, finally, *finally,* Leah left. And it was just him and Grace.

Silent.

In the hallway.

"So…" Kyle moved back onto his heels. He was usually pretty good with silence. Good with extricating himself from an uncomfortable situation. But apparently he wasn't all that interested in extricating himself.

She didn't smile and she didn't say anything. He took a hesitant step toward her. "Are you all right?"

She nodded, pulling her bottom lip between her teeth, which made him remember the moment before the phone call about the fire, which was not what he needed to be remembering right now.

She glanced down the stairs, then nodded toward her room. "Can I talk to you in private for a second?"

Since he didn't trust being able to speak like the damn twenty-eight-year-old adult he was, Kyle simply nodded and followed her to her room.

She stepped inside and let the bag slide off her arm and land with a thump on the ground. Slowly, she walked over to her bed, trailed a finger across the rumpled cover, not once talking to or looking at him.

It made him jumpy. Uncomfortable enough that the silence he was usually so good at was unbearable. "So, um, any news?"

She shook her head. "Police are looking for Barry. Fire investigator is looking for cause of fire." She kept her back to him. "It's fine, really. I mean, he had to know I wasn't there. Everyone in Carvelle knows I'm not home right now. So if he did do it, it's just petty revenge."

Kyle crossed to her. "Nothing about burning down your house is petty." Taking in her profile, he could see her throat move as she swallowed.

She expelled a loud breath. "No, I guess it isn't."

Since her voice wasn't steady, he knew he needed to soothe her. It was his first instinct, but he'd also become used to ignoring those instincts, so the move to touch her arm was a little jerky, a little rusty. Until she turned into him and her head rested against his chest; then it was no problem at all to wrap his arms around her and hold on tight. Nothing jerky or rusty about it.

She tilted her head up. Though her eyes looked suspiciously bright, no sign of tears was on her face or his shirt. "Before I kiss you, I need to say something."

He normally did quite well with surprising

information. So little about life fazed him. But this… "Um."

"You did something really sweet for me last night. Actually, a couple really sweet things, but mainly you went back to a place you didn't want to go, and chances are, it'll happen again. Not the fire stuff, I hope, but going back to Carvelle, being reminded of bad things. I…I don't know what happened to you when you were a kid, Kyle, but I know it was bad."

Kyle released her, took a step away. There were new things he was willing to do for Grace. Talking about that wasn't one of them.

"If you've changed your mind about…you know, where things were going last time, I understand."

Since that wasn't at all what he wanted, he opened his mouth to say so. But he didn't know how to verbalize it. Still, he stepped toward her again, knowing he needed to say something, to respond. To show…something.

"Just tell me and I'll, you know, back off. I can stay with my parents. I can—"

He couldn't take it. The way she wrung her hands, the way she tried to put to words something downright stupid. So he kissed her before she could talk anymore. He could feel the tension release from her body, his own tension at her bringing up his childhood disappearing.

She wound her arms around his neck; he pulled her close and forgot about pretty much everything else.

When she pulled away, just an inch, her lips curved into a smile. "I've decided to soak up all the good I can get, Kyle."

"That sounds very smart."

She chuckled, her breath fluttering across his mouth. "As much as I'd love to continue this, Jacob's going to be stomping up here momentarily. He's determined to be my 24/7 bodyguard now. I only got a few seconds of peace because he didn't want me to hear him call the police station for the eight millionth time."

Kyle's grip tightened around her waist. "When will they know for sure?"

Grace shook her head, leaned it against his shoulder. "I don't know. Barry broke parole by not checking in, though, so he'll go back to jail for sure. That's what matters. The police will find him eventually. The chances of him doing anything else are slim."

Kyle smoothed his hand over her hair, testing how it felt. Soft and silky, yes, but the action itself was new. He'd never offered someone physical comfort before. Never been the one to soothe. So the feeling was new. Nice.

"You know, you could tell Jacob that you'll take

care of the 24/7 bodyguarding and then we can just have, like, a 24/7 sex marathon."

Kyle choked out a laugh. "Well, that is an idea. I really don't think it's one Jacob will get behind."

Grace sighed. "I know. Does he have to be so unreasonable and overbearing?"

"He cares about you. He wants to protect you."

Grace tilted her head, studied him with serious brown eyes. "Do you care about me?"

It was surprising how hard one word was to say. "Yes."

"Do you want to protect me?"

Since she sneered at the word *protect,* he doubted going with a yes here was the right angle to take. "I want you to be safe."

"Isn't that the same?"

"No. I can't protect you from bad things, Grace." He smoothed one hand up her back, pushed some of her hair off her shoulder. "No matter how much I might want to."

"Why can't the rest of my family be as reasonable as you?" She traced her index finger over the bottom of his lip. "Let's stop talking about this."

"Excellent idea."

She smiled. He wanted her to keep smiling. To stop looking so sad and beat down. He wished there were something he could do to change things for her. He couldn't. But, hell, he could distract her, and himself.

This time the kiss was a little desperate, for both of them. Entwined in her, he could forget a lot. She made all the parts of his brain quiet. He would drown in that feeling if he could.

This time, it was his phone interrupting him. Slowly he became aware it was afternoon on a Wednesday and instead of being at his desk, doing the work he usually lived for, he was kissing Grace.

Well, it was a hell of a trade.

"You have to get back to work."

He didn't want to. It wasn't the first surprise of the day, but it was still a bit of a surprise. He'd rather stay right here and explore this almost normal guy he was finding behind all those walls he'd built up.

But he did have to get back, whether he wanted to or not. "Yeah."

She patted his cheek. "Well, get back to work, then."

"Tonight, um, we should…"

She raised an eyebrow and he had to clear his throat. Pathetic. He was bad at a lot of things, but usually not quite so clumsy at asking a woman out. "Go out to dinner."

"If my jail warden releases me."

"I'm sure you'll find a way."

She smiled, a wide, bright smile that made him feel like a hero. He ignored the voice that told him he'd never be a hero.

"All right. It's a date."

"A date." A date with Grace McKnight. Well, surely stranger things had happened. Somewhere.

"YOU SHOULD ASK Susan or Kelly. My date wardrobe is pretty limited." Leah stretched out on Grace's bed.

"You're closer to my size and closer to my comfort zone." Grace pawed through the messy pile of clothes Leah had brought after her last job of the day.

"Fair enough. If you're looking for my vote, wear the black T-shirt with my jean skirt and then the black boots."

Grace studied the outfit. "Awfully black."

"Black, gray and brown are what I bring to the table. You could wear colorful jewelry or that pinkish scarf."

Grace nodded, considering her options.

"So you're going on a date?"

"Yeah."

"With Kyle."

Grace pretended to be very interested in the floral pattern on the scarf. "That's the plan." Since Grace hadn't had a female friend in ages to talk to about this kind of thing, and hadn't exactly done the whole date thing in a while, she couldn't help but look at Leah. "You have some thoughts on that?"

Leah shrugged. "None of my business."

"Okay."

"But you do seem kind of like an odd couple. Kyle's so…bland. You're the opposite. That and the fact that I can't picture Kyle actually asking anyone out, it's kind of hard to figure."

Grace considered. "I lighten him up."

"Good. He needs it." Leah picked at the bedspread. "But what does he do for you? That's important, too, you know. At least, that's the lesson I'm trying to teach myself."

Grace considered. What did Kyle do for her? He understood, he comforted, he made her feel… special. Grace's mouth curved. "He does a lot for me, actually." Weird but true.

The bedroom door swung open and Jacob strode in. Grace pinched the bridge of her nose. This was getting old fast. Now she understood why Jacob never got angry. He simply wouldn't be able to handle it in a rational way. "What now?"

"You are not leaving this house."

"The he-man routine is really getting on my nerves."

"Your house burned down, Grace. The man who put you in the hospital is nowhere to be found and you want to go out with Kyle, *Kyle,* and make he-man jokes?"

Leah sat up on the bed where she'd been lounging. "Whoa. What?"

"Thanks a lot, Jacob."

Jacob spared Leah a brief glance. "Can you give us a minute?"

"Depends."

"On?" he ground out through gritted teeth.

"If Grace wants me to. This is her room. Not yours. And you're acting like an ass. Again. Maybe she wants backup."

"You know what, Leah? This isn't any of your damn business. Stop butting your big-ass nose where it doesn't belong."

Leah pushed off the bed and Grace wondered if Jacob saw the hurt on her face or if he was so caught up in his own idiocy he had no idea. She was guessing the latter.

Leah crossed to her, effectively creating a barrier between Grace and Jacob. "Do you want me to leave?" she asked earnestly.

Grace sighed. "Yeah." She offered Leah an impulsive hug. "Thank you, but I can handle him."

"Kick his ass," Leah muttered, sauntering out of the room.

"Okay, what the hell is your problem?" Grace flung the clothes onto the bed.

"You need to take this seriously, and you're not." He started pacing the room. "The police have nothing. Nothing. That guy is just…out there."

Grace tried to ignore the cold chill down her spine. "Yes. I'm aware. I was the one he beat the hell out of, if you recall."

"Yes. I do recall. I was the one in the hospital room while you were in a damn coma. So yeah, I understand. I won't let it happen this time."

For the first time, anger and frustration gave way to concern. This was so unlike her brother, so blown out of proportion. She expected worry. She expected Jacob to want her to stick close. She understood it all. She'd been down this road before.

What she didn't understand was the anger, the barely contained violence in his declarations. It wasn't Jacob.

"Jacob, you can't run my life. Even if I let you, that doesn't change or solve anything. We don't even know if this is what we think it is. It could all be a freak accident."

"Right. We should go around assuming it was a freak accident and going out on dates and being damned cavalier about it. How can you be this stupid?"

It took a lot of willpower not to smack him. To throw a fit and tell him to get out. People who never had to deal with what she'd had to deal with did not get to call her stupid, least of all her baby brother.

But he'd never, ever been anything but supportive up to this point, acting as interference between her and their parents. Giving her space. Treating her as he always had instead of like some fragile thing that would shatter. She held on to that little beacon of sanity.

"Jacob, you've never questioned my judgment before." She purposefully unclenched her fists. "This asshole you're currently being isn't you. This so isn't you."

He sank onto her bed. "If it takes being an asshole to keep you safe, then so be it." He clenched and unclenched his fists, looking as lost as she'd felt last night.

"You can't, though. Not really. You can't undo this or change it. What happened, happened."

"I can keep it from happening again."

"No, you can't." Grace sat on the bed next to him. She was beginning to understand. She'd felt this, too. The impotent anger. The feeling that if she did everything right it would be okay. It wasn't true. What had happened to her wasn't because of the choices she'd made. It wasn't because of anyone or anything except the choices Barry made.

That was really hard to swallow, but she'd had to, and Jacob did now, too.

"I don't want you to have to go through it all again." His voice was low and gravelly, his hands clenched in his lap. "I wasn't there the first time. I know I came home when you were in the hospital, but I went right back to school after. I was away and young and stupid and I didn't do anything to help. Seven years later and I didn't learn my lesson. I went out with Candy, I went on that stupid business trip. I wasn't here and—"

"Your being here doesn't change what happened. My house would have still burned down. The bottom line is, in a town like Carvelle, Barry knew I wasn't living there right now. If he did this, it wasn't to hurt me...physically anyway."

"God, this is so screwed up. You're comforting me. I'm sitting here making this about me again. And you... Christ, Grace. I'm sorry. I just want you to be happy and safe. Going out with Kyle..." He shook his head. "It's the wrong direction."

"It's my direction," Grace said firmly. "I need you to let go of being angry and let go of trying to control the situation. It can't be controlled. All we can do is...wait."

"I could hunt the jackass down myself."

Grace sighed. "Yeah. So could I. Believe me, I've thought about it. A lot. But I have to believe the police will find him and I have to live my life regardless. I'm not going to be reckless. You won't see me walking down any streets by myself at night, but I'm not going to let this take away every possible good. I can't let him do that again. I've come too far. If I can't have some semblance of normal..." Grace sighed. "What the hell is the point?"

"So you're going to go out. With Kyle."

Grace slid off the bed. "Yes."

"Because that's something good?"

"Yes. I think it could be."

"I don't think a date with a man like Kyle of all people is the best idea right now."

Well, so much for thinking she'd gotten through to him. "Should I remind you that you like Kyle?"

"Yeah, I do. He's my business partner and my best friend, but…"

"He understands." Grace picked at the paint on her jeans. "I know you want to. Mom and Dad want to. But you don't and he does, and I need that right now."

Jacob let out a breath. "You don't know him. Not really. Kyle is complicated and you don't need complicated." He moved off the bed.

"This isn't open for discussion."

"Grace—"

"You need to go apologize to Leah for being an ass before she goes home. You were awful to her and hurt her feelings."

Jacob's mouth went slack in surprise. Then he cursed. "She'll find a way to pay me back for that one."

"Not if you sincerely apologize. Now go. I have a date to get ready for."

Jacob grimaced. "For the record—"

Grace pushed him toward the door. "You've reached your advice allotment for the day. Now get out."

He grumbled but finally left, pulling the door closed behind him. Grace sank onto the bed, her clothes in her hands. The questions swirled through her brain. Was she being cavalier? Should she let her family lock her away until this was done? Should she put off pursuing anything with Kyle until this was all over?

But none of that felt right. She deserved something more. Finding the good. Someone who understood. A way to fight back the fear still threatening.

No, she deserved something, and this time she wouldn't take no for an answer.

KYLE WAS FAIRLY certain even his first date hadn't prompted this kind of all-encompassing nervousness.

Perhaps that was because he'd never spent much time dating people he connected with on a personal level. He usually dated career-focused women whose schedules rivaled his. That way, it was usually time that naturally ended the relationship rather than anything messy.

But Grace, even a simple date with Grace, had the potential to be messy. He was stepping into uncharted territory. Territory he'd promised himself never to walk. Territory he didn't think he even wanted.

Grace made him want it. She made all those feelings he'd been scared of for so long seem less scary and more enticing. More along the lines of something he didn't just want, but something he needed.

In a short time, she'd turned him upside down. He'd been afraid of that. The surprise wasn't that she'd done it. The surprise was that he liked it.

Quieting the nerves deep beneath a veneer of composure, Kyle stepped out of his room. He moved down the stairs, surprised when the nerves didn't disappear as they usually did when he focused. No, this time, they intensified.

Grace stood by the kitchen table, riffling through her purse. When she heard him enter, she looked up. "Hi." She smoothed her hands over her skirt.

Grace's normal wardrobe was jeans or sweats and paint splatters. He could count the occasions he'd seen her in something else on one hand. But today she was wearing a skirt that hugged the curve of her hips, showed off her long legs. Her hair waved to her shoulders, most of the color hidden underneath the top layer of rich brown.

Though he'd been less than kind about her wardrobe in the past, he found she didn't look any more or less beautiful dressed up. He liked her quite well either way. "You look lovely."

Her mouth curved into a smile. "Thank you."

"Well, I was thinking we could—"

"Knock, knock!" Mrs. McKnight bustled into the kitchen, Mr. McKnight at her heels. They carried KFC bags and smiles so fake it had to hurt.

Grace stared at them openmouthed for a minute

before managing a smile. "Mom. Dad. What are you doing here?"

"We brought dinner. Kyle, you're welcome to join us. We brought enough for an army."

"Honey, Kyle looks like he's going somewhere." Mr. McKnight's smile sharpened. "Night on the town? Big date?"

Kyle shared a brief glance with Grace; at her helpless look, Kyle shook his head. "No. Just back from a meeting, actually. I should go…"

"No." Grace clamped her hand on his arm. "Eat with us. You can go find Jacob and anybody else who's still around." Grace smiled brightly. A fake bright smile to match her parents'.

Because he didn't have a clue as to what else to do, Kyle nodded. "All right." He pulled his arm from Grace's grasp. "I'll see who I can round up."

"Wonderful." Mrs. McKnight was unpacking food onto the table, Grace watching as she chewed on her bottom lip. Then Kyle realized Mr. McKnight was glaring at him, and he moved into action.

Kyle crested the stairs. Since Jacob's office door was open and the lights on, Kyle went there first. Jacob was sitting at his desk, tapping fingers against the wood.

"Hey."

Jacob spared him a cursory glance. "Hey."

Kyle noticed the considerable chill, but tried to

ignore it. "Your parents are downstairs. I guess we're all having fried chicken."

Jacob swiveled in his chair, smiled. "Date ruined, then?"

"I guess so."

Since Jacob seemed awfully happy with that, Kyle stepped in front of him before he could exit the room. He considered his best friend, surprised things had turned, and so quickly. "Did—did you arrange this?"

"Arrange what?"

Kyle rubbed a hand over the back of his neck. Confusion. Discomfort. These were things that came with living life. Chaos. "Did you purposefully get your parents over here so Grace and I couldn't go out?"

Jacob was quiet for a long time. Long enough Kyle was convinced he had. Long enough Kyle realized Jacob's "I like you" speech from a few weeks back no longer applied.

"No, I didn't."

"You don't want me seeing Grace."

Again, silence was enough of an answer. He should go. Nothing about this conversation was headed in a place he could control, or really understand. His feet stayed rooted, blocking Jacob's exit.

"Didn't say that. She seems to think you understand her, and for now that's great."

"For now?"

"Yeah. I just… We've been friends a long time, Kyle. You don't date as often as me, but you're not exactly Mr. Reliable, and this is my sister. My sister who doesn't date much because some guy beat the hell out of her years ago."

"I would never hurt Grace."

"Not like that. But are you willing to completely change who you've been? Because while I know there's a decent guy under all your walls, you've never been willing to admit it to yourself before. She deserves a good guy."

Kyle didn't know what to say to that, how to explain he wanted to be what she deserved. Because even though he wanted it, Jacob's doubts were enough to bolster his own.

"I'm not trying to scare you off, because she seems to think you're important to her right now. I'm just saying, for our friendship, for our business, be very careful about this." Jacob gestured to the hall. "Going to get out of my way?"

Kyle stepped to the side, let Jacob pass. For a few minutes the words and doubts clouded his judgment, told him to go back to his office, to end this before things got more complicated and messy.

But the words ringing louder and louder were what Jacob had said about Grace thinking Kyle understood her, that he was important to her.

He'd never been important to anyone before. Except maybe Jacob, and even that wasn't the same as being important and needed and...wanted.

Kyle strode to the stairs. He wasn't giving up on that so easily.

CHAPTER TWELVE

GRACE PICKED AT the chicken on her plate. She was flanked by Dad and Jacob and had a feeling the move to have them seated on opposite sides of her was very purposeful.

Kyle was sandwiched in between Leah and Mom. Mom was going on about one of her current students while Kyle listened and responded patiently. He didn't look comfortable, judging from the rigid posture and the few bites of chicken he'd taken, but he was nodding and asking appropriate questions.

He was trying. It made her want to shoo everyone away and curl up in Kyle. She knew her family was trying, too. Trying to be all smiles and cheerful banter so no one would think about what was really lurking. It was nice, and it was better than lectures and directives, but it wasn't the same as Kyle's simple uncomfortable conversation with Mom.

Kyle was trying for her. Her family was trying for themselves. She couldn't blame them. She'd probably be acting just like Jacob if the situation were reversed, but it wasn't reversed. This was her life. And it was suffocating. The situation. Her family's reaction to it. The fact that there was no way to make either better.

"I thought we could go see a movie tomorrow night, sweetie. We haven't done that in ages."

"Oh." Grace wiped her fingers on her napkin and tried to smile at Mom. "I...um, have plans."

"I'm sure plans can be rearranged," Dad offered with a smile. Not a real smile, though. The weird, threatening smile he kept sending Kyle's way.

"She's coming to my book club," Leah piped in. "Susan and I started it and Grace wanted to join."

Both her parents looked relieved, and Grace would have to remember to thank Leah later. She'd go to a movie with Mom on another night. But she needed a break, and she needed Leah and Susan's "book club." It had been too long since she'd been at the gun range.

"What book are you reading?"

Grace coughed on a piece of biscuit, but Leah smiled brightly. "Oh, you know, that crazy sex book everyone is talking about."

It was Jacob's turn to choke on his food. Dad looked down at his plate uncomfortably, and it took every ounce of control for Grace not to bark out a laugh.

"Well… How nice." Mom's smile looked pained. "So how did your out-of-town meeting go, Jake? You never did tell us."

As Jacob started to talk about work, Grace

mouthed a thank-you to Leah, who winked in response. Grace's gaze moved to Kyle. He was staring at her. She smiled. He smiled.

God, he was cute.

Dad cleared his throat and Grace practically jumped. "So, Gracie, how many paintings have you sold now?"

And so went dinner, and the rest of the evening. It was nearly ten before she convinced her parents to head home.

"We can take tomorrow off and—"

"Mom, go home. Go to work tomorrow. Take *Dad* to a movie. We can do something this weekend, okay?"

Mom managed a wobbly smile. "All right. All right. Call me tomorrow, though?"

Grace nodded, accepted yet another hug from Mom, then Dad. Once they were out the door, Grace turned back to the living room. Kyle and Jacob stood, hands shoved in their pockets and a considerable distance between them. Leah was curled up on the couch, having fallen asleep sometime during the third round of Trivial Pursuit.

"Should I wake her up?"

Jacob picked up a blanket from behind the couch and put it over her. "Eh, let her sleep."

Then the three of them stood in the living room staring at one another. In silence. The only sound was Leah's heavy breathing and the occasional groan of the house.

"Well, it's late." Jacob rocked back on his heels. Looked expectantly at Kyle.

Grace nodded. "Yes. It is late. You should go to bed." Grace mustered up her best death glare, but Jacob didn't notice. He was too busy staring at Kyle.

Kyle let out an audible breath. "All right," he mumbled. "I think I'll head off to bed." Briefly, way too briefly, he touched her hand, squeezed. "Good night, Grace." And then he walked to the stairs and disappeared up them.

"You know you're still being an ass, right?"

Jacob smiled. "Brother's prerogative."

"And what exactly is your prerogative trying to prove? You like Kyle. A week ago you couldn't have cared less if I got involved with him. Now suddenly you and Dad are glaring at him and being rude."

"Maybe I do like Kyle, but that doesn't mean he's right for you. That doesn't mean you should be getting involved with someone with everything else going on."

"Oh, my God."

"I'm just saying—"

"Yeah, I'm not interested at all in what you're just saying." Grace turned on a heel. If she was going to get through however long it took for this whole ordeal to end, she would have to keep as much distance from Jacob as possible, or their once-close relationship would be gone.

Grace hurried up the stairs. She had planned on calling it a night, heading to her room, maybe indulging a little self-pity, but as she walked down the hallway from the front stairs, she had to pass Kyle's office. Which had a light on and the door cracked open.

Grace looked behind her. No Jacob to be seen. Grace slipped into the crack, doing her best to close the door silently.

"Grace—"

Grace put a finger to her lips. At this point, she wouldn't put it past Jacob to barge right in if he had in fact followed her up the stairs.

It was tempting to crawl into Kyle's lap, but he stood before she could act on the impulse.

"I feel like I'm too old to be sneaking around. Especially in my own house. Especially from your brother."

But he whispered. Grace smiled and moved so they were close enough he could touch her if he felt so inclined. She really hoped he was so inclined.

When his fingers lightly brushed the hair at her temple, she grinned. "So that was some date."

His expelled breath almost sounded like a laugh. "Yes, some date, indeed."

"When are we going to reschedule?"

"Perhaps when your family moves to Alaska?"

His hands smoothed over her shoulders, down her back, a delicious warmth following the movement as she had to step even closer. "I don't think they're going to give us much opportunity."

"No. Doesn't seem that way."

"I was thinking you could be my date to MC's anniversary party next Friday. Your family will be there, but by then everything should...die down."

She knew what "everything" was, and hoped he was right. Every time her phone rang she jumped with the hope the police had caught Barry. Or proved he hadn't done it and his disappearing meant he was dead in a ditch somewhere.

It probably made her a terrible person, but she was really hoping for the dead-in-a-ditch scenario.

"You don't have to, of course. I just thought—"

"It sounds perfect."

"Well, good." He smiled. She smiled, and then she had to laugh.

His mouth brushed hers. Lingered. The good kind of shivery feeling wiggled its way down her spine, so she pressed closer, as close as she could. "We could sneak into your room," she whispered against his mouth.

"The room in which I share a wall with Jacob?"

"We could sneak into my room?"

His breath sighed across her face as he pulled his head back a little. "Grace."

"I'm not used to a guy playing hard to get. I didn't really think that happened."

"I'm not used to…" He trailed off, cupped her face with his hands. "I'm not used to anything this important. I don't want to have to sneak, Grace."

That was nice. Sweet. One of these days sweet and nice wouldn't totally cut it, but for now it was really comforting.

So she kissed him again, sank into the feeling of nothing else mattering, and maybe one of these days it would actually be true.

Kyle squeezed her shoulders, then gently pushed her back a step, but then he rested his forehead on hers. "Good night, Grace."

Grace chuckled, took the last few steps to the door. "Good night, Kyle." She slipped back out the door and took a breath. The hall was dark; her room would be darker. Fear snaked its way around her lungs, but she pushed her legs forward, chanting her new mantra over and over.

Fear will not win.

KYLE DID HIS best to smile at the Martins, but they were driving him up the wall. Customers being overbearing or unreasonable didn't normally bother him. He usually had nothing better to do than sort out the problems and complaints.

Usually didn't live here anymore.

"I'm sure Jacob will be here momentarily."

"He's been missing a lot of meetings lately."

One. One meeting. If he missed this one, that would be two. Hardly a lot. Kyle smiled blandly. "Unfortunately, he's been dealing with a family emergency requiring some of his attention. Leah and Henry said everything went well at your meeting yesterday."

"Yes. I suppose." Mrs. Martin rolled her eyes to the ceiling. "Though I think we're paying a rather hefty sum, and that should give us the right to deal with the contractor directly."

Kyle's bland smile tightened. "Yes, of course. Why don't I go see if I can find Jacob. Can I have Susan get you something to drink while you wait?"

The middle-aged couple sighed together. "I'll take some coffee, black."

Mrs. Martin waved regally. "Nothing for me."

Kyle nodded and left the living room. He walked over to the formal dining room where Susan had her "office."

"Could you make Mr. Martin some coffee?"

"Jacob and Grace are in the kitchen." Susan chewed on her bottom lip and wrung her hands together. "With a police officer. Do you know what's going on?"

Kyle's heart stuttered for a second. Good news, he hoped hard for good news. "You can use the single-cup machine in Jacob's office."

Susan pressed her lips together. "The alarm thing, now the police. What's going on, Kyle?"

"Nothing. Nothing for you to worry about. If Grace wants to tell you, that's her choice. Now, the Martins are waiting, and they're in a pissy mood."

Susan glanced briefly at the kitchen, then sighed. "I'm going, I'm going."

Kyle took a step toward the kitchen, but it wasn't his business. It wasn't his place. Barging in there or even eavesdropping would be wrong, but it took a lot of willpower to listen to that reasonable voice in his head.

Before Kyle could decide the best course of action, Jacob stomped out of the kitchen, then stopped short when he saw Kyle.

"News?" Kyle prompted, unable to wait and let Jacob tell him of his own accord.

Jacob nodded. "The police said they found the stuff used to start Grace's fire in his trailer. Still no Barry, but all evidence points to his having done it."

Kyle's hands clenched into fists. "What can I do?"

Jacob looked at him, stared for a while longer than Kyle thought necessary. "She's not taking it well, but she didn't want me around." Jacob took a deep breath and loudly released it. "I'll take my meeting with the Martins. There's nothing else for me to do. Will you—" Jacob shook his head, practically gritted out the words "—check on her?"

Though it surprised him, Kyle wasn't about to ask questions. If Jacob was letting up, that was really all that mattered, especially if Grace needed someone.

"If she tells you to buzz off, you do it, got it? Only stay with her if she wants you to. Don't be pushy. And nothing overly friendly. Be her friend. That's it. A hands-off friend."

Kyle refrained, barely, from reminding Jacob that pushy was exactly what the McKnights had been for the past two days. He kept his mouth shut and nodded. "I can get Leah to take the meeting if—"

Jacob shook his head, pushing past him. "No. I'll do it. Maybe if I do it I won't want to punch something."

"I wouldn't guarantee it," Kyle muttered. He hurried up the stairs and down the hall to Grace's room. Her door was closed, so he knocked lightly on it. When there was no answer, Kyle struggled to decide what was the best course of action.

Just as he was talking himself out of barging into the room or knocking until she opened it, the door slowly creaked open.

"Hi," Grace offered. She'd been crying, but had obviously tried to hide the evidence. Then she let out a shaky sigh. "Well, I can tell by the pity on your face you already talked to Jacob."

"Yes."

She opened the door farther. "Might as well

come on in, then." She hugged herself as he stepped into the room and closed the door behind him. She walked over to her easel, keeping her back to him the whole time.

"If you don't want me here, I'll go. I just wanted to make sure you're all right."

She snorted. "All right? Yeah, I'm fantastic." She poked around at the brushes she kept in a cup on the tray of the easel. "Barry burned my house down and I'm perfectly all right."

"Grace."

She picked one of the brushes out of the cup and twirled it in her fingers. "But we knew that, right? I wanted to believe it was some freak accident. I kept saying, what if it wasn't him? What if? What if?" She threw the brush across the room, where it clattered against the wall and thudded to the ground.

Kyle's stomach pitched, as it always did when startled by violence, no matter how small. Luckily her back was to him, so she couldn't notice his body go rigid.

"Idiot. I knew. And now here it is, and damn it." She took the cup of brushes and heaved it against the wall.

Kyle swallowed down the discomfort jangling through his veins. "Grace." His voice was too rusty, too weak.

She pressed her palms to the wall, head hanging low. Kyle was too rooted to the spot to move, to offer comfort. He tried to work some words out, but he couldn't. Unease and a familiar fear worked through him. It didn't match the situation, but he couldn't convince his brain of that.

She turned to look at him and must have seen the discomfort on his face, because her anger seemed to leak out of her. Limply she leaned back against the wall and slid into a sitting position. "I don't want to be this girl anymore," she said, tears spilling onto her cheeks. "I don't want to be me anymore."

He knew the feeling so well it cracked his heart down the center. A painful, throbbing ache. But what could he do? The only thing that had ever made him feel like he wanted to be himself was MC and…Grace.

Since the violence had leaked out of her, he found he could move once again. He took a spot next to her on the floor and put his arm around her, drawing her close.

"I'm sorry."

"Sorry?" What possible reason could she have to apologize to him?

"I… I'm sorry for throwing things." She shifted so her eyes met his. Her fingertips brushed across his jaw. "It bothered you."

He looked away, trying to hold on to the feel of her hand on his face over the cold tension that wanted to creep into his muscles at the concern in her expression. "No. Of course not."

"I saw your face when I turned around. You were pale. You were..."

He didn't like the way she trailed off, as if she was going to say *afraid*. He hadn't been. Not afraid, only...surprised. He'd expected tears and he'd gotten rage and it had surprised him. That was all.

"I was, and am, fine. This isn't about me. It's about you."

He swore he could *feel* her gaze, as though it was a touch. He could *feel* her desperate attempt to search his face, his expression, and find some answer. An answer he could never, ever allow her to have.

"You don't have to do that with me," she said, her voice little more than a whisper. Quiet, but fierce. Determined. The core of Grace that was the center of why he cared for her, and the absolute reason why she terrified him.

"You don't have to pretend it's not there. Not with me."

She didn't understand. That was exactly what he had to do. To survive. To move on. To be him. This better version of himself. The version of himself that was almost worthy of her.

"You've had a rough day." His voice was rustier than he intended, and his muscles were tight with tension, but he forced himself to move. He ran a hand over her hair, her cheek, her neck. He kissed her temple and willed himself out of the equation.

This was about Grace. Not him. "Maybe you should lie down."

"You don't have to shut me out."

He forced himself to look at her, directly in the eye. To touch her face. The lie was hard, but the truth would be harder. "I'm not. I'm worried about you. Not wanting to be you." He brushed his thumbs across her cheeks, because that wasn't a lie. Those words from her did worry him, when he saw her as so brave and strong—braver and stronger than him—and she didn't want to be herself.

Yes, that killed him. Far more than an uncomfortable reminder of his volatile past.

Eyebrows drawn together, she studied him. He knew she saw a puzzle, and that she thought she could fit all the pieces together, but he'd never allow her to have those bad pieces of him, the ones with the jagged edges and violent images.

"But you understand how I feel, don't you?"

"Yes. Yes, I understand."

It seemed to appease her, because she rested her head on his shoulder and they sat there for a very long time while the world went on outside her bedroom door.

CHAPTER THIRTEEN

GRACE WAS A little raw and a lot angry. She didn't understand it, but that didn't mean it wasn't eating her alive. Something about the police confirming the fire was set by Barry, and still not having Barry in custody filled her with more anger than fear.

Crying on Kyle's shoulder had helped ease some of the self-pity. Vocalizing it and crying over it had taken away some of its power. But the anger…the anger still burned.

So Grace knew she had to act. Even if it was foolish. Even if it was a silly, empty gesture. She needed it.

She looked at her reflection in the hairdresser's mirror.

"Do you like it?" the perky, young stylist asked.

Gone were the colors and a lot of length. Gone was her natural brown hair. Instead she had a short black bob.

"I love it." She went through the steps of paying for her haircut and then walked out into the mall to find Leah. Of course, she hadn't gone far. No, no one who knew what was going on would let her out of their sight for too long. Leah was sitting on the bench just outside the salon, her nose glued to her phone.

"So what do you think?"

Leah looked up. "Holy shit." She pushed off the bench to study Grace's hair. "You look badass, Grace."

Grace smiled and touched the blunt ends of her hair. "Good. I like that. So should we head out to Shades? I'm ready to give old Betsy a workout."

"We still have about an hour. Mind if we go into Harpers? I need a damn dress for this stupid anniversary party next week."

"You know what, that's an even better idea because I need a dress, too." Grace smiled. If that was going to be her first "date" with Kyle, she would make sure in no uncertain terms that she wasn't looking for sweet or nice after the party. She wanted to be *wanted*. By him.

"Ugh. I hate shopping. I hate dresses." Leah pawed through racks. "I should just wear jeans and a T-shirt and tell your brother and his snide comments where to shove it."

"Why, what'd Jacob say?" Grace didn't naturally gravitate toward dresses, but with a specific cause in mind, it was kind of fun. She pulled three black dresses off the rack in front of her and draped them across her arm.

She was done with color for a while.

"He gave me this lecture about how it was going to be a fancy party with all our hoity-toity clients and maybe Susan and Kelly could help me find something appropriate to wear." Leah scoffed. "I'm an electrician, for Pete's sake. What the hell do I need with a fancy party?"

"Well, just think, if you wear something really elegant and fancy, you'll totally shut him up."

Leah stopped absently pawing through the selections and chewed on her bottom lip. "I'll just look stupid."

Grace shook her head and pulled a few dresses that she would have worn if she wasn't going for black. A royal blue, a poppy red, a flowery print. She shoved them at Leah. "You'll try those on."

Leah stared down at the dresses. "These are all… really bright."

"Go big or go home, Leah," Grace said, enjoying herself. She hadn't shopped with another female aside from her mom since high school. Mostly she'd rather spend money on art supplies than clothes, but this was a special occasion and it was fun having someone to boss around.

Besides, all her clothes aside from the ones she'd brought for her month at Jacob's were gone.

Leah looked down at the dresses, frowned. "I… can't wear low-cut dresses."

Grace shrugged, took back the floral print and picked out a few more dresses for her shopping companion. "You have to try them all on and you have to show me at least three."

"But—"

"I'm in charge. Embrace it." In charge. Because she couldn't be in charge of what was actually happening in her life, but she could be in charge of something silly like this.

Grace went through her stack of dresses. All but one fit well enough, but the one she gravitated to, the one that made her wince at the price tag but suited her new hairstyle perfectly, was exactly what she wanted. Black, sleek, sexy.

It might be a little short for a stuffy party, and the scoop neck might show off a little more than some of the older, rich clients would deem appropriate. The sleeves were long, though, and the black color meant that it didn't scream "look at me." She didn't imagine that her dad would enjoy seeing her wear it, but she couldn't stop looking at herself in the mirror when she was in it.

She looked hot. Powerful. Like someone she'd never, ever been. And that made the decision for her.

"Okay, I'm in one," Leah grumbled from the room over.

"Come out," Grace instructed, stepping out of her little cube.

"How about you come in?"

Grace chuckled and stepped inside the tiny

dressing room. Leah had on the bright red dress. It was long-sleeved, too, but the neckline didn't stray beyond her collarbone. The skirt was as short as Grace's, which made Grace a little more confident about her own choice.

"It's perfect. Classy, bright and it shows you actually do have a body under there. Jacob's eyes will pop out of their sockets."

Leah laughed uncomfortably, but she smoothed her hands over the dress and then smiled at her reflection. "Jacob doesn't, you know, look at me that way."

Grace shrugged, admiring her own reflection and how powerful she looked. "Maybe he will now."

"I don't want that," Leah squeaked. She smoothed her hands down the dress again. "But I look pretty good, don't I?"

"We both look amazing. Which means we owe it to ourselves to buy them."

Leah looked at the price tag and grimaced. "I hate to spend that much on something I'll never wear again."

"Hey, you never know. You could wear it to weddings or other parties or on a date."

Leah snorted. "Yeah, I attract a lot of men who take me to places I could wear this." She sighed and studied herself in the mirror one last time. "Thanks, Grace. I needed this. And now I kind of feel like a tool because you're the one going through…stuff, and I should be, you know, helping you."

Grace smiled. "It's fun. Having a friend who's a girl. I'm not used to that lately, so no thanks needed." It was nice having friends who didn't make a huge deal out of what happened. "Going through stuff" was Leah's first mention of it.

Where Kyle was comforting because he understood, a friend like Leah was comforting because she was a distraction. There was no reason to dwell on Barry.

Leah grinned. "Good." She wrinkled her nose. "Look, I don't do the whole hugging-people thing, but if I did, just know that I would hug you right now."

Grace laughed. "Thanks. Now let's go make our purchases and shoot some guns."

"I like the way you think."

They bought their dresses and headed out to the gun range. Susan was already there, in perfectly tailored jeans and a button-up shirt, loading her gun.

The range Grace had started going to after the first incident with Barry was in Bluff City. An inside range, there'd been a lot more hoops to jump through and people around. It had always been a nerve-racking experience. But Grace should have been doing this all along. Being outdoors, no hoops, just set up your own target and *boom*.

Leah and Susan set up the targets. More than one friend. Life was not all bad. Grace pulled out her holster, squeezed her hand hard around the handle. She would not let all the bad seep over the good.

"Whoa. Look at you," Susan said, shading her eyes against the slowly descending sun as she walked back with Leah.

Grace gave a little twirl that bounced her hair. "Like it?" She unsnapped the strap and began to load as Susan studied her.

"Well, it's a good look for you. It is strange, though."

"Strange?" Grace stepped up to the line and studied the target.

"It's just so not you. Dark and edgy and all."

Grace eyed the target. "Maybe it's the new me." She pulled the trigger, enjoyed the satisfying *zing* of hearing bullet hit target. Let Barry try to get near her. Just let him.

KYLE STARED AT the ceiling. His room was dark and he was exhausted, but he couldn't sleep. Though Grace had texted both him and Jacob that she was going to be at Leah's until eleven, he couldn't sleep knowing she wasn't home safe.

But he wasn't going to prowl the living room like Jacob, grumbling about Leah, ready to pounce the minute she arrived. Grace didn't need that.

Unfortunately, that was exactly what he *wanted*

to do, and trying to work had only given him excuse after excuse to wander downstairs with a question for Jacob. So he'd forced himself to get ready for bed and lie there, no matter how little sleep he got until he knew Grace was back.

Kyle glanced at the clock. Eleven-ten. Was she home and he just hadn't heard the door open? Quite possible.

Kyle clasped his hands over his chest, told himself he was not going to get up to check up on her. Unless he could come up with a really believable excuse.

No. No, not going to be that guy.

But his eyes didn't close, and his thoughts didn't shut off. He strained to hear any sound that might be the door opening or closing. Footsteps on the back staircase.

Eleven-fifteen. Kyle was about to say screw it and get out of bed when his door creaked open. Through a sliver of blinding light from the hall, he could make out Grace. She closed the door so quickly he only got a sense that she looked different without being able to pick out exactly why.

"Hi," she whispered. The lock on his door clicked loud enough to be a gunshot.

It took him a minute to make his throat push out the word. "Hi." It was dark in his room except for the glow of the clock and the shaft of streetlight from the gap between curtain and window. He could make out a shadowy figure and that was it.

But he could feel his bed dip, and then Grace's warmth next to him. He swallowed, remaining perfectly still because if he moved, any honorable intentions he had were toast.

She scooted closer, her shoulder brushing his, strands of her hair shifting across his face. Her fingertips tentatively touched his neck, tested the weight of her palm against his chest, then roamed up to his shoulder, as if she was searching for bearing.

Kyle was just searching for some semblance of control.

"Kyle." Her breath whispered across his cheek, and without thinking it through, he turned toward her. Her hand slid up his shoulder to his neck, and her lips touched his.

Screw control.

He pulled her to him so their bodies touched everywhere he could manage. He traced her lips with his tongue until she parted them, allowing entrance. She nibbled at his lip, pressed her leg between his.

Hell. He wasn't supposed to do this yet. The moment was supposed to be special and full of roses and romance and all that stuff he wasn't sure he was any good at, but he knew Grace deserved.

"Grace," he muttered against her mouth. "I—"

"I'm not taking no for an answer this time." Her

voice was breathless but determined. She pulled his mouth to hers again, a hard, demanding kiss that shattered any noble thoughts well and truly to dust.

"Well."

"Don't worry. I came prepared."

An uneven laugh escaped his mouth, which he then pressed to where her shirt met her shoulder. The kiss was half on skin, half on fabric. "Are you sure about this?"

Her arms tightened around him. "Yeah. Really, really sure." Good enough. More than good enough. Perfect.

He found her mouth again, eager and willing. It wasn't like that time before when they'd been interrupted. No, because now he'd already surrendered to Grace. There were no questions in his mind, or at least the questions were silent. Now he would just savor them together. Because he wanted it. Because she wanted it. Because it was theirs to have, no matter what baggage might take up space in his mind.

This wasn't about his mind. It was about her body and his heart and everything in between, but his brain certainly didn't have a say.

Kyle slid his hands under her shirt, taking his time smoothing his palms up the silky skin of her stomach, then the side of her breast. She pressed closer to him, hooking a leg over his until she'd shifted on top of him.

He could make out the outline of Grace taking

off her shirt, and he moved up into a sitting position, so she straddled his lap. He slid the straps of her bra off her shoulders, planting kisses along her arms as she arched against him.

She pushed his hands away, finding the hem of his shirt and pulling it over his head. Her mouth explored his neck while his hands explored her back. He could hear only the sound of their breathing and it made it feel as if nothing else in the world existed.

He unclasped her bra and she let it fall. Kyle moved his mouth across her collarbone, then down, finding her nipple with his mouth and using his tongue to trace its outline. Grace groaned, clasping her hands around his neck and pulling him closer. He wished he could see her, but maybe that would break the illusion that this was somehow right.

So right.

"You have to be quiet," Kyle whispered against her skin, running his knuckles over her sides, smiling as he felt her skin break out in goose bumps.

Taking a lazy path across her chest, Kyle found her other nipple, gave it the same teasing attention, Grace grinding softly against him until it was him who had to bite back a groan.

He tangled his fingers in her hair, realizing there wasn't quite enough of it. "You got your hair cut."

"Mmm."

He kissed the corner of her mouth, her chin, fingers tracing the waistband of her jeans. "Let me see."

"Later." Her hand found the waistband of his sweats, sneaked its way down until it brushed him. He whistled out a breath. When she took him in her hand, he groaned.

She clucked her tongue. "Quiet. Remember." Her hand stroked the length of him as she bent forward to kiss him. Was that why she was so different? Because even with her hand around his dick, when she kissed him it felt like more than just a fun trip to release. It felt more like showing her what she meant to him, too.

He undid the button on her jeans, pulled down the zipper. He couldn't maneuver his hand inside, so he tugged at her waistband. Taking the hint, she moved off him for a second, and after some rustling was back straddling him in only her panties.

Though he was desperate to be inside her, to feel the joining of their bodies on that purely basic level, he also wanted the moment to last.

He traced his finger along the waistband of her underwear, then down, cupping her until she whimpered. He slipped his finger underneath the soft cotton, then bit back a groan as his finger found her wet. He teased her there, and she returned the favor until they were both breathing heavily into the otherwise silence of the dark room.

She moved away and tugged at his sweats until

he arched up enough that she could pull them and his boxers off. She removed her panties and crawled back, over him this time, and grasped him again, rolling on the condom.

When she lay next to him, he lifted up over her, wishing he could make out more of her face. Wishing he could see everything, because this was perfection. Romance or not, it didn't matter. Not with the right person.

He eased into her and she expelled a little sigh, pulling him down so that he was crushing her into the mattress. And then she held him there, as if she wanted to savor a little, too.

She kissed his collarbone, his neck. "This is exactly what I wanted," she whispered.

Nothing had ever meant this much. No moment. No person. It shook him right down to the core of everything he thought he understood. She moved against him, and he met her urging with slow, unwavering thrusts. He wanted to draw out this moment for as long as was possible.

Nothing in his life had ever been perfect, but this moment was. It always would be.

She held on for dear life as they moved together, and so did he. He whispered her name as her breathing hitched, her movements became more frantic. Kissed the spot just behind her earlobe, let his tongue slide down her neck.

She pushed hard against him, a lengthy sigh escaping her mouth, and he couldn't hold back his own release. He pushed into her and held on as the overwhelming sensation blasted him.

She relaxed beneath him, sighing contentedly as her fingers danced up and down his back.

He wasn't sure how he understood this would be a culminating moment in his life, he only knew it was.

CHAPTER FOURTEEN

GRACE ROLLED OVER and into solid male. Since that was such a foreign experience, her eyes popped open immediately. And then her mouth curved into a smile as her eyes met a pair of very blue ones.

"Good morning," Kyle offered, placing his phone on the nightstand next to his head. He was sitting up against the headboard, torso bare.

"Morning," Grace returned, making no bones about admiring all that yummy muscle. "Shirtless is a good look for you."

He made a scoffing noise, then reached out and touched the ends of her hair. "It's short and black."

"Yup. Don't like it?"

"Of course I like it," he murmured, rubbing the ends between his fingertips. "I might miss the color."

Grace laughed, inching closer. "You didn't like the color."

"That's not true."

"Kyle, you don't have to lie."

"I'm not lying. I liked it just fine. It suited you. It suits you. I just…" Wrinkles creased his brow and he brushed his thumb across her bottom lip. "You scared me. Color. Life."

Grace curled up next to him. "And I don't scare you anymore?"

He let out a breath that might have been a laugh, rested his arm across her shoulders and pulled her closer. "I don't know about that. Maybe I'm ready to face my fear."

She kissed his shoulder, then rested her cheek there. Fear lurked outside this room, but for as long as she could savor the moment, fear—his and hers—could stay locked outside that door.

Kyle rested his cheek on the top of her head and entwined his fingers with hers. They sat, quietly soaking in each other's presence.

This was the most intimate she'd been with a man. She'd slept with a couple guys before her incident with Barry, but she'd always been living at home and hadn't ever spent the night in a man's bed.

Grace wasn't sure if it was sad or nice, but she closed her eyes to just embrace the moment, live in it, wallow in something that felt absolutely right.

Kyle's thumb traced her tattoo. "You never told me about yours," he murmured against her ear.

For some reason, it warmed her even more that he wanted to know something about her. "It's a Native American morning star. My grandma Davenport grew up on a reservation and she had this purse with this design beaded in. She said it was her prized possession because the morning star represented strength and bravery."

"That suits you."

Grace didn't know about that. "She used to say symbols had power. So I wanted something powerful to remind me to be strong and brave. I needed that." Some of the joy at memory faded at the past tense. "Need it, I guess."

Kyle's finger traced the diagonal again. "Symbol or not, you are strong and brave, Grace."

Emotion clogged her throat, so she only burrowed closer. It was nice someone thought so. "Do you remember any of your grandparents?"

His body tensed and Grace frowned. It was a rather innocuous question for him to get tense about, but maybe his grandparents were as awful as his parents had been.

But he didn't say anything. Instead, silence stretched out, and Grace grew tense enough to match him.

"No," he said at length.

Not exactly the look into his past she'd been hoping for, but at least he'd answered her. With Kyle, that was actually something.

A loud bang on the door caused her and Kyle both to jump. "Christ, Kyle," Jacob yelled. "The phone is ringing off the hook. Susan has the day off and you choose this as the one day you sleep in." The pounding started again. "Are you dead or something?"

Kyle clamped his hand over Grace's mouth as she began to giggle. "I'll be right there. Just give me a second or two."

Jacob said something she couldn't catch, then cursed. "There's the damn phone again. Be in my office in five."

Grace watched Kyle scurry into action, muttering to himself as he flung open his closet and pulled out some khakis and a polo. Grace loved watching him get dressed. Quickly, precisely, all focused Kyle.

Until he pulled a pair of socks out of his drawer. Suddenly he stopped all his frantic movements and turned to her, perfectly folded over socks in hand. "I'm sorry."

"For? I'm just enjoying the show."

He shook his head, looked worriedly at the door. "I forgot Susan and Kelly were heading to Sioux City today to meet with their surrogate. I have to get to work. Any other day I'd—"

Grace rested her chin on her knees, raised one eyebrow at him. "You'd what? Play hooky? I find that hard to believe."

"Fair enough." He crossed over to the bed and sat next to her. "I'd consider it, though."

Grace kissed his cheek. "Very sweet of you." She lingered, inhaling the scent of his soap or shampoo or aftershave or whatever was piney and decidedly male. She pressed her lips to the corner of his mouth this time, then the other corner, then the other cheek.

He groaned. "I have to go to work."

"Mmm-hmm." She slid into his lap, sank her mouth to his. His hands came up to her shoulders as if to pull her away, but they simply slid down until they rested at the small of her back.

"Killing me," Kyle murmured against her lips.

"That's the point." She gave him one last peck, then slid off his lap to look for her clothes. "All right. Do you want me to go first or should you?"

"If Jacob's gone, why don't you?" Kyle grimaced. "I'm going to need a minute to think about the appropriate kind of pipes for a century-old house."

Grace chuckled, pushing her legs into her jeans from last night, then pulling her shirt over her head. "If you find my bra, consider it a souvenir." She loved this feeling. In-control, sexy, adult Grace. Who didn't have to worry about a crazy ex-boyfriend.

Since she didn't want to be that girl, she'd be this woman instead.

"Grace."

His expression was suddenly serious and it had her stomach doing flops and jitters. "Yeah."

"Last night." He frowned, rubbed a hand over the back of his neck before pushing off the bed.

"Last night was very…special." He grimaced again. "That sounds terrible. Last night was…"

Grace crossed to him, gave him a quick peck on the lips. "Perfect."

His mouth curved and he pushed a strand of hair out of her face. "Yes. Perfect."

"And if you want a repeat of perfect, just know I'll be keeping my bedroom door unlocked." She grinned and sauntered to the door, biting back a chuckle as Kyle groaned and stared at the ceiling.

Grace stepped into the hallway, pulling the door closed as quietly as she could, and then bumped right into a scowling Jacob.

It took everything she had not to laugh at the anger emanating off him. "Thought you went to answer the phone."

Jacob didn't soften or falter. "You slept with him."

"Yup."

He shook his head in disgust. "Unbelievable," he muttered, and then turned around and stalked down the hallway.

Childish and petty as it may be, she stuck her tongue out at his retreating back. She was not going to let Jacob ruin any of the good she was squeezing out of life.

KYLE WAS JUST about caught up with all the phone calls he'd missed that morning, guilt and irritation threatening to ruin his good mood. But he thought of Grace in his bed and smiled as the caterer droned on about the menu for next week's party.

Mostly worth it. He couldn't afford to linger in bed like that a lot, but once or twice wouldn't kill him or MC. In fact, it would be downright good for him.

He finally wrapped up the call, pulled up today's schedule on the computer and formulated his afternoon to-do list. He was feeling good enough about life that he found himself whistling, and then he laughed because he'd never really known himself to whistle.

Kyle checked the news and the whistling stopped. One of the leading stories on Bluff City's news website was a piece about Grace's fire and Barry's being wanted for questioning.

Kyle's stomach turned. How easy it had been for him to put the threat of Barry on the back burner when he was enjoying life for once, but he doubted Grace felt the same. As happy as she'd seemed this morning, surely this whole thing was always in the back of her mind.

He thought about last night, about being with Grace. Maybe, just maybe, Kyle had been a distraction and nothing more. But she'd sat with him that morning, hand in his, head on his shoulder. He had to believe she felt at least a little of what he did.

Kyle x-ed out of the website. He would keep

Grace safe and happy. Barry, wherever he was, wouldn't get close enough to threaten her ever again.

Surely there was something he could do to make sure of it. Maybe if he talked to Jacob, they could figure something out. Something that wouldn't smother her, but would keep her mostly inside the house for the next few days. Maybe something with her painting.

Kyle left his office, descended the stairs, found Jacob pacing the rarely used sitting room. When Jacob saw Kyle, he practically growled.

"You slept with my sister."

Kyle pinched the bridge of his nose. Well, that was fine. Not having secrets about him and Grace was for the best. Jacob would have to get used to it, and maybe if he realized they were good together, he'd get over this misplaced anger.

"Yes, I did. But that's really not your business, Jacob. Considering you were all but giving me your stamp of approval a few weeks ago—"

The blow was so unexpected, so out of left field, Kyle barely had time to flinch before Jacob's fist connected with his face. Kyle stumbled back a few steps, nausea mixing with the radiating pain of bone-on-bone connection.

He closed his eyes and saw his father, so he purposefully opened them back up. Focused on Jacob.

His best friend. Who had just sucker punched him in the face.

"You stay away from my sister. A few weeks ago was different. Now she's scared and in danger and you're taking advantage of her. You go near her again, and…and…"

Kyle closed his eyes, no longer reminded of his childhood. No glimpses of his father now, because his best friend's treating him like this was bad enough all in its own.

He clenched his fists, because if he looked at Jacob the violence he felt in return might escape, and he wouldn't let anyone, *anyone,* make him that person again. Dad was the sole owner of that title.

Jacob pushed him against the wall and Kyle's eyes popped open. "Do you understand?"

Do it. Don't do it. Do it. The chorus was loud and painful as he waited for Jacob's next move, arms and jaw locked tight.

Jacob's face was twisted with fury, his breath coming in short, heavy bursts. "I should kick your ass."

Kyle jutted out his chin. "Go right ahead. I'm used to people whaling on me because they don't have their own shit together."

Jacob's fighter's stance slumped and Kyle took the opportunity to walk past him. He needed to get ice on his cheek before a mark showed up, because the last thing he was going to do today was explain to Grace that her brother had punched him.

His arms shook as he pulled a towel out of the drawer, shook so badly he dropped ice while trying to wrap it in the towel. *Pathetic.* After all, he should be used to this. He should know exactly how to act.

But violence outside of brief, infrequent interactions with his father had been out of his life for ten long years, and now it was back, both from someone else and zinging through his own veins. It all mixed with a jumpy stomach and searing headache, so Kyle climbed the stairs, went to his room and crawled into bed.

He held the ice to his cheek, willed the ice to freeze every part of him. He looked over at the rumpled pillow Grace had slept on last night.

He cared about Grace. He liked her, wanted her. He wanted to soak up her light and warmth. Even with her dark hair and her small fit of anger the other day, even knowing she was still struggling with her own ordeal, he wanted what was between them to grow. To be.

And it killed him that it put him at odds with his oldest friend, the one person who had been a constant in his life.

But Jacob couldn't offer what Grace could, and Kyle couldn't let Jacob stand in the way of something good. Something right.

GRACE TRIED TO think of anything else, but something about being in the dark, lying in bed, made her brain, which had behaved itself all day, suddenly give her fits.

When she closed her eyes, she saw the fire, or worse, Barry. When she opened her eyes she thought of everything she'd lost. Her stored paintings. Scrapbooks from high school. Her first and only love letter.

All the power and anger she'd stored up the past day had melted away. In the dark, alone, she felt weak, afraid, empty.

She willed herself to believe she'd wake up feeling better, or Kyle would come to her as she'd suggested that morning. She willed herself to believe this downtrodden, pathetic feeling wasn't permanent, wouldn't dog her forever.

Barry would go back to jail eventually. *What if they never find him?* They would. He wasn't that smart. Anyone who left evidence of starting a fire in their own place couldn't escape the police forever.

Barry would go back to jail and everything would be fine. *Except you don't have a house to go home to.* Maybe she could get a job in Bluff City, pay rent to MC, really start living. *Until Barry gets out again.*

The tears ran down her face, the wet, pathetic drops sliding down her cheek, neck and then onto the pillowcase. She should get up and paint. She'd been able to lose herself in painting all day. She should keep going until she was too exhausted to function. Then maybe her brain would shut the hell up long enough for her to sleep.

She should go find Kyle. Be proactive. Like she'd been last night. What was wrong with doing the initiating all the time? Nothing, if it got her what she wanted. A distraction. Actually, Kyle was more than that. Sex with him was, like he'd said this morning, special.

Three precise raps sounded at the door, followed by it creaking open and Kyle whispering her name.

Thank God. Thank *God*. She hadn't thought last night, and now she wouldn't have to think again. "Come in." The door closed, and since her eyes were adjusted to the dark she could see his outline slowly move toward the bed.

"It's late. I thought maybe you had changed your mind."

His breath was audible in the silence of the room. "I thought maybe...I shouldn't. There's a lot to do with the party and..." He trailed off.

"So what changed your mind?" she asked when he never offered an explanation.

"I just wanted to be with you."

It soothed some of the pain away. That someone just wanted to be with her, even though something horrible had happened. Even though she was in danger, someone needed her. Just another thing Kyle offered no one else could.

Though she'd been crying and didn't want him to see that, she also didn't want him to trip and send Jacob running. "Come here. You can turn on the lights."

"No. No, that's okay." Footsteps, rustling, then he was in bed next to her, pulling her close, burying his nose in her hair.

Grace squeezed her eyes shut, snuggled closer. When his fingertips brushed her face she winced. There was no way he'd mistake the wetness on her face for anything but tears.

"You've been crying," he murmured, kissing her temple, smoothing a hand down her back.

"Just a little."

He didn't ask her what was wrong or tell her it was going to be okay, he just held her, rubbing calming circles over her back. Which almost had her crying for a completely different reason.

"I'm glad you came," she mumbled into his chest. At first it felt silly to say, awkward and pathetic, but he sighed against her neck and some of the tension she hadn't noticed in his shoulders relaxed.

Maybe it was something he needed to hear. That she wanted him there, needed a comfort only he seemed able to give. And the way he held on to her, just a fraction tighter than necessary, made her think maybe he was sad, too. After all, the way Kyle could be, had been, she doubted he had too many people telling him they were happy he was around.

"I'm just glad you're here," he murmured against her ear before kissing the sensitive spot just behind her earlobe. "I might not stay tonight. I have to be up early. Really early. But I wanted to be with you for a little bit."

Then he kissed her temple, her nose, moving his face until they were nose to nose, forehead to forehead. She could barely make out the features of his face, the square jaw, the high cheekbones, imperfect nose. Handsome and kind and a little wounded himself.

He brushed his thumb across her jawline, his fingertips glancing her cheekbones. All light, feathery touches like a blind man might touch a beloved object.

Grace's stomach flipped as if she was on the incline of a roller coaster. Her heart shuddered when he kissed her forehead. As though she was precious, important, loved.

Frightening and wonderful and dizzying to think that might be the case. Since she didn't want to dwell on the frightening, just the wonderful, she wound her arms around his neck. "Make love to me, Kyle."

His mouth met hers, soft but maybe a little desperate. And it was right. Even if things weren't, this was. His hands touching her skin, his tongue skimming her lips. She yanked at his shirt until he pulled away and discarded it. Then he pulled her shirt off and they both groaned as his palm found her bare breast.

Then they both laughed breathlessly as they shushed each other, shedding the remainder of their clothes. He shifted on top of her, the hard lines of his body pressing her into the mattress, his thumb brushing her nipple until she arched up against him.

Everything about him was long and hard and perfect. She clutched his shoulders as his mouth lavished attention on her breasts, then her stomach, then lower. He kissed the insides of her thighs, then licked and nibbled and sucked until she was nothing more than a quivering mass of need.

Then he touched her, slid a finger inside, slowly moving in and out until the climax ran through her like a delicious wave of heat. Kyle took his time kissing his way back up her body, so that by the time his mouth was on her neck, she wanted more. So much more.

"I have condoms in the nightstand."

His weight shifted, and she heard him briefly shuffle through the drawer until he was above her again, resting between her legs, slowly entering her. Their breaths escaped in twin gusts of satisfaction, of rightness. And then he loved her exactly as she needed him to, slowly and intimately until they grasped each other through their climaxes.

His weight shifted to the side, but he held on, keeping her close. "We're going to have to do this in the light some time. I want to see you. Us. I want..." He let out a frustrated laugh. "Okay, I'm shutting up now."

"Why?"

"I sound like an idiot," he muttered, rubbing a hand across his face.

Grace nestled her nose into the curve of his shoulder. Soft skin over hard muscle. "You sound like exactly what I need."

"Good." He kissed her temple. "Give me a second." He slipped out of bed, moved across the room, fumbling in the dark. The distinctive sounds of tissue leaving its box followed by the rustle of the garbage can liner echoing in the silence. When he returned, he didn't slip back into bed.

He sighed heavily. "I should go back to my room. If your brother..." He grunted. "We need to..." Another incomplete sentence, another frustrated sound.

Grace sat up in bed, worrying her bottom lip between her teeth. "Are you and Jacob not getting along? Is it making work too hard? He's getting so worked up about this. I don't understand. He was fine with us, like, a week ago. I don't know why Barry changes it. I'll talk to him." She wouldn't be the reason Kyle and Jacob were on uneven footing. Even if it was Jacob's fault for being an idiot, she didn't want to play the role of Yoko Ono, either.

The bed shifted. "Everything is fine." He pulled her against him so they sat together against the headboard, much as they had that morning.

"Everything isn't fine if you're worried about him seeing us together. He knows. We shouldn't have to hide it. Is he making things hard for you? That isn't right. And it's my fault, so I'll talk to him and make sure it's okay."

"Everything will be fine with me and Jacob, I promise. Once everything blows over with… everything, it'll all go back to normal."

Normal. Back to normal. As much as she wanted everything to be normal, she didn't really want to go back. "Not everything, I hope."

His fingers entwined with hers and he kissed the back of her hand. "You're right. Not everything."

Grace nestled back into Kyle's chest, but she still chewed her bottom lip. Things were hard enough without her family making things worse. And she shouldn't have to wait for the whole Barry debacle to be over—if it ever would be.

She deserved a relationship. She deserved *this* relationship. So did Kyle. And they both damn well deserved everyone to be on board with it.

That was something she could control, or at least try to.

CHAPTER FIFTEEN

KYLE WASN'T SURE if it was noble, cowardly or just necessary to sneak out of Grace's room early the next morning before the sun rose or she woke up enough to see the shine of bruise on his cheek. He just knew he didn't want to have to explain when she'd already spent time last night worrying about him and Jacob getting along.

Nothing she, or he, could do until Jacob decided to stop being unreasonable.

Jacob was being unreasonable, right? Kyle carefully closed Grace's door behind him and walked as soundlessly as possible down the hall. All the while, a niggling insecurity tapped away at his brain.

Maybe Jacob was right. Maybe in some twisted way Kyle was taking advantage of Grace. Taking advantage of her bad experience so he could have something he'd always deep down wanted. Someone to look at him as if he mattered, as if he was important, as if he was loved.

Maybe it was all fiction. His mind reasoning and justifying to make his actions seem noble rather than questionable.

He gathered his clothes for the day and slipped into the bathroom. When he looked at himself in the mirror, he saw someone different from the man he'd been for the past ten years. There was no blankness in him now.

He felt things. Good things. If he could quash the bad, everything would be fine. So he refused to entertain the doubts another second. No old insecurities allowed. Not after the past two nights. Grace accepted him as though he meant something and that was...

Something.

Kyle studied the faint bruise. The ice had helped, but it was still visible to anyone staring at his face, which Grace was wont to do. If he stuck to his office for the day, kept busy until Grace's mom picked her up for their movie night, maybe tomorrow it wouldn't be noticeable.

Kyle let his head droop. *Asshole*. He didn't want to keep something from her, but he didn't want to make things worse with Jacob or between Jacob and Grace. So he had to choose asshole A or asshole B. Keeping scarce for a day or two while the bruise faded, when she had plans anyway, seemed like the better option than creating a bigger rift between siblings.

So that was what he would do. One little lie for the sake of the greater good couldn't be *that* wrong.

Kyle ran through the shower and got ready for the

day. He'd already knocked out half his email and half the payroll for the month when Jacob stepped into his office.

His posture was stiff, his usual easygoing expression granite. "I'm running to the bank for Susan. Anything else that needs doing while I'm there?"

How had things flipped? How had it gotten so he'd gained something special but lost the anchor that had brought him here? Kyle didn't know. Didn't know how to change it. "Not that I can think of."

"Are you sure? You've been pretty busy not working and not doing what you should lately."

The slight made him feel tired. The childish prodding was so unlike Jacob, even Kyle couldn't keep his mouth shut about it. "So this is just how it's going to be? Because I'm…"

Because he what? He could finish that sentence with "sleeping with Grace," but it was more than that. This wasn't a few nights of sex. Kyle felt as though he'd finally found someone he could be with for a very long time. Finally found someone he could trust himself to love.

Because he loved Grace? Yeah. Too soon and really frightening, but it was a truth he couldn't deny. Still, while those words might ease some of Jacob's misplaced anger, he couldn't be the first to hear them from Kyle.

"Because of Grace and me," he finally finished. Lame, but the best he could do in the circumstances.

"Yeah." Jacob sneered. "This is how it's going to be. As long as I think you're going to hurt my sister, this is exactly how it's going to be." He ran an agitated hand through his hair. "I shouldn't have hit you. That was wrong, but I still think you and her together, right now, is wrong."

Kyle knew it was the closest he was getting to an apology, and that was fine. As he'd said the night before, he was used to it. Maybe not from people he trusted, but until Grace, Jacob had been the only person he trusted. Maybe he could only have one trustworthy person in his life at a time. Some curse or punishment for his own violent tendencies.

"She's dealing with a lot, and you're taking advantage."

"Regardless of what she's dealing with, she's a grown woman. She can make her own decisions." That was true. Grace knew what she was doing. What was happening between them was happening because she wanted it as much as he did. That wasn't taking advantage. It wasn't.

"She's going through something bad. You really think you made the best decisions right after your parents went to jail?"

Kyle pushed back from his desk. Jacob didn't know the whole story, but he knew enough to poke at old wounds. "I was eighteen. And maybe I spent a few nights at the wrong end of a bottle, but I got my act together. This… Grace… It's different. You can't compare me then to her now."

"Maybe you're Grace's wrong end of a bottle."

Because it scared the hell out of him that it might be true, his fists itched to connect. They weren't going to keep doing this. Not this. He had to put a stop to it. "You don't need to pick another fight or try to justify what you did. I didn't tell her you hit me. Everything will be better if we forget it ever happened. So your lame apology is fine and enough. It doesn't change my feelings toward Grace any more than anything you're saying does." If he said it, it was true, right?

Jacob's brows drew together. "Grace doesn't know I hit you?"

"I'm not going to be the one to cause her more problems."

Any glimpse at a possible truce evaporated into a scowl. "And you're saying I am?"

Kyle sighed. When was this going to resolve itself? "Well, you're not helping."

"Maybe *you're* not helping."

If he'd had siblings growing up, maybe he would understand this petty fighting. If he'd had a different life, maybe he could keep engaging in it. He couldn't do either. "I'm done getting in pissing matches with you. You want to be silent business partners, I can do that."

"Fine." Jacob hesitated at the door, but Kyle

didn't know how to bridge this gap between them. This was new. Untested. Kyle could only handle so many new things at a time.

Jacob finally disappeared and Kyle looked at his computer. The numbers and columns that had once made sense now jumbled in his brain.

He'd worried he wasn't right for Grace. Before the fire, he'd wondered why she couldn't see that. Why she made him feel when no one else did. He'd thought there was a connection, even beyond that similar traumatic past.

Now Jacob's words rang in his head. Maybe Kyle was Grace's mistake. Her version of something bad for herself.

Kyle pounded a fist onto the desk. He wouldn't think that way. Wouldn't think that little of himself or her.

But Jacob's words lingered.

GRACE PACED IN front of the doors that led to the second-story porch. She was going to paint there, damn it.

But the thought of sitting on the porch alone, even on the second story, even in the bright afternoon light, even with Kyle and Susan inside and Mom texting every ten minutes, had her shaking with fear.

"My life. My life. My life."

What a joke.

She had her gun in its case in her bag of supplies. She had the confidence that she was making her own decisions, her own life, but she didn't have the belief that Barry couldn't touch it.

Power, weak and unsteady, tried to push over that depressing thought. Though her whole body was practically shaking with fear and nauseating dread, she pushed the door open. On unsteady legs, she stepped onto the porch with her things.

It took a lot of breathing, a lot of very specifically not looking beyond the balcony's rail, but she set up her easel and paints. Once everything was set up, she took a long, deep breath, and then forced herself to look out over the street.

Houses. A short row of parked cars. Trees beginning to leaf, lawns beginning to green. A picture-perfect world. Nothing to be afraid of.

Her hands still shook, but she wouldn't let that stop her. Even if this painting ended up being an unusable mess of shaky strokes, at least she was doing it—doing something.

Though her heart continued to pound in her ears, her arms began to strengthen. The more she looked out over the street and houses below, the more she felt like she was accomplishing something. Getting over something.

Barry wasn't winning. He wasn't.

The sound of a car door slamming punctuated

e easy silence, making Grace jump, a dark blue
plash of paint going across the sunny sky she'd
en painting. She swallowed and looked below.

A man strode out of a car parked against the
urb. He stalked toward the house. She couldn't
nake out the man to identify him, but her mind
whispered her worst fears.

Grace whimpered, her legs almost giving out
s she grasped the railing. She squeezed her eyes
hut. This was like the gym. It wouldn't really be
im. It would just be an MC client. It could be any-
ody. Not Barry. There would be no way he was
ust walking up to the house. Didn't make sense.
Wasn't possible.

She just had to stay calm, reopen her eyes. And
on the offest of all off chances it *was* Barry, she
vas on the second story. What could he do? Unless
e had a gun. *No. No. Not him. Not again.*

Since no sounds rang out into the quiet afternoon,
Grace reopened her eyes. Her whole body shook
and her lunch threatened to revolt, but as she fran-
ically scanned the street unable to breathe, she realized the man below was Henry, Jacob's plumber.

Blond hair, smaller frame, tan skin. He didn't
ook a damn thing like Barry as he disappeared
around the corner of the house.

Tears spilled over her cheeks. Relief? Continued
ear? Utter despair that this, this was her life again?

She didn't know. She only knew she wanted to
back into her safe little room, under the cove
Forever.

Don't give up. But she began to toss her suppl
willy-nilly into the bag she'd used to bring the
out. *Pathetic.* But she left the painting "to dry" a
would come get her easel later. Or have someo
else bring it in.

She tripped on her way to the door, righted h
self. This was just a process. First step was getti
outside. Tomorrow she'd try again. Take long
Baby steps. Wasn't that what her therapist had a
ways said? Step two tomorrow.

Even the thought of it made her sick. She stur
bled inside, hurried down the hall.

Don't let him win. Don't let him win. Oh, but it
be so much easier to let fear take over. Easier
hide and cry and wait for everything to resolve
self, for however long it would.

"Grace?"

Grace stopped halfway down the hall and fun
bled with the disorganized array of stuff she wa
carrying. Paint was probably seeping over ever
thing in her bag, but she didn't care. She didn't ca
about anything except hiding.

"Hi. Hey." She tried to look casual, but with h
breathing unsteady and her brain a jumbled mes
of fear and adrenaline, she didn't know what tha
might look like.

Kyle frowned as he crossed to her. "Are you all right?" He scratched a spot on his face, rested his hand awkwardly over his cheek.

"Yeah, yeah." Grace mustered the fakest, brightest smile she could manage. "I was just painting, but I remembered...I'm supposed to go to a movie with Mom tonight." In five hours. "So I was going to clean up and, um, head out to Carvelle." How? She didn't own a damn car, and was she really going to take a cab?

Kyle studied her, so she stared at the collar of his blue shirt. No fading, no wrinkles. Everything about it was crisp and perfect and put together. Kyle to a T.

She wished his composure would rub off on her.

"Did something happen?"

"Huh? No. Everything's fine." She attempted to look at him again, managed to get her eyes to focus on his forehead. As long as she didn't meet his eyes, she'd be okay. So she stared at his hand resting on his own face.

His brows drew together, worry creasing his forehead. "If something is wrong..." He trailed off, pursing his lips together.

"I'm just jumpy, you know?" She looked at the wall behind his shoulder, grimacing. "I am fine. Really." He was silent. A little standoffish. The awkward silence reminding Grace of her first days here. She met his gaze. "Are *you* okay?"

He managed a small smile. "Of course."

Grace frowned. His "of course" seemed less than convincing.

"I have to get back to work. A lot of things to catch up on."

As he passed her, she grabbed his arm. When his hand left his cheek, she noticed a mark. Frowning, she held on tighter as Kyle tried to tug his arm back into place. The mark was slightly bluish-purple and it hadn't been there the last time she'd seen him. Which wasn't last night, because she hadn't actually seen him through the dark last night.

Grace reached out and touched the bruise. "What happened here?"

He stiffened. "Oh, um, I don't know."

It was strange to realize he was lying. Strange because it was probably the first time. As far as she knew. A sobering, uncomfortable thought. Maybe he lied to her all the time and she'd never caught him in one. She pulled her hand away. "People don't usually get bruises on their faces without knowing what happened."

He rubbed the back of his neck. "Clumsy, I guess." This time it was him not meeting her gaze.

Grace's heart sank at another lie. "The last thing you are is clumsy, Kyle." His blue eyes sharpened on hers, guilt blanketing his expression so deeply it made her stomach cramp. "What happened?"

she asked, her voice demanding, but not as steady as she had hoped.

"I don't want to keep you from meeting your mother. We can talk about this later." He nodded as if it would convince her the mark on his cheek was unimportant and caused by himself rather than someone else.

"Don't lie to me, then try to shoo me away." Hurt and anger crawled inside all the hollow spaces panic had left in her chest.

His expression went pained, maybe a little panicked. "It really isn't important. Forget about it."

"You don't get it. It's…" Grace shook her head. This was not what she needed. She wasn't going to get upset over something stupid when she had enough real things to be upset over. If he wanted to keep something from her, that was fine and dandy. She didn't have time for relationship problems, didn't have the energy for it when so much else was testing her. She wasn't going to cry over yet another man, no matter how deeply she cared for him. "Never mind." She pushed past him.

"Grace."

"I'm not going to stand here and listen to you lie to me," she muttered, striding away until she put two and two together. Her stomach clenched and she turned back to face him, praying it wasn't true. "Did Jacob do that to you?"

He opened his mouth, but no sound came out.

Anguish lined his face, but finally he nodded, almost imperceptibly.

"When?" Her stomach turned, tears burned her eyes. "Why?" She shook her head in disgust. "Well, I think I know why, but how did it happen? What is wrong with him? I never thought he'd go this far. I'm so sorry. I don't know why he's acting like this."

"Don't worry about it. Everything is fine. He just got a little angry over…things, and, it's fine. Really. Don't be upset over something that isn't important." He reached out to touch her but she stepped away.

"When did he hit you?" It was just as important as why. Not for her anger toward Jacob, but for how angry she was going to be at Kyle.

Kyle closed his eyes, leaned his back against the hallway wall. "Yesterday."

"Yesterday. He did that to you yesterday and you didn't tell me? You snuck into my room at night, snuck out before sunup and you didn't tell me." Grace clenched her hands into fists. "And you were going to keep it from me."

"I didn't want things to be worse between you and Jacob." He opened his eyes, his slumped stance going from defeated to a straight-backed defensive. "So yes. I was going to keep it from you. It was something small and inconsequential and Jacob apologized for it. Mostly."

"Hitting someone is not inconsequential. Apologies or not," Grace said through clenched teeth, doing everything in her power to keep the tears from falling. "You of all people should know that as well as I do."

His whole face fell. "I—I'm sorry. I just didn't want you to be upset."

Grace snorted. "Good job. You really accomplished that now, didn't you?" This time when she walked past him, nothing was going to get her to turn around. She was going to go to her room and indulge in crying over everything, *everything,* because damn if she didn't deserve it.

"Grace." His footsteps followed, but she would not be deterred.

"I want you to leave me alone right now."

His footsteps abruptly stopped. She entered her room and slammed the door behind her. In one quick motion she dumped her bag on the floor and climbed up into her bed.

Half of her wanted to laugh. She was crying over some silly little fight with her...well, whatever Kyle was to her. All the while a man who had once beaten the hell out of her, had recently burned her house down, was on the damn loose.

Way to focus on priorities, Grace.

She closed her eyes, but focus wouldn't come. Emotions swept through her, but thought was gone. She was too tired. Just bone-dead exhausted. Too many emotions. Too many things she was trying to control, to accept, to deal with.

Too many people letting her down.

Grace lay in bed for a long time, not crying, not thinking, not sleeping, just feeling a giant void inside of her grow until it got harder and harder to breathe.

A knock sounded on the door, quickly followed by the creak of it swinging open. Not Kyle come to apologize again, then. No, her brother.

Grace swallowed. The void evaporated because, in the light of everything that had happened to her and Kyle in their lives, what Jacob had done was downright inexcusable. "Hey. I was going to go into town and get some lunch. Want to join me?"

She looked at him from beneath her covers, just stared until his smile faded and he fidgeted where he stood.

"What's wr—"

"You hit him." Grace pushed into a sitting position. "You *hit* him."

Jacob scowled. "He told me he didn't tell you. Asshole. I can't believe—"

"Stop." Grace's voice echoed with anger and hurt and the surprise on Jacob's face was pronounced enough she got angry all over again. Didn't he even feel the least bit ashamed for his actions?

"I have been proud of you since you were born." Grace looked at her hands. A tear spilled over, rolled down her knuckles. "I have been your biggest cheerleader. Never in my life have I been ashamed of you, Jacob. But this… I am so damn ashamed I could throw up. You should know better. You should *be* better."

She couldn't bear to look at him, but his silence was something. Hopefully the harsh words knocked some reason back into his thick skull.

"I'd like you to leave me alone. Mom's picking me up at five and I think I'll just stay with Mom and Dad tonight. I don't know if I'll come back."

"You have to come back. It's safer here. You'll go crazy there." His voice cracked. Good. She hoped he went to *his* room and shed a few tears over his shitty role in all this.

"The police are keeping an eye on Mom and Dad's, on Barry's trailer, on Carvelle in general. All you offer is an alarm and, at this point, I'm not sure it's worth it. Mom and Dad smother me, but they'd never take their fear and anger out on someone who didn't deserve it. No matter how angry I am with Kyle, he doesn't deserve what you're doing. Maybe it'll be better if I'm not around."

"Gracie—"

"Please go. I'd like to be alone."

Alone, so the people who were supposed to care about her and be honest with her and not hurt her couldn't dig this wound any deeper.

CHAPTER SIXTEEN

GRACE WOKE UP in the paneled and purple room of her youth. Her muscles ached; from what, she had no idea. Actually, everything kind of ached. Muscles, head, heart.

She buried her head in the pillow, the distinct smell of the weird generic laundry detergent Mom always bought overpowering everything else. Maybe if she inhaled the smell enough, she could travel back in time to when it was so a part of her everyday life she didn't notice it.

Back in time before the past few weeks. Back in time before she'd ever gone out with Barry. Back in time before she'd given up on college.

Frustrated with herself, Grace rolled back to face the ceiling. She stared at the bumpy white surface and took deep, cleansing breaths.

She couldn't go back in time. She was who she was, bad decisions, bad luck and all. If she wanted to go to college now, she could. If she wanted a relationship, she could patch things up with Kyle. There was plenty of life right within her reach, even if it didn't erase all the bad.

But working for it seemed way beyond her energy level at the moment. Actually, everything, including getting out of bed and facing her overly fake, cheerful parents who had no doubt skipped work again seemed beyond her energy level.

When her door creaked open, she quickly closed her eyes, hoping Mom or Dad would think her asleep and leave her alone. At least for another hour. Or two.

"Gracie?"

At Jacob's voice, Grace sat up in bed. "What are you doing here?" She glared at him, but the expression softened when she saw how pale and disheveled he looked. Almost like he was sick.

It didn't matter. He was still an asshole.

He inched into the room, looking uncertain and not at all steady. "So I guess Mom didn't tell you I got trashed last night and had to call Dad for a ride home?"

"No, she didn't." And apparently Grace had slept through it all. Well, that was something. She'd slept well and dreamlessly. Miracle of miracles.

"And that he brought me back here and Mom spent thirty minutes at 3:00 a.m. psychoanalyzing me while I puked my guts out on the yard."

It wasn't funny. It shouldn't be funny, but, damn it, the picture of Jacob throwing up on the lawn while Mom gave one of her guidance counselor lectures was just too great not to find some amusement.

"Yeah, laugh it up." His mouth quirked into a smile briefly before it fell again. "The worst part was she was right. Which means I've been wrong. Which sucks."

Grace looked away from his earnest searching of her face. "Wrong about what exactly?"

"This thing with Kyle...wasn't really so much about Kyle as it was about me not dealing well with anger. You know I don't get angry often, but how can I not be angry about this? And how can I not be angry about not being there for you and doing things the way I should have?"

He paced the room, running his fingers through his hair, then grasping it in his fist. "And since I couldn't actually go be mad at Barry, and I didn't want to be angry at myself, it all kind of morphed into being pissed at a guy who doesn't deserve it."

His hands fell to his sides, and he looked at her imploringly, pleadingly, the way he used to when he was begging for a favor. Because she'd so rarely been able to tell him no.

"I'm sorry. I screwed up. Can you forgive me?"

Grace studied her hands. "I guess that depends. I'm not the person you punched in the face."

"I know. I owe Kyle an apology, too."

She picked at the hem of her sweatshirt. "I don't want to be the reason you guys aren't friends."

"You're not. I am."

Grace let out a breath, surprised when some

of the weight in her gut lifted. "I guess I can forgive you."

"Good." His relieved exhale was loud and lengthy. "And you'll come back and stay with us? For as long as you want. Even after they get Barry. You can stay until you rebuild your house or whatever. Stay forever if you want."

Grace pulled her bottom lip through her teeth. "I...don't know."

"Come on. You belong there. Everyone loves having you around, and with the painting stuff you'll be right there if a client ever wants to buy something."

"Have you even talked this over with Kyle?"

Jacob rolled his eyes. "Grace, he's gone over you. I've known the guy half my life and I have never, ever, even for a sliver of a second, seen him like he's been the past week. I don't need to ask him. I already know the answer."

Grace fidgeted. She liked living with Jacob. She liked the house, the company. She liked that the house was big and her parents weren't tripping over themselves to make her happy. She had friends there, and Kyle...

Except, she wasn't totally sure where she stood with Kyle or vice versa, and she wasn't totally sure she had the energy to figure it out.

"Just think about it. I'm going to go drink about a gallon of water, maybe eat some plain toast or something. I've got to be back at noon. You want to come, I'll give you a ride. If not, I'll come get you anytime you want. Okay?"

Grace nodded.

Jacob stepped over to the bed, kissed her forehead. "I love you, Gracie."

Grace managed a smile. "Love you, too."

Jacob left her room, and Grace sat chewing on her lip for a long time. There were really two choices here. Hide from the life she'd started to build or fight for it.

She kept choosing fight and getting knocked back down. But maybe that was life. Maybe it was just a series of knocked-back-downs. And the good parts were all in the getting-back-ups.

She wasn't sure if that was depressing or life-affirming. Either way, she'd head back to Bluff City with Jacob. And maybe, just maybe, she'd get back up again, even if the next fall was inevitable.

WORK WAS STILL WORK, and thank God for that. Disgruntled clients, Kyle understood. Payroll, spreadsheets, timetables. All things he excelled at. Every mundane business-manager task totally doable.

Not doable? Stop worrying about Grace. If she was okay. If she was coming back. If she would forgive him. If this was ending after only just getting started.

He should have never gotten into this mess.

Which was laughable. Would he take it back? Not on his life.

He should call her. Maybe a text. Or email. Or just go to Carvelle. Or he should grow a pair and make a decision instead of letting his mind race in idiotic circles.

Good luck with that, pal. Idiotic circles had been the name of the game for the past two days.

Kyle leaned back in his chair, squinted at the clock. Nearly one. Hopefully the rest of the crew had cleared out of the kitchen so he could eat lunch in peace.

Of course, that wasn't the case. Luck was not on his side these days. All three MC women sat at the table oohing and aahing over the ultrasound picture Susan and Kelly had brought back from their trip. Since Kyle had already been through the particular brand of torture of trying to figure out what to say about a black-and-white squiggle that looked like a gummy bear, he tried to back out of the room.

"Quick! Put the ultrasound away. It's Kyle Kryptonite." Leah made a big production out of hiding the picture.

Kelly turned to smile at him. "He did an almost passable impression of a man who cared this morning. I was very proud."

Since he was already found out, and his stomach was growling, Kyle moved stiffly to the refrigerator.

"Man, Grace really is rubbing off on him. He laughed at one of my jokes Friday. It was like being beamed to an alternate universe."

Kyle stiffened, but focused on getting out the ingredients for a sandwich so no one would notice his discomfort. After all, his normal predisposition was stiff; how would they notice any difference?

"Where *is* Grace, or Jacob, for that matter? I wanted to introduce Grace to the Martins today when I drop off the paintings, and Jacob is supposed to come with me."

Kyle froze at Kelly's question. He opened his mouth to come up with some plausible lie. "Well…" Nothing. "I'm not sure."

"Oh, man. He screwed things up already." Leah slapped the table. "Grace texted me that she was staying at her parents' this weekend. I just thought it was to spend time with them, but look at this guy. He's being all shifty."

"I most certainly am not." Kyle straightened.

"But you did screw things up."

He looked down at the half-assembled sandwich. Not worth it. "You know, someone should cover the phones. This *is* a place of business. Not a slumber party."

"That means he did. He totally screwed things up." Leah clucked her tongue. "Well, you'd better fix it. We like New Kyle a lot better than Cyborg Kyle."

Kelly and Susan nodded solemnly. Kyle shook his head. What the hell was happening? A few days being involved with Grace and suddenly these women felt the need to poke into his private life? There was something to be said for not having a private life to be poked into.

Unless…they had advice.

Idiotic. Stupid, foolish thought. He was not going to ask these three women for relationship advice. Who was he, some kind of…of…normal human being?

Kyle sighed. "So what do you suggest?"

The women looked at each other, brows furrowed. Kelly tapped her chin; Leah studied the ceiling.

"What do you think? Heartfelt apology and flowers?" Susan asked. But she wasn't consulting him.

"I don't know." Leah frowned. "Flowers are kind of cliché, don't you think?"

"Anybody ever brought you flowers?" Kelly demanded.

"No." Leah sighed almost wistfully. "Flowers. Definitely."

They looked at him expectantly, as though he was supposed to drop everything and run to the florist right this second. "You don't even know how I screwed it up."

"You didn't do anything despicably horrible, did you?"

Kyle rubbed a hand over the back of his neck. Was this really happening? "No…not despicably horrible."

"Then flowers and a heartfelt apology should do it. Not just 'I'm sorry,' though. You know, explain why you were wrong, how you won't do it again." As Kelly spoke, Susan and Leah nodded like sage bobblehead dolls. "The understanding of how you were wrong is the most important part. The flowers just get your foot in the door."

Kyle opened his mouth to seek advice on what kind of flowers, but the sound of the back door opening and closing stopped him. And then Jacob and Grace stepping into the kitchen froze him.

"Well, there they are," Kelly greeted them, all smiles.

Kyle wished he could muster half of her casualness. Instead he could barely hear Jacob's response because his heart was beating too hard in his ears.

What was he supposed to do? He had no idea.

Kelly chatted about the meeting with the Martins until Grace agreed to go. "Okay" was the only word she spoke. And she didn't once look at him.

Jacob, on the other hand, couldn't seem to stop looking at him. Kyle didn't know whether it was good or bad that Jacob's expression was missing its threatening quality of late.

Kelly was still chatting with Grace, and they

ended up disappearing upstairs. Leaving an uncomfortable silence among the four remaining.

"Can you guys give me and Kyle a second? Alone?"

Susan and Leah exchanged a look and Kyle hoped, perhaps childishly, they'd say no. No such luck. They picked up their lunches and exited the kitchen, chattering about Susan and Kelly's trip to Sioux City.

"Um, look, I just need a minute or two of your time."

Kyle stared at the sandwich he'd been making. What other choice did he have? "All right."

"Mom said something to me last night that... Well, it's really gotten me thinking." Jacob sighed and sank into a chair. "The thing is, I don't get angry often. You know me. Most things just don't get to me."

Kyle grew more uncomfortable. He didn't want to talk about this. He'd rather they just forget the past few days and move on. Better than apologies and not knowing what to do with them. "You don't have to—"

"Man, let me apologize. I screwed up. Royally. Like, biggest screwup of my life here. It wasn't about you. Really. I was angry. At myself for not being here. At Barry for...everything, and since I couldn't do anything about it...I found a target."

Kyle shrugged. "Maybe you weren't totally

wrong." That was what he was wrestling with, wasn't it? That Jacob had been right and Kyle would wind up being bad for Grace. He'd lied, maybe in the name of something good, but he'd lied. What other bad things would he do without thinking?

When would the little pockets of violence he couldn't keep under wraps make an appearance and remind Grace and Jacob that he'd come from the same place as Barry?

No. No. He was *not* Barry. No matter how he screwed up, he wasn't that kind of man. Maybe not good, but not bad, either. Not after all the work he'd put into being something different from his parents.

"No. I was wrong. Whatever ends up happening between you and Grace, it isn't my business. I'm staying out of it."

"Really? Just...like that." It was hard not to be skeptical no matter how sincere the apology seemed.

"Let's just say I never want to have to tell my mother she's right about my psyche ever again." Jacob rested his head in his hands. "And I really never want to be this hungover again."

Though Kyle was having trouble wrapping his mind around it, he also wanted this whole ordeal over. Over, over, over. "So we're good?"

"I want us to be."

"Well, good."

"Yeah. Good."

Awkward silence settled. Kyle stared at his shoes. Things might be "good," but he wasn't convinced they would be back to normal anytime soon.

Jacob cleared his throat. "Well, I'm going to go get ready to head over the Martins'."

Jacob left and Kyle turned back to his sandwich. Though it was only half-made, he went ahead and put the top piece of bread on and absentmindedly took a bite.

He was standing in the middle of a silent kitchen, alone. For ten years this had been his normal, what he wanted. Silence and alone had been easy, controlled and comforting.

How had it become the opposite? What had unwarped and untwisted in his brain and heart for him to wish the noise back? The conversations, the prodding.

Footsteps sounded on the back stairwell. Voices drifted into the kitchen, then silenced as the back door opened and closed.

Kyle chewed on the last of his sandwich. He didn't have to be alone. Not if he didn't want to be. Despite his best efforts, there were people who cared about him, if he was brave enough to let them.

Kyle jogged upstairs, grabbed his wallet and keys.

He had flowers to buy.

GRACE STEPPED INTO her room at MC and sighed in relief. Somehow, this little green-and-purple Victorian room now felt more like home than anything else.

Probably because her house in Carvelle was a bunch of blackened boards now. She wasn't going to think about that. Not until the insurance company made her.

It was nice to have a bit of work to keep her mind off the whole thing. Meeting the Martins had been nerve-racking and downright strange, but Kelly had coached and prompted her enough that she'd made the best of it.

She'd sold two more paintings, and now had a commission for the third.

Grace took a deep breath and smiled. Getting back up. Soaking up the good. She would keep doing it, keep doing it, keep doing it. What other choice was there?

Professionally, she was better off than she'd ever been. So it stood to reason that personally she was kind of a mess.

After a weekend away, her anger at Kyle had turned inward, and she flip-flopped back and forth trying to decide if she'd overreacted. If it had been the adrenaline of seeing Barry where he wasn't that had fueled her "walk away" reaction.

But he'd lied.

But he'd been trying to protect her.

But she didn't want to be protected.

Except part of her did.

Grace flopped face-first on her bed and screamed into the pillow. She knew how unfair life could be. Had seen some pretty low lows in unfairness. So why was something this minuscule in the face of true misery so difficult to deal with?

Grace's phone went off and she dug it out of her pocket. A text from Leah. We need you in the kitchen.

Grace let out a breath. *We.* Her mind stupidly jumped to the conclusion that *we* might include Kyle. Leah and Kyle weren't exactly hanging out after business hours, unless maybe it had something to do with the party on Friday.

Uncertain and idiotically nervous, Grace moved out of her room and down the back stairwell. When she stepped into the kitchen she was met with candlelight.

And Kyle.

Her heart flipped.

"Hi," he offered, standing next to a fully set kitchen table, two plates full of some kind of pasta. A bouquet of tulips in a vase in the middle.

"Hi. Leah texted me..."

"I know. I thought perhaps you might not come down if I asked you, so I employed a little help."

"You... This is for me?"

He nodded.

Grace didn't know what to do with her hands, or with herself for that matter. She couldn't find all the right parts of her brain to figure out what this meant.

"I wanted to apologize for what happened last week."

"This is an apology?" A dinner with candlelight and flowers. This stuff happened in movies and in books and to people way more sophisticated than her. This did not happen in Carvelle or Bluff City, Iowa. It just…didn't.

"No, this is a romantic gesture so that you allow me to offer you an apology."

"Oh."

"Sit down?" He gestured to a chair. "Even if you end up not accepting the apology, the meal is still for you."

"Oh." Could she be any lamer? With halting steps she moved toward the chair, and not at all steady, lowered herself into it. Dinner smelled like heaven. "Spaghetti and meatballs. That's my favorite."

"I asked around," he said simply. He stood in front of her, studying her face until he sighed. "Grace, I'm sorry I lied to you. It was the wrong choice."

When she didn't say anything, he faltered a little bit, but then pressed on. "It will be my first instinct to try to protect you. To keep you safe. No matter what outside factors apply, your being safe and happy will always be my priority." He pushed out a breath. "And that's what I thought I was doing, keeping you from something that would have bothered you. I see now that it's not the same."

It was the perfect apology. Truly perfect. Impeccable word choice, flawlessly earnest delivery, plenty of eye contact. Not a "but" in sight.

If she had any sense in her head, she'd jump into his arms and take him to a room with a locking door and let dinner get very, very cold.

Instead she felt silly and inadequate in the face of his perfect words and perfect apology.

"You know, it really doesn't seem fair you can apologize off the cuff like that. I've been thinking about how to apologize and I really just don't know how." Grace fiddled with the napkin on the table before sneaking a glance at him.

His eyebrows drew together, mouth quirking to the side. "What would you have to apologize for?"

Grace looked at her plate. The food he'd prepared or bought, it really didn't matter. "I don't know. Maybe I overreacted. I was all hopped up on freaking out over yet another Barry moment of fear. And I've never really done this before. I mean, I went on a few dates with Barry when I was twenty-three. And then I kind of didn't do that. At all." Grace dared to look up; Kyle's expression was still confused. Which meant she had to keep explaining all the weird things she wasn't sure she understood herself.

His perfect words ringing over and over in her head. Why couldn't she have a practiced speech?

"It's just...all I have are these kind of immature relationships to go off, and I'm not sure what the right moves to make are. Then add at least half my brain space is being taken up by worry and trying to be brave. I...I just think I might have screwed up, too." Grace looked back down at the plate. This was not going well.

"So...just so that we're moving forward on the same page. This thing between us is a mature relationship?"

"Well, what else would it be?" She glared up at him. Mr. Perfect should be making this easier, not harder.

"I don't know." He rubbed a hand over the back of his neck. "Maybe just a distraction."

The laugh bubbled up over the self-pity and irritation and uncertainty. "Oh, honey, if I wanted a distraction, you'd be, like, the worst choice. Unless by distraction you mean so busy trying to loosen you up and figure you out that I don't have time to worry about my own problems."

"I'm not really sure how to take that." He pulled a chair over, sat so they were just a few inches from face-to-face, just a few centimeters from knee to knee.

She wanted to reach out and touch him but wasn't sure if they were on even ground yet. "It's a compliment. You're not a distraction. You're very important to me."

"Good. You're very important to me, too."

"Good."

Silence settled. Awkward. Grace tried to come up with a million things to say other than a desperate "I love you" she wasn't altogether sure about. Did she love him? Maybe. But what if she was wrong? She'd never been in love before.

All she knew was she liked him. She was attracted to him, both physically and because of the man he was, what he'd overcome. He complemented her. She complemented him. There had been a sense of rightness in being with Kyle.

Was that love?

Kyle's hands took hers, gently, as if he would let her pull them away if she wanted. No, she didn't want to. Not at all.

"I just want us to be an 'us,' and for us to be okay."

And that was what she wanted, too. She leaned forward, keeping her hands in his as she pressed a kiss to his lips. "I want that, too." She kissed him again. "No more lying, and we will be."

He nodded, a slow smile curving his lips. "Good."

Good. Yes, it was. And yes, it would be.

CHAPTER SEVENTEEN

GRACE STARED AT the computer, her finger hovering above the mouse, the arrow sitting on Send. Intimidating.

What's the worst that could happen?

Well, the art gallery seeking a receptionist could laugh at her sad little résumé. Of course, since she was sending it via email she'd never know that. Really, the worst that could happen was they never called her for an interview. Surely she could survive that.

So she clicked Send, and promptly felt sick and wished it back.

"Grace?"

She jumped in the chair of Jacob's desk, looking guiltily at Kyle standing in the doorway. "Oh, hey."

"What are you up to?"

She waved him away, clicking out of her email. "Just random stuff. Um, job hunting, I guess. You know, almost anything is better than going back to Cabby's."

"So you're looking at…jobs in Bluff City?"

He still stood in the doorway, leaning against

the frame. Maybe they were both pretending. Him pretending not to be fishing. Her pretending not to be intimidated by making life choices that were different than she'd anticipated. That might end in failure.

"Yes." She forced herself out of the chair and across the room. "I mean, who knows how long I'll be here with the house issues, and Barry, and... everything. And when I do have to go back to Carvelle... Well, it's only twenty minutes away."

"Right. Of course." That tense smile. Uncomfortable robot Kyle.

Oh, what was he thinking in that complicated brain of his?

He cleared his throat, focused on her face. "I do like you being here," he said carefully, the robot melting off him even if his discomfort didn't.

Yeesh. He really could say the sweetest things. "I like being here, too."

"Good." Then he took her hand, tugged. "Come with me."

"Where are we going? I was hoping we could make out in Jacob's office."

He shook his head, pulling her into the hall. "That would be a no."

"Fun hater."

He led her down the hallway to the attic door. Grace had never been up there. She hadn't ever seen anyone go up there. She only knew it was the attic because she'd once asked Jacob where the door led.

"Can I ask why you're taking me up to the attic?"

"It's a surprise."

"I'm not sure I like attic surprises." But she followed him up the short staircase. Late-afternoon sunlight poured in through a series of octagon windows along the far wall. The floor was paneled in whitewashed wood, but on the window side a huge drop cloth covered the ground. The walls were filled in and painted a creamy white, and lights hung from the rafters.

Then she noticed her easel was set up. And there was a long table with all her paints and supplies. A chair. Plants. One of her paintings hung along the nonwindowed wall.

She could barely force the words out of her tight throat. "What's all this?"

"A gift."

She blinked. It was like a studio. A much nicer version of her basement, or what had been her basement, back in Carvelle. Better lighting, prettier surroundings, not burned to the ground. "A gift?"

"Jacob brought up that it may be a while before you can rebuild your house, if that's what you decide to do. And we all wanted to make sure you'd feel comfortable staying here. For as long as you wish."

"All of you?"

"Yes, Leah wired special lights." He pointed at the ceiling. "Jacob moved all your stuff and did the floor and walls. Kelly and Susan decorated, obviously. Henry's working on getting a sink up here, though it's not done yet."

"You all…" Grace swallowed, looking around the little studio they'd built her. As if she belonged here. With them. God, could that really be possible?

She turned to Kyle. He was still standing by the stairs, hands in his pockets, a smile on his face. Pleased that she was pleased.

"And it was your idea." He'd mentioned everyone else, but she knew. This had to have come from him.

"Well, we all contributed."

"It was your idea. You brought me up here alone because it was your idea."

"I… Yes." He gave a little nod of admission. "I suppose I came up with the idea, and they might have made me show it to you alone. Apparently they didn't trust you not to shower me with kisses of gratitude. Which I wouldn't mind, by the way."

She walked over and threw her arms around his neck because this—this was amazing. As if he hadn't already done so many things for her, this… The words *I love you* were on the tip of her tongue, the feeling so big and huge she could barely contain it.

But she didn't know if he was ready to hear it.

Ready to believe it, not when he so easily resisted the credit he deserved. So she pulled back, keeping her arms around his neck, looking him right in the eye, and swallowed. "Thank you. You have no idea how much this means to me."

His hand moved down her back, a gesture of intimacy, but then he shrugged. "It's just a little thing."

"It's a huge thing. A monumental thing." She kissed his nose and released him, turning to the studio again because she couldn't resist. This was hers. They'd made it for her. Her fingers itched to paint. Right now, with the late afternoon making everything glow orange.

She turned to Kyle. "You know what? I want to paint you."

His eyebrows shot up. "Me? Now?"

"Yes, you. Remember, I said you'd be a good subject. I wasn't lying. Or trying to get in your pants. At least, I wasn't only trying to get in your pants."

"Grace."

"I don't do many faces, but I need to expand my repertoire. So grab that chair, move it next to the plant and sit."

"You have sketched me before."

"That was just a caricature. This will be a real painting." She pointed at the chair, gave him her best menacing look. "Butt in chair. Now."

"And I don't suppose telling you I have work to do is going to deter you?"

"Not in the slightest."

He pressed his lips together, but it wasn't an expression of irritation. More like trying not to smile. She really liked that she could make him smile, laugh. He needed to do it. Far more often.

Well, she'd get right on that.

"I am staying one hundred percent clothed during the painting portion of the evening," he announced, settling himself on the little blue armchair in the corner of the studio space.

She burst out laughing, so unexpected was the joke, told with a straight face. Loved him. She really, really did. "Aw, come on, just lose the shirt?"

"Not on your life."

"You know, I might have shirtless you memorized. I'll just add it in on my own."

"You had better not."

She went to collect her paints, but she got sidetracked because he was sitting on the chair. He was going to pose for her. He'd come up with this place for her. This was…important. And she couldn't let him joke that way, no matter how much she loved to see him joke.

She stood before him. Even if she didn't think he was ready to hear words of love yet, maybe she could ease him there. With the truth he seemed so reluctant to see. "You are such a good man, Kyle Clark."

His expression, the set to his shoulders, it all

changed. Tensed. Hardened. "I wouldn't go tha
far." His gaze went somewhere beyond her and al
the ease left him.

It reminded her of the night she'd called him he
knight in shining armor and he'd said that was th
last thing he was. Could he really not see himsel
clearly? All that he'd done for her? The way all hi
little gestures added up to this beautiful canvas o
small but amazingly important deeds?

She slid onto his lap, touched his face. "You are
so good, and someday you're going to have to ac
cept that." Before he could argue, she pressed he
mouth to his, let all that love she felt pour into the
kiss. Into him.

She'd make him accept it. Believe it. And maybe
just maybe, love could give them what they both
needed.

KYLE HAD NEVER been so happy to get to a Friday
before in his life. Never looked forward to a week
end where he didn't have to think about work.

He smiled a little to himself. Get through to
night's party and he had forty-eight uninterrupted
hours to spend with Grace.

Life certainly could change in an instant.

Kyle finished the month's schedule, hit Print,
then looked at his rarely used personal calendar.
Maybe he could actually work out a day or two to
take off later in the month. Surely the police had

o find Barry soon, and once Barry was locked
way maybe he and Grace could go somewhere.
Take a short little vacation where they could both
elax and not have to worry about interruptions or
ecurity alarms.

Kyle laughed at himself. At this rate, Grace was
going to kick him to the curb for being *too* needy.

As he glanced at the calendar on the screen, his
aughter stopped, died along with any lighthearted
happiness he was feeling.

Under May 20, in the computer's tiny font, were
he words he dreaded every few years.

Dad's release.

Kyle kept meticulous check, because he'd grown
tired of Dad showing up at his door unannounced.
Now he knew ahead of time. About two days after
release, Dad would show up at MC, pretend they
were old buddies and ask for money.

Kyle had tried to be out of town in the past, but
Dad always came back. So instead, he kept track,
made sure Jacob was busy or out of town, then
tried to find a way not to be sucked into the trap.

But it went down the same way each time. Dad
showed up, pretended they had a relationship not
based on violence and hate for about five seconds,
before reminiscing about his son holding a gun to
his head. He poked and prodded until Kyle threw a
punch, years of control out the window with a few
nasty comments.

In the aftermath of a bloody fight, Kyle forke
over whatever money he could spare and sent Da
on his way. Some mix of guilt for knowing he'd a
most killed him once, knowing this man brough
out the monster in him and the disgusting hope Da
would use the money to buy and overdose on som
drugs, or at the very least land himself back in jai

Kyle's stomach turned in slow, nauseated rolls
He x-ed out of the calendar.

He couldn't let Grace see that part of himself
He couldn't. He would have to find a way to fix it
Make it not happen. Sure, he'd been trying for ter
years to defuse the bomb that was his father, bu
now he had a real reason. Grace. He had to find a
way to keep Dad out of the picture, to keep the bac
away from all the good he'd found.

Still two weeks before he had to worry abou
that. He'd figure something out. Some way to keep
Grace away. To keep the violence away. To—

The knock on the door caused him to jump in his
chair. He couldn't find his voice, but Grace pushed
in without waiting for a "come in" anyway.

"I've got something for you." She smiled brightly
paint splotches over her hands and shirt. She held
up the painting to one wall, then another. "You ge
a Grace McKnight original. Free of charge. I was
going to put it up for sale, but it reminded me too
much of you."

The painting in her hands was small compared

to most of the other ones he'd seen of hers. Not much bigger than a piece of paper. It was almost a perfect representation of the view from the top of the bluff they had hiked up. Before the fire. Before they were them.

Before she'd wiggled her way into his heart so deep he'd do just about anything to keep her there. Including believing he could find a way to circumnavigate his father this time. Believing he could hide the violent part of himself away from Grace, because if she ever saw it...

He couldn't even let himself think what might happen, what kind of person that would make him.

"It's lovely," he managed, though his voice wasn't steady.

She rested the painting in front of some accounting books on his shelf. Backed away. Then she slid onto his lap and studied her painting, as if that was the most normal thing to do. "There. Move some of those books and keep it on the shelf like that. A little lesson Kelly taught me on giving a bookshelf dimension." She kissed his nose, and he held on. Held on to that one good thing.

He had to find a way to head Dad off at the pass. He wasn't coming to MC this time. Not with Grace around. Kyle would figure something out. Figure some way out of who he was, who his father could still make him be.

"You okay?"

He knew he was holding on to her just a hair too tight, but she felt good and right and he didn't want to lose that right now. So he nodded against her shoulder while the voice in his brain he wanted to silence whispered a question he wouldn't allow himself to dwell on.

How many times would the answer to that question be a lie? When they'd already agreed no more lying?

"Stressed about the party, aren't you?" She popped off his lap to stand behind him and rub his shoulders, rubbing the guilt in deeper with each massage.

"You know what you need?"

"I was thinking about going for a run, actually."

"I have a better idea. We'll call it a different form of cardiovascular activity." Her hands traveled past his shoulder, inching down across his abs until he huffed out a laugh.

"The door is open." And he didn't deserve this. Or her. Not with his father's reappearance looming.

You will handle it. You will absolutely handle it. Because Grace is yours.

"I can close it," she whispered in his ear.

He wanted to find humor, to believe he was in control, so he pulled her into his lap. She smiled at him. Beautiful. Happy. Perfect.

"I'm going to do whatever it takes to protect you." It slipped out. A misstep. She was frowning

ow and he'd ruined it all. Which seemed about
ght.

The threat of his father ruined everything.

"I don't need you to protect me." She rubbed her
alm against his chin, frowning. "I just need you
) be you." She framed his face with her hands.
What's bothering you, honey?"

Honey. No one had ever called him that, called
im any kind of endearment before. It was wrong
) break his promise. Wrong to keep a secret, to lie,
ut this one was important. Imperative.

"I'm just…worried about the party." He cleared
is throat. "I want you to be safe."

"I will be." Her whole brow furrowed, she kept
ubbing her palm against his cheek. "It's a party.
)ur first date." She smiled brightly, but he knew
t was forced. Saw the determined glint behind it.
"It's going to be a good night. And I know I'll be
afe because once you see the dress I'm wearing,
'ou won't be able to look anywhere else."

He took one of her hands, kissed it. He had to
emember the plan. What he'd promised himself
)ack at that trailer park the night of Grace's fire.

He'd bury the bad so deep it would never see
daylight. He wasn't Barry, because he would never,
ever hurt Grace. He wouldn't let the violent, evil
part of him win. It wasn't lying. It was survival.

And he'd always been a survivor.

GRACE SAT ON her bed in a fluffy robe, trying to w
herself to get ready and stop wallowing in self-pit

But Barry was supposed to be in jail by no
and every lead the police found ended up being
dead end. They couldn't even determine if he'd le
the state or not. All they knew was he was still o
there. Somewhere.

She hoped he was dead. She hoped to God h
was dead.

But until they knew that for sure, here she wa
being a burden again. Though Jacob and Susa
tried to wave it off as no big deal, Grace knew tha
because of her, extra precautions were in place fo
the party tonight.

People had to bring their invitations to get in
which Jacob assured her was just because rich peo
ple liked the thrill of feeling exclusive. They'd hire
an independent security guard, which Kyle had ex
plained was in case any guests got rowdy.

Yeah, right.

It was because of her. Because the security sys
tem wouldn't be on the entire time as it usually was

Their excuses were thoughtful, but she wasn'
an idiot. Kyle's bizarre statement about protecting
her. All this dumb party stuff. She was the reason
for their extra work. For their worry, and as swee
as it all was, it made her feel like crap.

A few knocks, her door swung open and Kelly

Susan and Leah streamed into her little room with bags and hangers and laughter and friendship.

"Here comes the getting-ready brigade."

The heaviness on Grace's heart lifted just a little. "I didn't realize there was going to be a brigade."

"Leah told us you got her to buy a dress. So we're making her do a grand reveal."

Leah wrinkled her nose. "I'm not wearing it. I'm protesting."

Kelly waved her off. "Don't be stupid. We'll wrestle you into it if we have to. In fact, we want to see it immediately."

Susan began to chant "strip" and Grace happily joined in. Self-pity be damned. She was going to have fun tonight. Like she'd told Kyle. This was a party and their first official date, so she was damn well going to enjoy herself no matter what precautions were in place.

Leah huffed, muttered a few choice obscenities, then tossed her dress bag over her shoulder. "I'm going to change in the bathroom."

Susan booed her as she disappeared, then grinned at Grace. "All right. Let's see your pick."

Grace pulled her dress out of the closet and Susan and Kelly dutifully turned around and studied some artwork on the walls as she changed.

"All right."

Kelly turned and let out a low whistle. "Damn, girl. Are you trying to give Kyle a stroke? I'm not sure he's ready for this kind of thing. Although he has dropped the cyborg routine rather quickly. Still, this might short-circuit him."

Grace smoothed a hand over the front of the dress. She could go for a little short-circuiting. Especially after the weird moment this afternoon. She didn't want worry—his or hers—she just wanted a little fun. It was amazing that a simple change of wardrobe and a few friends could knock self-pity to the curb.

Leah hurried into the room in her red dress with her other clothes bundled up in front of her. The door slammed shut and the whole room fell silent. Kelly's and Susan's mouths just dropped.

Leah scowled. "Well, somebody say something, for chrissakes."

"Holy shit," Susan said on an exhale. Then she turned her reverent gaze to Grace. "How on earth did you get her to buy that and then wear that?"

Kelly had the same wide-eyed kind of awe on her face. "Grace. Mother of pearl. You must have some voodoo magic. I've never even been able to get her to wear a cheapo jersey dress."

Grace grinned. If anything had ever made her feel like part of the group, this was it. Knowing she'd helped do something Kelly and Susan hadn't been able to do in however many years of friendship with Leah.

Even if she went back to Carvelle and Cabby's

and her old life when this whole Barry debacle was over, she'd still have friends. And Kyle. And this life full of people not only who mattered to her, but to whom she mattered.

Leah fidgeted, pulling the hem of the dress down. "I don't wear this kind of crap because I look stupid."

"You look great," Susan said with the wave of a hand. "Freaking amazing. And if half the guys at the party are drooling all over you, you'd better buy Grace a nice thank-you present." Susan shook her head. "How did you do it, Grace?"

Grace shrugged. "It probably helped that my house had just burned down. A lot of sympathy points." There. She'd even kind of made a joke about the fire. Barry could play the bogeyman in all her dreams from here to eternity, but he wasn't winning everything.

KYLE HELD THE CLIPBOARD, physically checking off all of the to-dos as Jacob verbally listed them. Guests would be arriving any minute, and it seemed everything was in place.

The party had not been his idea, but it made good business sense, so he'd gone along with it. The house looked great and the potential for a few more houses on their schedule was large.

Besides, surviving as a business for five years was an accomplishment to be celebrated. He sighed.

If only this kind of celebration didn't leave his shoulders stiff and his nerves twitching.

"The security guy's here?"

Kyle nodded. "He's going to watch the back of the house. Henry will be on front-of-the-house duty. Your parents are on Grace duty the first hour, then Leah, then me, then you."

Jacob scratched a hand through his hair. "All right. We should be good, then."

Female laughter on the stairs grabbed both men's attention. Kelly and Leah walked down first, Susan and Grace right behind.

"Christ," Jacob muttered, and then his jaw just kind of hung down. Kyle followed his gaze. Well, Leah certainly looked different, but the way Jacob stared at her made Kyle wary.

"I wouldn't suggest looking at Leah that way."

"Huh?" Jacob huffed out a breath. "I'm not looking at her any certain way." He crossed his arms over his chest, but his eyes didn't leave Leah and her red dress. In Kyle's mind, only bad things could come of that.

But Jacob was keeping out of his business with Grace, so Kyle would keep his mouth shut.

Speaking of Grace… She was walking behind Kelly so he couldn't really get a good view until the group of women reached the bottom of the stairs and scattered.

And then just about everything in the room disappeared. Except Grace.

She walked up to him, all skin and black dress. Dark and sexy with a very self-satisfied smile. "Hi," she offered.

It took a considerable effort to move any muscle in this face enough to work out a response. "Hi," he finally managed.

"I'm *right* here," Jacob muttered. "Could you maybe save those kind of looks for... I don't know. Not around me?"

Grace made a shooing motion with her hands. "Then go away."

Jacob grunted, but then he disappeared.

"I hate to fish for compliments, but do you think I look okay? I mean, I know I look good, but do I look like I'll fit in with the party? I don't want to stick out."

It amazed him she could possibly have any doubts about how perfect she looked. Room empty or full of clients, she looked exactly like she belonged.

"If you stick out, it's only because you'll be the most beautiful woman in the room."

Her lips curved into a smile, something a little shy that curled into his heart and got lodged there, making him completely forget about everything else.

Until Mrs. Martin's voice interrupted the peace

of the room. "Grace, darling, don't you look lovely!
Have you finished our painting yet?"

Grace was swept away, and more and more people swept in. Congratulations were offered, food
was circulated, music was soft in the background.

Despite being engaged in multiple conversations
with clients and suppliers, Kyle's eyes never left
Grace. And more often than not, her eyes remained
on him.

He could do this thing. He could live this life.
Once he found a way to defuse the bomb that was
his father, everything would be fine.

GRACE RETURNED TO the main room, freshly armed
with a few more business cards. It hadn't been that
hard to hand them out, really. Mrs. Martin had in-
troduced her around the party as though she'd personally discovered her. When she handed her card
to a few people later in the evening, she didn't even
feel weird or pushy about it.

She stopped at the entrance, her old friend unease settling through her limbs.

All night, she'd had to fight this feeling. This old
niggling worry that even if no one looked at her
funny, she didn't belong. With her parents gone already and the rest of MC mingling throughout the
crowd, Grace felt like little more than a believable
fake among faces of the real thing.

These people talked about vacation homes, the

stock market, restaurants she'd never even dreamed of going to. They commented on the wine, the fancy food Grace had wrinkled her nose at for being too fussy and weird.

She might look the part, she might have handed over business cards with ease, but she was an impostor, and it was an exhausting disguise.

Grace searched the room for some hiding place or dark corner. Any space that might allow her to fade into the background and wallow in her insecurities without putting them on display.

"Thank God you're back." Leah grabbed her arm and hung on for dear life. "You don't leave my side until Handsy McGee over there leaves."

Grace glanced over to where Leah gestured. A middle-aged man was staring at Leah all too fervently.

"Who is it?"

"He works at Abesso Lighting. Apparently now that he knows I have a decent rack, thanks to this idiotic dress, he's all over me." Leah shuddered.

"Let's go sit," Grace instructed, nodding toward the love seat in the far corner. Very few people were in that area, and with Leah by her side she could pretend that she wasn't feeling out of place.

"Drinks first." Leah dragged her to the hired bartender and asked for two glasses of the sweetest wine he had, and then led the way back to the love seat. "Much better. I do love to people watch."

Grace looked out over the groups of people. Even sitting next to Leah, the unease continued. It was a little like high school, being self-conscious and being so sure people noticed that unease, though they likely didn't.

"What's up with you? You're all mopey for a girl who's been disgustingly happy all week. Kyle screw things up again? He's probably going to do that a lot, but give him a break. He's not like your brother. Girls aren't a revolving door for him."

"No, it's not about Kyle." Grace sighed, fiddling with the stem of her glass. "I don't really belong here."

"Who does?" Leah surveyed the crowd of people. "You think I do? Remember just how much it took to get me into this dress? This is all your brother's realm, and Kelly and Susan. The rest of us put up with it because we have to."

"Kyle fits right in."

Leah rolled her eyes. "Kyle is an excellent actor, I'll give him that, but he doesn't like this stuff any more than we do. This is the first event we've had where I've seen him genuinely smile. And that smile is always for you, Grace."

Grace fidgeted, not sure what to say or how to explain that this was separate from Kyle.

"You know, our second year we threw a New Year's Eve party. A lot like this, but on a smaller

cale. Just trying to impress some people. You
know what Kyle did?"

"Leah—"

"He filled drinks, he checked food trays, he went
and got brochures if someone asked. He did whatever he could to not be involved, all while acting
like he was. So look at him tonight."

He was talking with Kelly and a couple Grace
didn't know. He looked…relaxed, she decided. And
then she realized despite the fact that he talked to
those people, his eyes kept venturing back to her.

"I think it's pretty amazing. That you can effect
that kind of change in someone. Impressive, really.
Not everyone has that ability. In fact, I'd venture
to say most people don't."

Grace didn't know what to say. On one hand,
yes, Kyle had changed in the past few weeks. He'd
opened up a little. She knew that had to do with
her, even if she didn't know how. Maybe it wasn't
so much her as it was someone simply seeing the
man beneath his mask. Maybe anyone could have
done it.

Or maybe not. Maybe the commonality of violence in their pasts was what had broken down
those walls and barriers. So maybe it was her.

Not that she'd broken down all his walls. There
were still things that caused him to shut down
or back away. But she'd done more than anyone,
including Jacob, in ten years.

"There's that smug lovey-dovey look," Leah said, slapping her on the shoulder. "Oops, he's coming over. I'll make myself scarce."

"Leah, you don't have to—"

But she was already jumping off the couch, and in no time at all Kyle took her place. "Everything okay?"

Grace nodded. "Just a little partied out. Maybe hungry. Everything has some weird soft cheese on it."

Instead of looking insulted or condescending, he pulled a granola bar out of an inner pocket of his suit jacket. "That's why I carry these."

Of course, it was one of his healthy fruit-and-nut bars, but it was still better than stinky cheese and wine.

"Gimme." She snatched the bar and he laughed. Once she had a free hand, he took it in his. As she munched on his granola bar, he brushed his lips across her knuckles, an absent gesture of affection. It, along with Leah's words, prompted a very strange realization.

This was her life. Her real, adult life. It was a weird, out-of-body thing. Of course she knew this was her life, but she felt as if she was seeing it from the outside.

It wasn't what she'd planned or expected, but it wasn't pathetic, either. In the past few weeks, she'd managed a lot of things she hadn't since the whole Barry incident.

She was dating. She was being more proactive in selling her paintings. She was living with fear. Not in spite of it, but actually with it. And still moving forward. There was no need to feel out of place. Even if she didn't have a stacked bank account or a million fancy cocktail dresses, she had the things she'd worked her ass off for, and those things made up a life no one could take away from her.

Grace leaned into Kyle. Maybe he wasn't an open book. Yet. But she'd get there. They'd get there.

CHAPTER EIGHTEEN

"WELL, IT WAS quite a party."

Kyle figured that was the highest of the highest praise from Mrs. Martin, or she was very, very drunk. Either way, she was leaving. Kyle smiled and waved as Mr. Martin ushered her out the door.

Last guests gone, he turned to survey the damage. Not too terribly bad, but there was a lot of cleanup to do. He looked at Grace in her black dress and thought about how badly he didn't want to do cleanup.

"I have an idea," Susan offered, kicking off her heels. "We leave the mess for tonight. Kelly and I will come back tomorrow morning, with doughnuts, and we'll have a little cleanup party. I'm not sure I can face doing this right now."

"Sounds good," Jacob replied.

All eyes turned to Kyle.

"What say you, boss? Can you handle a little mess for a few hours while we mere mortals sleep?"

Kyle smiled. Since sleep these days included being in Grace's bed, what once would have driven him crazy was barely a blip. "Sure." He looked at the damage again. Okay, maybe more than a blip.

Grace smiled at him as Susan, Kelly and Leah gathered their things and chattered out the door.

He'd deal.

"We could go ahead and clean up and call them in the morning and say not to bother coming over," Jacob offered.

Kyle opened his mouth, trying to formulate some excuse, but what would be the point? Whether they spent a few hours cleaning or not, he still wasn't planning on sleeping alone tonight.

"All right," Grace agreed with a little sigh. "Let me go change into something a little more cleanup friendly."

Well, that was unfortunate. He'd worked up one or two fantasies about tonight and that dress.

The security alarm beeped as someone entered the code, then Leah stumbled in, dripping wet. "My car won't start," she grumbled. "And it's raining cats and dogs. Someone give me a ride home?"

"Why can't Susan and Kelly drive you?" Jacob was quick to say. A little too quick, but Kyle was trying not to notice Jacob and Leah's weird vibe, hoping it would resolve itself without him having to step in.

Leah glared at Jacob. "They're already gone, moron. You think I wouldn't have thought of that?" She grumbled something else under her breath.

Jacob took a few odd steps away from Leah. "Just crash on the couch. Nothing you haven't done before."

"I can't stay. I'm dog sitting for my neighbor. She dropped him off at my place before she left this afternoon, but I promised I'd be home by eleven-thirty to let her out. Besides, I'm soaking wet and there's no way I'm wearing this damn dress for another hour, let alone many."

Jacob looked back at Grace and Kyle, possibly hoping one of them would offer. Uh, yeah, no.

"Fine, fine, fine. I'll drive you home." Jacob sighed, muttered something about a pain in the ass. Leah followed him to the door. After Jacob had exited, Leah turned and winked, her irritation melting into a smile. "Enjoy a little alone time, guys." Quickly she closed the door.

Kyle set the alarm, then turned to Grace surrounded by the debris of a party. It was hard to notice what would usually drive him nuts while she was wearing that dress. "I feel like perhaps I should clean up, but…"

Her mouth curved into a smile. "Alone time is very rare."

"Yes, it is."

"We should take advantage of it."

He nodded, still standing way too many feet away from her. "Yes, We should."

Grace sauntered across the room, smoothed a

hand over his tie, then grasped it. "Come on, honey. I have plans for you before Jacob gets back."

Kyle gladly followed. "Plans?"

"They involve lights and not shushing each other when we make too much noise."

"Very exciting plans."

Her laugh was low and husky. Since she was pulling him by the tie, he sped up his pace and then slid an arm around her abdomen so as they walked to the stairs her back was pressed to his front.

Such a comforting feeling, to know she fit against him. To know she wanted to.

She reached the staircase and turned to face him. Standing on the bottom step, she was just a hair taller than him. She rested her arms on his shoulders, took his mouth with hers.

Kyle was sure he'd never tire of sinking into this kiss, of holding her against him. He trailed his hands down her sides, then her hips. When he reached the hem of her skirt, he tugged up, and her lips curved against his.

Feeling unbelievably light and happy and *right,* he banded his hands under her butt and lifted. Not needing any instruction, she wrapped her legs around him so that he could essentially carry her up the stairs.

She laughed breathlessly against his neck. "If we fall and break something, it's going to be really embarrassing."

He dropped her onto her feet when they reached the top. Any laughing was over. Her mouth was hungry on his, her hands deftly removing his tie, unbuttoning his shirt.

He slid his palms down the curve of her back. She could leave her dress on for just a little bit. Backing her into her room, she tossed the tie aside, then pulled his shirt off him.

And for the first time since they'd been together, the lights didn't go off the minute the door was closed.

Hallelujah.

For a second, he let himself stand there and just look. The black hair and the black dress weren't the image of Grace he would ever first conjure up. It was too dark and edgy, but it was still sexy as hell.

She toed off her heels, then stood in front of him, her smile all self-satisfied. He brushed a strand of hair from her temple.

"Did I tell you that you look absolutely beautiful tonight?"

The self-satisfied smile grew. "You may have paid that compliment once or twice."

"It bears repeating."

"You know, I look pretty good without my dress on, too."

He chuckled. "I just bet you do."

She turned her back to him, tilting her head to the side so the blunt ends of her short haircut were out of the way. Slowly, enjoying this form of anticipation torture, Kyle pulled the zipper down.

He traced the bare V of skin the zipper freed, down the smooth skin of her neck, over the strap of her bra, to the curve just above her butt. Still behind her, he kissed the base of her neck, pushing the fabric farther apart and a little off her shoulders.

He trailed kisses down her spine, then back up, his hands roaming anywhere he could reach, smoothing, exploring.

"God, I love that."

"Love what?" he murmured against her neck where he knew she was ticklish.

She laughed, turned to face him, dropping the front of her dress and then wiggling out of it so she stood in front of him in simple black underwear.

Simple black underwear on Grace was about the sexiest thing he'd ever seen.

"All the little touchy, kissy stuff. You're really good at it."

Her hands began to slowly, excruciatingly slowly, fiddle with his belt buckle. "Touchy, kissy stuff."

"Mmm-hmm. To be fair, you're really good at everything, but you happened to be doing the touchy, kissy stuff at the time, so I thought I'd compliment you on that."

Kyle lowered his forehead to hers. "Can we please stop saying *touchy kissy?*"

She laughed against his mouth, his belt dropping to the floor. Quickly followed by his pants. He stepped out of them as she led him to the bed.

Much better.

She flopped onto the bed, pulling him on top. Mouths and bodies fused. His hands roamed the soft, pale skin of her arms, her abdomen, her thighs. He nudged the bra straps off her shoulders with his chin, kissed along the top of her bra cups.

She trailed her fingers across his body, exploring dips, tracing along angles and curves. He unsnapped her bra and pulled it off, planting kisses across creamy white breasts until he was as breathless as she was.

She pushed at his boxers, taking the hard length of him in her hand. Kyle bit back a groan as she stroked.

"Grace."

She released him and he almost whimpered, but got distracted when she pushed off her panties.

"I know we should take our time and all, since it's so rare to be alone. But, jeez, just hurry, okay? We'll do slow and lazy some other time when we have to be quiet."

Kyle reached over and pulled open the nightstand drawer, but what usually held just a bottle of lotion, a flashlight and a box of condoms now had an extra, menacing addition.

All good feelings ground to a screeching halt. "You...have a gun." It was painted the same design as her tattoo, but it was a gun. Real and there and frightening.

"Yeah." He could feel her shift on the bed, some of the breathlessness leaving her voice. "Sorry, I don't usually keep it there, but with the party going on I didn't want it in my purse. I figured with the room locked, that was the safest place to put it. No one would be able to get to it except me."

He couldn't stop staring at it. Frozen, vision tunneled so that it was hard to remember or take in anything besides the deadly weapon in her nightstand. All the fun and pleasure of just a few minutes ago sucked out of the room so quickly he was dizzy.

Or maybe that was just the gun.

"I'm not, like, a big gun person or anything. It just makes me feel safe, you know?"

He tried to nod or agree or do anything other than freeze and stare and be transported back to a moment he relived so many times it was a wonder it still gripped him, completely and unrelenting.

"Sorry. Does that bother you?"

She touched his shoulder, and it helped dislodge some of the paralyzing fear and ice and sick emotion. "Yes." He cleared his throat. "No, I mean no. Of course not. I'm sure you're very responsible with it." He shook his head to dislodge the image of a time long ago and a gun in his hand. The heavy feel of—

"Kyle?"

"What? No. I'm fine."

"You really don't seem it. Do you want to go to your room?" Her fingers entwined with his. The smell of paint and perfume just barely infringing on the smell of booze and trailer.

"No. I mean, it doesn't matter. Whatever you want."

"Kyle."

Finger on the trigger, ready to pull and end it all.

"Kyle, look at me."

It wasn't easy to separate past and present. In fact, this was the hardest it had been in a long time. He managed to move his gaze to Grace. The dark brown of her eyes, the worry lines creasing her forehead, the faint color of red lipstick that had faded since the beginning of the evening.

"Talk to me." So earnest and caring.

But he had promised himself to bury it. Bury the bad, the evil, and ignore the horror that lived inside him. It was the only way to have Grace.

"I'm sorry. It took me off guard is all." Kyle closed the drawer, willing his hands to be steady. "Everything is fine."

"Kyle, you didn't get the condom."

Right. "Right."

She touched his arm before he could open the drawer again. Her face hovered in his vision, and

he tried to focus on it and her and anything but his
pounding heart and the sick feeling in his gut.

"I need you to tell me what's wrong."

She was in bed with him naked and he was losing
t, that's what was wrong. He swallowed down the
sick fear, focused on control. It was a little rusty,
but ten years of honing that kind of emotional dis-
connection was still there, just waiting to be used.

"I'm sorry. Guns just make me nervous." Which
wasn't a lie. They did. Nervous about what he might
do with access to one if his dad showed up. Kyle
forced his lips to curve upward. "Took me a little
by surprise, but I'm fine now."

Her eyebrows drew together and she pulled her
bottom lip through her teeth. "Do they bring up
bad memories or—"

He silenced her with a kiss. Nothing passionate,
just a quick peck. "I'm okay. Really." This time
when he pushed his mouth into a smile, he willed
himself to believe it. Everything was fine because
Grace was here, and he wouldn't jeopardize that
with the whole ugly truth.

"We can talk about—"

"Let's save talking for another time." He willed
himself to forget, to reengage in the moment. He
smoothed a hand down her arm.

She crawled into his lap, kissed him on the forehead, the nose, the mouth. "You can talk to me,
you know," she said earnestly, massaging at the

tension in his shoulders. "About anything. Nothing will change the way I feel about you. Nothing that happened to you could do that."

Kyle nodded, even though he knew there was no way in hell he would ever talk to her about this. About then. It wasn't to be talked about. It was to be buried and forgotten. That was what had gotten him here, had gotten him her. Pretending those first eighteen years were nothing, and all he'd built since that was everything.

Letting those two versions of himself out would change things, or he wouldn't have had to bury the old version.

She hugged him, and he rested his cheek on her shoulder. His body, his mind, his heart relaxed. This was it. That thing he needed to overwhelm the bad, to make it go away. Her and this and love. "I love you, Grace."

She stilled for a fraction of a second, then pulled back from the hug and touched his mouth with the tip of her index finger. She smiled, traced his bottom lip. "I love you, too."

Her lips touched his gently. Something soft and caring rather than meant to end in sex, but when the image of the gun popped back up in his mind, he squeezed his eyes shut and deepened the kiss.

GRACE LAY IN the dark, tracing the shadows and light in the room. Sleep had never come to her,

ven hours after Kyle's breathing had slowed into
estful sleep.

Her mind kept turning over the moment he'd
een her gun. How pale he'd gotten, how unre-
ponsive he'd been, like someone transported to
nother place.

She'd offered comfort, and he'd taken it, but he'd
never explained himself. Never opened up. And, as
she'd lain in the dark, every other instance where
ne'd clammed up popped into her mind.

It was a switch; anytime she asked him about the
past, she'd always known that. He'd always been
that way. So it wasn't so much a surprise as a dis-
appointment.

Because he'd said he loved her just moments
after shutting her out of part of himself. Grace
didn't know how to handle that, to process it.

The relationship was new, yes, but the feelings were real and deep. Still, she hadn't spilled
her guts over everything in her life. A lot, but not
everything.

Maybe he just needed time to warm up to the
idea of sharing. If even his oldest friend didn't
know everything that had happened to Kyle, why
should she expect a few weeks and love to make
him spill all his guts to her?

She was expecting too much. Rehashing traumatic events wasn't easy. She knew that better than
anyone. It wasn't as though she'd told him the de-

tails of what Barry had done to her. Kyle knew it had been a severe beating, just as Grace knew that Kyle's parents had treated him badly.

How could she expect more?

There was a difference, though. Tiny, but bothersome. If Kyle asked her, she would tell. She'd asked him to talk to her, and he'd all but refused.

She squeezed her eyes shut, listened to the sound of his even breathing, pressed her nose against his arm.

Time. Time would make it okay. Time would make everything okay.

It had to.

Sometime later, she finally fell asleep, but it was fitful. Snatches of senseless dreams. Just splashes of color and light and pricks of pain. Nothing concrete. Nothing meaningful.

When she woke up, her eyes were gritty and her throat was sore. She felt vaguely achy and not at all a happy woman in love.

Kyle kissed her temple. "Morning."

Grace took a deep breath, soaked in the feel of his skin, the smell of him, in her bed, with her. It was enough. She'd had so little for so long, he was enough just the way he was.

"Morning." She snuggled in, willing away the niggling part of her brain insisting something wasn't quite right.

His finger stroked up and down her arm for a

w minutes and she held her breath, hoping maybe
e'd say something. Maybe he'd just needed some
me before he explained himself. Maybe—

"Well, I want to get an early start." He kissed her
gain, then slid out of bed. "No sense in waiting
round for people to start showing up." He pulled
n a pair of sweatpants that had somehow found its
ay into her room over the course of the past week.

Grace sat up in bed, watched him pull the shirt
ver his head. He seemed relaxed and easy and she
vanted to feel that way, too. She wanted to wal-
ow in happy and love, but she couldn't quite make
hat step.

"Kyle, about last night..."

"I'm going to go run through the shower. You can
leep a little longer if you want. It's awfully early."

"Kyle—"

He gave her an absent kiss. "I'll be downstairs
vhenever you're ready to help." He left the room
s though it was normal to leave someone with half
a sentence unsaid.

Grace flopped back on the bed. Maybe she just
nad to accept that this part of him was closed off,
ind maybe that was for the best. The only way he
could cope. She could almost understand that.

It was the "almost" that was a problem.

KYLE FELT THE weight of Grace's uncertain stare the
entire morning. While everyone else ate doughnuts

and cleaned up, chatting cheerfully about memorie
over the past five successful years, Grace watche
him. As if she stared long enough she could unloc
his secrets and figure him out.

He wasn't going to let that happen. Instead h
put on his best normal-person disguise and chatte
and laughed right along with his coworkers.

Screw the past and any memories that made the
future more daunting.

Of course, he couldn't quite manage that yet
He had to take care of his father. Something wit
money, of course. Maybe a preemptive visit. He'c
never tried that before. So surely if he tried this
kept Dad away...then everything would be fine.
He'd really be able to bury it all and Grace would
never see a glimpse of it.

The niggling worry that he was kidding himself
was quickly and ruthlessly pushed away. He'd spent
ten years working on controlling every impulse and
emotion. Grace had tested that, yes, but only because he'd wanted the end result. Her.

Since he didn't want this result, letting the ugly
part of himself loose for all to see, or for even one
to see, he could control it. Absolutely.

Unless dear old Dad detonated that bomb before
Kyle had a chance to defuse it. But that wouldn't
happen. The walls of his jail cell would keep him
and Grace safe. For now.

"I think it's clean, boss," Leah said.

Kyle looked down at the spot on the rug he'd been scrubbing. Gone. Long gone by the looks of it. Kyle forced his mouth to curve upward despite his utter lack of feeling behind it. "Of course."

Anything could be erased with enough work.

CHAPTER NINETEEN

GRACE WAFFLED BETWEEN her grand plan to get Kyle to open up and keeping her big mouth shut. Accepting that this was the way things were. He kept a part of himself closed off. No big deal. She could accept that, couldn't she? That she loved the man in the present, and that maybe the man in the past didn't matter.

Grace shifted in bed. Maybe if they were two people who hadn't been shaped by their pasts it wouldn't matter, but it did. It just…did.

Surely if she gave him a piece of herself, he'd do the same. He'd feel safe enough to do the same. This wasn't about *if* he would open up, it was when.

Grace took a deep breath and let it out. And if he never shared, what then? Did she give up? On understanding him? On them? Pretend it didn't matter or keep trying?

Damn it. She didn't know. It was only moderately less frustrating than thinking about Barry, but at least it didn't give her nightmares.

Kyle slipped in the door, dressed in track pants and a T-shirt. Grace smiled a little because she'd once thought he'd never deign to wear something so casual, even to bed.

"Sorry, got caught up with an email. You could have gone to sleep."

"I like falling asleep with you."

It was easy to say things like that to him because he seemed so genuinely pleased in return. As though no one had ever said nice things to him before. The thought that very few probably had made her incredibly sad for him.

Kyle had once told her that what had happened to them wasn't the same, and he was right. He'd had to grow up in a world where the people who were supposed to love and protect their children didn't, and that was a different kind of pain, a different kind of trauma from what she'd gone through. She wasn't sure it made hers better, but it made it different.

It made her wonder if she had any business being here, trying to reach him, trying to understand, but he slid into bed, his arms cool against her blanket-warmed skin. Easy to curl up in him because she was safe here. With him. It wasn't something to take for granted or give away so easily.

Or push away.

Leave it alone, the careful part of her mind instructed. The part of her brain that kept her from taking any chances, kept her from trying for anything more than survival. It was a part of her brain that she'd never listened to when it came to Kyle.

So why was she now?

He pressed a kiss to her hair. "Ready to turn out the light?"

Her mind went in circles. It would keep doing that, too, until she did something decisive. She toyed with the collar of her shirt, knowing she had to do it. She owed it to herself, to her happiness, to *their* happiness. "You know that night I had a nightmare and you came into my room?"

He tensed almost imperceptibly, just a slightly harder edge to the set of his shoulders. "Yes."

"You were up. Did you have a nightmare, too?" Grace forced herself to look into his eyes, but he wasn't looking at her.

"I don't recall."

"I still have them. I, um…" Grace swallowed. "You know, sometimes it's nonsensical stuff, but sometimes it's a lot like reliving that night." His face remained impassive, unreadable, but the tension in his shoulders stiffened degree by degree. "I can feel every punch, hear every curse, and the fear that I'm going to die still overpowers every second until I wake up." She didn't have to force the waver of her voice. This wasn't easy to talk about, but if he had the same issue, they could talk about it together. Share coping mechanisms or even just support.

He didn't say anything. Not a word. She couldn't

ven hear him breathe. Some little piece of her
eart cracked off that he couldn't give something.

And then his breath came out in a whoosh.

"That's hard," he said finally, smoothing a stiff
and down her hair.

"I wonder what's worse sometimes." Grace
ressed her nose to his arm, hoped fervently for
omething, anything to come of this. "If you expect
t. If you know it's coming, or for it to come out of
he blue. I'd seen Barry get irrationally angry, but
ot violent."

His silence persisted, but his hand rubbed up and
down her arm. He wasn't stopping her. That had to
mean something.

"He was nice enough, but I knew something
didn't feel right about him or us or whatever, so
when I tried to break it off I figured it'd be no big
deal. I'd never dreamed of him being angry enough
to…" Grace had to take a deep breath. If anything,
this was a reminder to be patient with him. This
was hard. So hard to talk about, and she'd been
through therapy, had a supportive family. What
had Kyle had?

"It's not even that he was in love with me or
anything. He just started going on about how girls
didn't break up with him. He was in charge, and
he got angrier and angrier until when I started to
leave, he snapped."

"Grace."

Was he trying to get her to stop, or was it jus
a sympathy "Grace"? She didn't know, but she'
gladly stop talking about it so the images would
stop stabbing at her. Grace squeezed her eyes shut
tried not to see Barry's fists or feel the shock o
that first blow. "Do you have nightmares ever?"

That heavy silence again. What was she doing'
What was she going to get out of this? Painfu
memories and a door slammed in her face. So wha
was the damn point?

"It's not something I feel comfortable discussing, Grace."

He talked like that and reminded her of the man
who'd always looked down his nose at her. "Fine."

"I'm sorry if that bothers you," he said carefully,
and she noted he didn't pull away physically. That
was something. "It's the way I have to live."

If she could find the right words to make him
understand she wasn't trying to pry or make him
relive… She was trying to understand. "I just want
to get to know all of you."

"There are parts of me not worth knowing."

He said it so easily, she had no doubt it was an
ingrained belief. She didn't know what to do with
that, how to combat it. Like telling him he was
a good man and having him so easily dismiss it.
She just didn't know how to fight those sad ingrained beliefs.

She curled into him. "I love you." Damaged parts

and all. When would she learn she couldn't heal someone else's pain any more than someone else could heal hers?

But what if neither of them ever healed? Could they really build something lasting with so many issues between them? And how long would she have to wait to find out?

He held on tighter. "I love you, too." And his hold didn't loosen for a very long time.

GRACE STARED AT her phone that refused to ring aside from texts from Mom and Dad. They'd laid off the calling, and she had to be grateful for that. She couldn't even be angry with them over the texts, considering...

Barry was still out there. The police were still clueless.

Her life was on hold. Stuck in limbo. Waiting for Barry to be caught. Waiting for Kyle to open up. Waiting and waiting and waiting on everyone else.

Powerless.

Once again her life had become all about the things beyond her ability to control. And she hated it.

Grace looked at her phone again, and then purposefully pushed it deep into her purse. This interview might be stupid, a waste of everyone's time, really, but she wasn't going to cancel it. She was going to try for something that was at least a little in her control.

She had to start acting as if…as if it didn't matter what the police found or what Barry might do. She had to start taking the reins of her own life.

If anything in the past few weeks, that was the lesson she'd learned. Other people might be able to affect her, but they couldn't control her any more than she could control them.

So she was going to start controlling what she could.

Grace hopped off her painting seat and headed downstairs. She'd find the first available driver to get her to town and she was going to start planning the rest of her life.

Leah was walking into the kitchen the same time she did. "Hey, are you busy?"

Leah pointed to the refrigerator. "Just going to grab some lunch."

"I'll buy you something from Farillo's if you can drive me over to State Street by eleven-thirty." She'd been hemming and hawing with herself for two days over this getting a surprise callback on the résumé she'd sent out to the art gallery for a receptionist job. A shot in the dark. The interview offer was a shock, so much of one she'd spent the past two days thinking about canceling. Forgetting it. But she hadn't, she'd been rendered immobile with indecision, and now she was glad.

This might be stupid, but it was hers. All hers.

"Ooh, Farillo's. Sure thing. When do you want to head out?"

"Ten minutes?"

"Sure. Just gotta be back by one."

Grace nodded, then took off on her mission. She ran through the shower, ridding herself of all signs of paint splotches, then dressed in her best pair of black pants and her nicest shirt. She grabbed the art portfolio Kelly had had her make back when the Martins first showed interest, and marched back downstairs.

She tried not to think about her résumé. It was pathetic. Fifteen years at Cabby's. But that showed she had loyalty and assistant managerial experience. She wasn't going to let the pathetic part of her psyche talk her out of this one. Besides, they'd called her. This was on them if she turned out to be not what they wanted.

If all she got was a resounding no, so be it. A no sure as hell couldn't kill her. Kyle kept shutting her down and out; what was a job turning her away?

Leah let out a low whistle. "I didn't get the dress-to-impress memo. Honestly, I'm not sure you want to be riding in my truck dressed like that."

"It's okay. I'll put a towel down. It's really not that big of a deal." Grace had to work hard not to fidget with her shirt, with her purse, with her hair as they stepped outside.

"You're wearing black pants. In my world, that's a level-eight big deal."

"How many levels are there?"

"Level one is pajamas. Level ten is that idiotic red dress." Leah hopped into the driver's side, pushed some trash onto the floor, then helped Grace put a towel down on the dirty passenger seat.

"I know Jacob gives you a hard time about things, but he's right about your truck."

Leah laughed. "I'm a pig. What can I say? Now, don't think I'm letting you off the hook that easy." She maneuvered her truck onto the road, headed for State Street.

Headed for the future.

Drama much?

"What am I driving you to?"

"Lunch."

"Grace."

Grace placed the portfolio on her lap, swallowed down the nerves. They were stupid. Barry's threat was something to be nervous about. Being in love with Kyle was a definite cause for worry. A job interview for a job she wouldn't get? Nothing to concern herself over. She'd just consider it practice for the future, not this one little job opportunity.

But it was at an art gallery. In Bluff City. It was like a symbol. If she got this, she really did belong here. She really did have control of her life.

And if she didn't...

"Earth to Grace."

Grace forced herself to smile. "Sorry. I'm a little nervous. I have an interview. A…a job interview. It's at an art gallery."

"Oh, man, how perfect. Does that mean you're staying in Bluff City? That'd be awesome."

Staying. An idea she'd had in the back of her head since Jacob had suggested it. She'd loved living in Carvelle, but she also liked being here. Close to friends. Friends who had made her an art studio. She'd really felt like an adult for the first time here. Like she was building a life, not just skating by. "I think so. It's not as if I have a house to go back to. At least not for a while."

"And it wouldn't have *anything* to do with the cyborg you've recently turned into a real boy?"

Grace chuckled, but it was a sobering thought. "I'll admit, when I first started thinking about staying, it had a lot to do with Kyle, but it's more than that. You and Susan and Kelly and feeling… I don't know. Carvelle has been my whole life. It might only be twenty minutes away but who I am is already determined there. Here, it's like I get to be who I want to be. You know?"

Leah was quiet for a few minutes. "Yeah. I actually do kind of know." Stopped at a red light, Leah tapped her fingers on the steering wheel and stared hard at the road ahead.

Grace got the impression there was some puzzle

piece she was missing. Something that had happened to Leah, and that was what she was thinking about now. The same feeling she got when Kyle closed down and shut her out.

"Do you think you can ever really know someone? Totally? Or does everyone have some secret side of themselves hidden away and we just have to accept it?" Maybe she really did just need to be okay with not knowing everything.

"I don't know that we have to accept it." The light turned green and Leah inched forward. "But I think we all have things under the surface no one else can ever really understand."

Grace didn't know what to say to that, or how to feel about it, but the idea that she didn't have to accept it rattled around in her brain. Was that what she'd been doing? Accepting Kyle's refusal to let her in? She'd tried, but then she'd backed off.

Maybe she just couldn't back off.

When the art gallery came into view, she knew she couldn't dwell on that, on him right now. One life step at a time.

Even though it was a receptionist position, she wasn't qualified. No college degree, no receptionist experience. All she had was a sad little résumé and a reference from Kelly and her manager at Cabby's.

Leah brought the truck to a stop right outside the pretty little brick front building that was State Street Art. "Grace?"

"Yeah."

"Go kick some ass. Then I'm buying *you* lunch."

Grace mustered a smile. Maybe she wouldn't get the job, but at least she'd have tried. And there were always more jobs in Bluff City. There'd been an ad online for a cashier at the craft store. Sure, it wasn't anything like being an electrician or an accountant or even a professional artist, but it was *something*.

So, yeah. She was going to kick some ass, and make this life what she wanted it to be. No matter what.

CHAPTER TWENTY

"WE NEED TO TALK."

Kyle swiveled in his chair to see Grace standing in his office doorway. Her expression was grave and she was dressed in black pants and a silky purple top. Aside from the dress she'd worn to the party, he'd never seen her nearly so dressed up.

He'd also never seen her look so...intimidating. Maybe at one time he'd been a little bit afraid of her, of the threat of her making him feel anything, but this was different.

This was a little as though he was going to be taken to task by a stern teacher, and he wasn't quite sure where he'd misstepped to earn it.

"About what?"

"You."

Ah, that did not sound good. At all. He wasn't sure what exactly had changed since this morning, but apparently something had. She had that battle light in her eye, the kind that said she wouldn't surrender.

He wasn't sure he was ready to face it. "I have a few hours left of work. Do you think it could wait?"

Her eyebrows drew together and she studied him. Everything about her was grim and serious and his heart twisted. "Everything is all right, isn't it?"

He'd been holding her off, and he'd sensed her dissatisfaction with it. He just needed more time to figure out what to do. Maybe if he told her about the appointment to see his dad in jail without going into details.... Maybe if he gave her a little glimpse without showing the monster within.

This relationship thing was all about balance. Finding the right amount of things to reveal without taking that one step too far that would make her afraid or uncertain.

He'd find that step. He just needed a little more time.

"I think we really need to talk about...well, the future. If it's really important that we wait until tonight, I can. But I'd prefer to talk about it now."

The future. Yes. He could talk about that, even if the formal, grave way she spoke made him nervous. She wanted to talk about them. The future of them, and that was good. So good he relaxed and opened his mouth to agree with her, but Susan appeared at the door.

"Um, Kyle?" She wrung her hands together, a gesture so unlike her his stomach turned, though he wasn't sure why.

"I'm sorry to interrupt. There's a man at the door for you."

Kyle frowned. "I'm not expecting anyone."

"He said his name is Tony and you'll know who that is. I… Do I need to call the police? He seems a little threatening.…"

It couldn't be. It couldn't possibly be. He had a meeting at the prison tomorrow and his dad wasn't set for release for another four days. It couldn't be. No. Impossible.

"Kyle?"

He stood, legs shaky and unsure. "I'll take care of it," he managed in a rusty voice he could barely hear over his heartbeat. *Can't be. Can't be. It simply can't be.*

He pushed past Grace, ignoring her questioning glance. He got to the hallway, then turned to both women staring at him quizzically. "Stay here."

"Do I need to call—"

"Just stay here," he snapped, striding down the hall, his heart racing, his breath coming in slow, shallow puffs.

This couldn't be happening. It couldn't be happening. But when he unlocked the front door and opened it, there he was.

"Sonny boy. Fancy meeting you here." Tony didn't look particularly like a drug addict might. He didn't scream "abusive, negligent, sorry son of a bitch of a father" at first or even second glance. He didn't look like a man who'd been to prison more times than Kyle could count. In newish jeans and a faded black T-shirt and work boots that had likely seen zero hours of actual work, he looked like any man you might pass on the street. Short hair, clean-shaven.

Until he smiled, and the rotted teeth and ugly sneer gave a peek at who Tony Clark really was.

In a dream world, Kyle could just clock him right now, right in the nose. Pound in his face until this never ever happened again. How had this happened? Kyle had a plan. How on earth had this happened?

"Your release isn't until next week. I checked myself. I—"

"Good behavior and politics, boy. A lethal combination." He smiled again, making Kyle's stomach turn.

Remembering where he was, Kyle glanced back at the house. Grace was inside. Grace, whose abusive ex was still on the loose. Who wanted to talk to him about him. Who looked so serious and...

He had to nip this in the bud now. Now. No punching. No violence. None of Dad's usual tricks could work. Not with Grace so close. Kyle could not let that happen.

"How much do you want?"

Dad's eyebrows raised. "Straight to the chase, eh? A refreshing change not to get all your pansy-ass whiny bullshit about how I don't deserve a dime from you." He glanced at the house, too, predatory blue eyes taking in every inch.

"How much?" Kyle demanded, hating that he saw himself in those eyes, that face. He might not have his father's thick build, but the face? Too many similarities to name.

"Now, that *is* a question, isn't it? How much money is enough restitution for almost committing patricide?"

And he wished he had. He didn't want to think of how Grace might react to that. She might keep a gun for her own safety, for protection, but how would she feel knowing wanting to end his father's life wasn't about either of those two things?

It was about revenge. "Impressive vocabulary. Use jail time to catch up on your reading?"

Dad's smile dimmed. "Be careful who you fuck with, son. Haven't I taught you that lesson yet?"

"How much do you want? I'll hand it over right now. The longer you make me wait, the less you get." If he pretended that he was in control of the situation, maybe he could be. *Just keep pretending until something goes right.* That was how he'd gotten here, gotten everything, by pretending he was someone else, not born of this man, not capable of all the violence he felt when he looked at him.

Dad tapped his chin, eyes still watching the house. Kyle's muscles tensed, bunched, itching for action. He wanted to push his father away. Physi-

cally remove him right this second, but…Grace was
right inside. She might hear and then see.

How could he get his father out of here without drawing any attention? How could he protect
everything he wanted so desperately?

"I'll give you all my cash, my personal credit
card, my debit card. Everything, if you leave right
this second."

"Seem kinda desperate, sonny."

The door opened and Grace stepped out. Not inside anymore. Right there at the top of the stairs,
only a few feet away. Something exploded in his
chest. Painful and real. He couldn't inhale, not with
her right there.

How had he ever thought she could be something he deserved?

"Kyle. Is everything all right?" Her tone was
concerned, but more than that she moved toward
him, as if she would somehow protect him.

But the closer she got, the less he could protect
her. The less he had a chance to still come out of
this okay.

"Everything is fine. Please go back inside."
Away. Far, far away from this, from him. The real
him, the one he couldn't pretend not to be in front
of his father.

Dad's eyebrows rose. "Well, well, well."

"If you want the money this time, you will leave
right now." He said it as low as he could, hope-

ful Grace wouldn't hear. Maybe if she didn't hear, things could be okay. Maybe if Dad walked away. He just had to go, and Kyle would fix everything.

"Will I?"

"Take another step and you're not getting a dime." He could feel the seconds ticking, the pressure building, and when it exploded he'd be left with nothing.

"Do I need to call the police, Kyle? I'm going to. I'm going to—"

Kyle spared Grace the briefest of glances. "Everything is fine. Don't call anyone. Just go inside, please."

"Kyle's having a chat with his dear old dad. Who are you, sweetheart? Girlfriend? You're the McKnight girl, aren't you? The one who got beat up?" Dad moved toward Grace, but Kyle stepped in his path.

"Get the fuck out of here right now," Kyle growled. He wasn't going to resort to violence. Not in front of Grace. Never in front of Grace. But it was building, boiling in his veins, his heart.

Dad would not get near her. Not now. Not ever. No matter what.

"Kyle."

He turned to face her completely then, because he didn't know how long he would last. How much Dad would poke at her to get to him. "Please, just go inside. I am begging you." And he was begging.

Through the tightness in his throat, the constricting of his chest, through the tensed muscles and clenched fists. Begging, *begging,* her to not see the inevitable.

Because he was fighting it, but the ending *was* inevitable. Maybe Grace seeing this side of him was inevitable, too. Maybe losing everything was just so damn inevitable there was no point fighting it.

Grace opened her mouth to say something, but his father was behind him, talking first. Crowding him, baiting him.

"Pretty little thing. Nice rack, too."

Kyle tried. He tried so hard to rein it in, to control himself. This was what Dad was after. Reaction. This was what Dad wanted. Him to get angry enough to fight him. Him to get angry enough to want to kill him. Again. That was what Dad lived for, and Kyle would not give him the satisfaction, not with Grace watching.

"Turn around, honey—let me get a look at your ass."

Kyle squared and used every last ounce of force to knock his fist into his father's face. It only took a second, possibly two, to understand he'd ruined everything.

Everything. And there was no way to pretend enough to ever get it back.

CHAPTER TWENTY-ONE

GRACE WATCHED IN horror as Kyle turned and smashed his fist into the older man's face. She winced. She couldn't believe… But there it was right in front of her eyes. Kyle doing to his father what Barry had done to her.

The ugly thought made her sick enough that she pressed a hand to her stomach, her back to the house. There it was. Instead of just dating a man who used his fists to show his displeasure, she'd fallen in love with one.

Kyle's father cackled out a laugh, blood dripping down his chin. Grace had to look away. God, this wasn't happening. But when she closed her eyes, she saw Barry. Barry's fist hurtling toward her.

God. *God* help her.

There was another crack of bone against bone, a grunt that sounded suspiciously like Kyle. Grace forced herself to look. Now there was a trickle of blood coming from Kyle's nose.

She stepped toward him before stopping herself. He was in a punching match with his father, and he didn't look to be at all ashamed of it. In fact, if looks could kill…Kyle's father would be long gone.

A chilling thought.

"I'm not doing this with you again. I'm not." His voice was rough and gravelly; his chest hitched a breath in and out.

"Funny. I got blood on my face and you got some on yours. Seems like you're doing it again just fine. Got a gun lying around you can point at my head like old times?"

Grace's body went ice-cold. Whatever had gone on in that trailer during Kyle's childhood was even uglier than she'd imagined, if this conversation was any indication.

But of course, she didn't know for sure because Kyle had never told her.

She reached for her phone to call the police, but when no more punches were thrown, she paused.

Kyle pulled his wallet out of his pocket and threw it on the ground in front of his father. "Take whatever and leave, or I will call the police." He trudged up the stairs, toward her, never making eye contact. "Please go inside first," he said, so quietly she could barely make out the words.

She didn't know what else to do. She certainly didn't want to stay outside with Kyle's father any more than she wanted Kyle to. So she stepped inside, Kyle at her heels.

What did she say? What could she possibly say

in this moment to make it...something other than heartbreaking and painful and downright frightening.

"Should I call—"

"Everything is fine, Susan. Would you please give Grace and me a minute?" He sounded so damn weary, she wanted to soothe him.

Until the picture of his fist connecting with his father's chin flashed across her vision.

Kyle sank into the couch, cradling his head in his hands. "I'm so sorry, Grace. So sorry you had to see that. No apology will ever be enough." His voice broke, but he didn't look at her. Didn't make a move to reassure her. He just sat there, and she didn't know what to do.

Because the sad state of affairs was she didn't know him. Not really. She thought she'd fallen in love with him, but he'd never let her see all of him, so he felt like little more than a stranger now.

After a few silent minutes, he looked up. The blood under his nose was smudged across the palms of his hands, his eyes blue and intense, shiny with what she suspected were tears.

Her heart broke.

"You're afraid of me."

And then it broke even more, because she didn't know what she was. "You would never hurt me." That, she supposed, was the difference here. Though the event had reminded her of Barry, there were some things she knew Kyle simply wasn't capable of.

Or thought you knew.

"No, I would never hurt you, Grace, never like that." His throat convulsed and he shook his head. "But I am capable of hurting people. More than capable. I...can't seem to help myself."

"He said..." Part of her was trying to excuse him, to make it okay. But how could this be okay? Her throat and eyes burned as she tried to make any sense out of any of it. "He was trying to get you to hit him."

"Yes. He always does, and he always wins. Always."

Always. As if Kyle didn't have a choice in the matter, but of course he did. Everyone had a choice.

"I'm sorry you had to see it. I'm sorry I didn't think... I should have known. I should have predicted this. Letting myself love you was a recipe for disaster from the beginning, and I knew, but I wanted you too badly to really think."

"You could have..." What? What could he have done? Told her, she supposed, but would that really change this reality? "You held a gun on him. That's...why my gun freaked you out."

Kyle stared at his blood-streaked hands. "Yes." He cleared his throat. "When I was eighteen. One of his and my mother's bouts got more heated than usual. I put a gun to his head, but the police came before I could…"

Relief washed through her, because there was a reason. He had a reason. She stepped toward him for the first time. "So you were protecting her."

"Don't." He shook his head and his look stopped her cold. "Don't try to make it noble. It's not. I wanted to kill him. I wanted to end it. I wasn't protecting anyone."

The way he said it, as if he hadn't just *wanted* to kill him, but still wanted to. She knew that feeling, the deep-seated, haunting fear it wouldn't be over until the bad guy was gone. All the way gone. "I…I understand that, Kyle. Me, of all people. I understand that."

"Yes, I suppose you do, but that doesn't change anything."

"Maybe—"

"If we were together, this wouldn't be the last time he sought me out, goaded me into that. It won't ever be the last until he's dead. So even though I'd never physically hurt you, every time he came by would be a reminder that you have been hurt like that, and I am capable of it, even if it isn't against you. Barry and I are cut from the same cloth."

"Don't say that." She didn't want to believe it. Couldn't. Maybe she didn't know all of Kyle, but she knew enough to know he wasn't Barry, or his father. Maybe he wasn't perfect, but he wasn't them.

"I thought if I was cold enough, detached enough, it wouldn't happen. I could control it. My reaction to him. And then I thought if I locked the bad away enough, drowned it in light and good and you, I'd be able to control it. But the truth is, if I couldn't stop myself for you, in front of you, nothing can stop it. I certainly can't. Today proves I can't, and I can't possibly love you and want you to be a part of that. And I do love you, Grace." His voice cracked again and he covered his face in his hands.

It felt as though the universe had yanked her off the path she thought she'd been on. Like when Mom had gotten sick, like after Barry. She'd been traveling this path, then, yank, new path. New hurt. New pain.

One minute she'd been confronting Kyle about telling her the truth about what kept him so tight-lipped about the past, the next that path was laying a cold dose of reality on both their laps.

"I'm sorry. I'm sorry I didn't… I thought I could be someone you deserved, but the truth is, it's not enough. I'm not enough and I never will be no matter how hard I try. I'm sorry I let it get this far."

Dread pooled in her stomach, a hard, heavy weight, tears burning her eyes, her throat. "I don't want this to be over." She swallowed down the lump in her throat. Even after seeing all that, even though she wasn't sure exactly what she *did* want, she wasn't ready to lose Kyle, even with blood on his hands and face.

"I don't either, but...can you really live with the reality of the situation?" His blue eyes met hers briefly, searching maybe for some answer. Then he shook his head. "I can't. I can't live with knowing I'd expose you to that every few years. I'm sorry. I can't. I thought I could, but I can't. How could you want a future with someone who'll remind you of the worst thing that ever happened to you?"

She didn't have an answer for that question, a rebuttal. He was right. How could she want that?

Something hard and painful pressed against her chest. This was it. How could this not be it? She wanted to argue with him, to tell him he absolutely was enough, and they could find a way through this.

But at the moment, she didn't know how, and she couldn't find her voice to argue with him. Or maybe there were just no words to argue.

He stood. Swallowed hard enough she could see his Adam's apple move. "I'm so very sorry you had to see that, that I frightened you or hurt you. I'm going to go clean up. If you'd like me to stay elsewhere, I will. I don't want to make you uncomfortable."

He was talking to her as though she was a stranger, and she felt like one. She felt as if she didn't know him at all. As if they'd never kissed or